BlindSide

Why everyone loves James Patterson and Detective Michael Bennett

'Its breakneck pace leaves you gasping for breath. Packed with typical Patterson panache . . . **it won't disappoint**.'
Daily Mail

'It's no mystery why James Patterson is the world's most popular thriller writer. Simply put: **Nobody does it better**.'
Jeffery Deaver

'No one gets this big without **amazing natural storytelling** talent – which is what Jim has, in spades.'
Lee Child

'James Patterson is the **gold standard** by which all others are judged.'
Steve Berry

'Patterson boils a scene down to the single, telling detail, the element that **defines a character** or moves a plot along. It's what fires off the movie projector in the reader's mind.'
Michael Connelly

'James Patterson is **The Boss**. End of.'
Ian Rankin

PERSONNEL FILE

Req #: 2014-PL-10945
File #:

TO BE FILLED IN BY IMMEDIATE SUPERIOR:

Detective
MICHAEL BENNETT ☑

6 FOOT 3 INCHES (191CM)   200 POUNDS (91KG)
IRISH AMERICAN

EMPLOYMENT

Bennett joined the police force to uncover the truth
at all costs. He started his career in the Bronx's
49th Precinct. He then transferred to the NYPD's
Major Case Squad and remained there until he moved
to the Manhattan North Homicide Squad.

EDUCATION

Bennett graduated from Regis High School and studied
philosophy at Manhattan College.

FAMILY HISTORY

Bennett was previously married to Maeve, who worked as a
nurse on the trauma ward at Jacobi Hospital in the Bronx.
However, Maeve died tragically young after losing a battle
with cancer in December 2007, leaving Bennett to raise
their ten adopted children: Chrissy, Shawna, Trent, Eddie,
twins Fiona and Bridget, Ricky, Brian, Jane and Juliana.

Following Maeve's death, over time Bennett grew closer to
the children's nanny, Mary Catherine. After years of on-
off romance, Bennett and Mary Catherine decided to commit
to one another, and now happily raise the family together.
Also in the Bennett household is his Irish grandfather,
Seamus, who is a Catholic priest.

☐ AMENDED REPORT

PROFILE:

BENNETT IS AN EXPERT IN HOSTAGE NEGOTIATION,
TERRORISM, HOMICIDE AND ORGANIZED CRIME. HE WILL STOP
AT NOTHING TO GET THE JOB DONE AND PROTECT THE CITY
AND THE PEOPLE HE LOVES, EVEN IF THIS MEANS DISOBEYING
ORDERS AND IGNORING PROTOCOL. DESPITE THESE UNORTHODOX
METHODS, HE IS A RELENTLESS, DETERMINED AND IN MANY
WAYS INCOMPARABLE DETECTIVE.

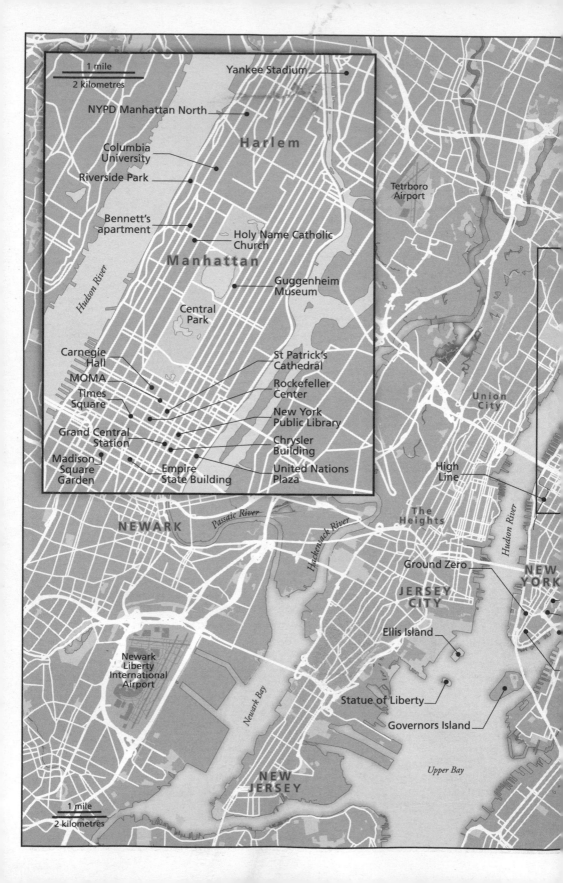

1 mile
2 kilometres

Yankee Stadium

NYPD Manhattan North

Harlem

Columbia
University

Riverside Park

Tetrboro
Airport

Bennett's
apartment

Holy Name Catholic
Church

Manhattan

Guggenheim
Museum

Hudson River

Central
Park

Carnegie
Hall

St Patrick's
Cathedral

MOMA

Rockefeller
Center

Times
Square

New York
Public Library

Grand Central
Station

Chrysler
Building

Madison
Square
Garden

Empire
State Building

United Nations
Plaza

Union
City

High
Line

The
Heights

NEWARK

Passaic River

Hackensack River

Ground Zero

NEW
YORK

JERSEY
CITY

Ellis Island

Newark
Liberty
International
Airport

Statue of Liberty

Governors Island

Hudson River

Newark Bay

NEW
JERSEY

Upper Bay

1 mile
2 kilometres

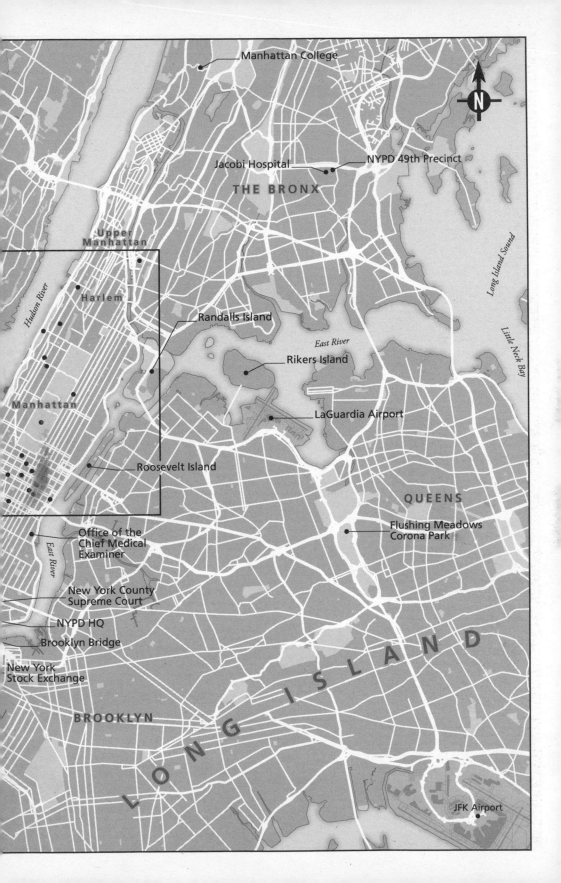

Manhattan College

NYPD 49th Precinct

Jacobi Hospital

THE BRONX

Upper
Manhattan

Harlem

Randalls Island

East River

Rikers Island

Roosevelt Island

LaGuardia Airport

Manhattan

Hudson River

East River

Office of the
Chief Medical
Examiner

QUEENS

Flushing Meadows
Corona Park

New York County
Supreme Court

NYPD HQ

Brooklyn Bridge

New York
Stock Exchange

BROOKLYN

LONG ISLAND

Long Island Sound

Little Neck Bay

JFK Airport

N

BlindSide

JAMES PATTERSON

& JAMES O. BORN

CENTURY

1 3 5 7 9 10 8 6 4 2

Century
20 Vauxhall Bridge Road
London SW1V 2SA

Century is part of the Penguin Random House group of companies whose
addresses can be found at global.penguinrandomhouse.com

Penguin
Random House
UK

First published by Century in 2020

www.penguin.co.uk

A CIP catalogue record for this book is available from the British Library

ISBN 9781780899343
ISBN 9781780899350 (trade paperback edition)

Printed and bound in Great Britain by Clays Ltd, Elcograf S.p.A.

Penguin Random House is committed to a sustainable future
for our business, our readers and our planet. This book is
made from Forest Stewardship Council® certified paper.

BlindSide

CHAPTER 1

I DID EVERYTHING I could to distract Lucille Evans from noticing the bloody footprint. A responding patrol officer had tracked the blood into the hallway. One look at the scene inside and the veteran needed to run into the street. I didn't blame him one bit.

The forensics people were in the small, two-bedroom apartment on the third floor of this building on 146th Street near Willis Avenue in the Bronx. The scene was so horrendous that the local detectives had called me to help even though it wasn't technically considered part of Manhattan North Homicide's usual territory. Two of the local detectives had lost it. It happens. It's happened to me over the years. I lost it once at the scene of a murdered girl. Her stepfather had bashed her head in for crying because she was hungry. She reminded me of my own Shawna, staring up through blood splatters. When I heard her stepfather

3

in the other room, talking with detectives, I snapped. It almost felt like another being possessed me. I burst into the room, ready to kill. Only the fact that my partner at the time, Gail Nodding, was as tough as nails and shoved me back out the door had kept me from killing the creep.

Now I considered this bloody scene. Who wouldn't be affected by the sight of two bodies with bullet wounds in their heads? Large-caliber wounds. Not the usual .38s or 9mms used in the city. The bodies frozen in time. A mother trying to shield her little girl. I wanted to bolt home and hug my own children. But I had work to do.

I had my hands full with the sixty-five-year-old woman who merely wanted to say good-bye to her daughter and granddaughter.

Mrs. Evans tried to push past me to open the simple wooden door with the number 9 hanging upside down. The threadbare industrial carpet didn't give my feet much traction. My semi-dress Skechers were more for walking comfort than for wrestling.

Mrs. Evans said, "Let me pass, young man. I have to see my babies." She wasn't loud. She wasn't hysterical. She was determined.

So was I.

I said, "Ma'am, I'm not in charge. But I do have kids. I know loss. You don't want what you see inside that apartment to be your final memory of your daughter and granddaughter. Please, I swear to God, you'll get your chance to say good-bye."

She stared me down as hard as any drug dealer ever had. But I was resolute. I'd already seen the horror behind the door. I wasn't about to let this elegant, retired teacher see it, too. Her daughter, still in her nurse's uniform from the Bronx-Lebanon Hospital. The left side of her face missing from a single, devastating gunshot. Lying over her daughter. A nine-year-old with a hole in the side of her head. This time, too, the girl reminded me of my Shawna.

The whole scene had shaken me to the core. Never believe a cop when he or she tells you they've seen it all. Nobody ever sees it all.

Mrs. Evans cracked. Tears started to flow. It'd finally hit her with full force. Two of her greatest treasures had been taken from her. Her watery eyes looked up at me again. She simply asked, "Why?"

She started to weep. I put a tentative arm around her. She fell into me and I hugged her. I remembered how I'd felt when Maeve, my wife, died. That was a slow death from cancer. It still tore me to pieces.

This poor woman had been blindsided.

I eased her onto one of the cheap plastic chairs a detective had set up in the apartment's hallway. A little African American girl peeked out of one of the doorways down the hall. The light at the end of the hall near the stairs flickered.

Why would someone shoot a nurse and her little girl? Why did someone like Mrs. Evans have to suffer through this? How would I hold it all together?

I had to. It was my job.

CHAPTER 2

THE UNIFORMED CAPTAIN from the Fortieth Precinct erupted into the hallway from the stairs. I knew the tall captain from my days on patrol. He yelled down the hall to the NYPD officers working diligently, "Let's move this along, shall we, people?" Then he saw me.

I had just gotten Mrs. Evans seated. A young patrol officer stepped over and offered her a cup of cold water. She was starting to get that glazed look family members have after a murder.

The captain marched toward me and said, "This ain't Manhattan North. What are you doing here? Trying to steal a stat?"

Sometimes cops embarrass me. Yeah, it's a job, but it involves people. People with feelings. I kept it professional and said, "Just helping out, Captain Ramirez."

The captain was almost as tall as me. He wore his dark hair slicked tightly against his scalp. There were definite cliques inside the NYPD. Divisions happen in all large organizations. The simple old Irish-versus-Italian rivalry had given way to a much more complicated system. Ramirez identified strongly with the Hispanic clique and didn't give a crap if I was Irish, Italian, or black. I wasn't Hispanic so he didn't cut me any slack.

The captain barked, "Then help clear this scene. We got shit breaking all over the Bronx. There's a goddamn protest about the price of housing. In New York. You think they'd realize housing prices are going to be crazy."

I motioned toward Mrs. Evans, hoping this moron would get the hint. It was a foolish hope.

The captain said, "How much longer will this take?"

I eased us away from Mrs. Evans. When I leaned in close to the captain, I said, "This lady's daughter and granddaughter are in that apartment. It'll take as long as it takes. We gotta grab the asshole who did this. Don't you agree?" I'd spoken very slowly so nothing I said could be misunderstood.

The old-school captain locked me in his gaze. It was nothing compared to Mrs. Evans's stare down. Then he said, "Okay, hotshot. I'll get the manpower from somewhere else."

When I stepped back to Mrs. Evans, she said, "Oh, dear Lord. I have to tell my sons."

I decided to walk her the two blocks to where they lived. I needed the break.

CHAPTER 3

IN A SIMILAR apartment to that of their sister and niece, I helped Mrs. Evans break the news to her two adult sons, who both worked for the city and seemed like sharp young men. They took the news like anyone would. They were shocked.

The larger of the men, a good six feet five inches and close to three hundred pounds, started to wail and put his head on his mother's shoulder. She stroked his neck and spoke to him like she would to a toddler, in a soft, soothing voice. A mom's power never really diminishes, no matter how big a child grows.

I told them the lead detective would be down to talk to them at some point. They'd have questions about why someone might do this.

The older of the two brothers, a bus mechanic, said, "This is not a bad neighborhood. Not *too* bad. Who would do something like this?" He had the distant stare of a man in over his head.

That's the way it should be. No one should be used to tragedy like this. Not even a cop.

I gave them a card in case they needed anything. I felt confident Mrs. Evans would be most comfortable if she stayed here with them tonight.

The clear, cloudless skies and afternoon sun did little to lift my spirits. I barely noticed passing cars or the other normal rhythms of the city. I walked with a measured pace, trying to give myself a little time before I went back to the crime scene. All I could see in my head was a mother lying on top of her little girl. The left side of her face a massive hole leaking blood. The apartment a shambles.

No witnesses. No suspects. No hope.

I looked up at the sky and spoke to Maeve. I did that quite a bit. This time I said, "I hate that you saw stuff like this, too. A nurse's job is harder than a cop's in some respects. I miss you, Maeve."

Sometimes I swear I can hear a faint answer. It's easy and convenient to claim it was the wind or a distant radio. But it happens occasionally. Today I thought I heard, "Love you." And no one can tell me I didn't hear it.

I swung into a bodega and grabbed an ice-cold grape Gatorade. I'd briefly considered buying a beer, but they still needed me at the apartment. The radio behind the counter was broadcasting a news brief about the murders. That would attract more curious onlookers. The day was not getting any better.

The clerk looked at me and said, "Tough day?"

"Does it show?"

"Gatorade is on me."

I thanked him, more for a quick jolt of humanity. Then

dropped two dollars on the scarred and nicked counter before I headed back out.

I was still a block away from the apartment building and the growing crowd of onlookers. I had parked my city-issued Impala over here in case I needed to get away quickly. Experience has taught me that if you park too close to a scene, you can get boxed in.

Suddenly I had an uncontrollable urge to speak to Mary Catherine and the kids. As many of them as I could get on the phone. They were what kept me sane. If I ever needed a connection to my real life, it was right now.

Leaning against my car, I took a swig of the Gatorade and set it on the roof. I fumbled with my phone.

While I considered whether I should call Mary Catherine's cell or the home phone, someone said, "Let's make this quick."

I looked up into the barrel of a pistol.

CHAPTER 4

THE YOUNG BLACK man's hand trembled ever so slightly. There was no doubt the barrel was still pointed at my face. But he was new to this kind of stuff. That made him more dangerous. He had no idea what could happen.

He repeated, "Let's make this quick."

I didn't hesitate. I immediately reached into my sport coat for my personal wallet. My police ID was in my back pocket. At the moment, he thought I was just a citizen out for a stroll. I'd be happy to let him keep thinking that.

I can't count the number of times I've heard the wife of a murdered robbery victim say, "A lousy wallet wasn't worth his life." No way I was going to put Mary Catherine in that position.

I held up my wallet to show it to him and said, "Here, it's yours." I'd seen enough bloodshed today. I just wanted him to walk away. A few bucks and some credit cards aren't worth anyone's life. I figured this was over. There was no one on the street near us. He had no reason to hang around. Everyone could have another day on Earth.

Then I heard a second voice from across the narrow street. A tall, skinny man came out of an alley between an empty storefront and a ninety-nine-cent store. He wore a crazy heavy jacket with an odd, fur-trimmed collar. The man had an angry tinge to his voice when he said, "What chu doin', RJ?" He glanced at me. "You finally joinin' up? Good man."

The second man was about thirty. His pupils were black circles covering most of his eyes. But drugs were the least of his issues. His head swung in wide arcs as he glanced in every direction. His left hand had a constant, jittery movement. His tongue played with the gold grill across his front teeth. He was a walking advertisement for one of the antipsychotic pharmaceuticals advertised on news channels and ESPN.

The man said, "Lookee here, dressy." He stayed in the street, on the driver's side of the car. He stared straight at me and said, "You going out, Pops? Nice jacket. Not too hot, nice dark blue. Too bad you're too wide. Jacket would never fit me."

Why did he have to come and stir shit up?

The younger man, RJ, who still held me at gunpoint, turned to his friend and said, "I got his wallet. Let's go."

The man in the fur-trimmed coat said, "Somethin's not right about him. He's taller than us. That's enough to shoot his ass right there."

RJ said, "I got money, cards. It's cool."

"It ain't cool, RJ. It's a lot of things, but it ain't cool. He don't care nothin' about us. And he don't *mean* nothin' *to* us. Go ahead, show him how little he means to us."

RJ was torn. I could see it in his face. He wanted to leave. But this new guy, he wanted to see something happen. He wanted some excitement on a weekday afternoon.

The new man stepped to the front of the car and let his coat fall open. I could see the Colt stuck in his waistband. I thought about the head wounds at the crime scene I was just at. It was a big caliber. Probably a .45. That was not a common gun in the Bronx. I wanted to fix his face in my brain.

The man snapped, "What chu starin' at?"

I didn't answer. I did a quick scan to see if I could find any blood spatter on the cuffs or collar of the heavy coat he was wearing.

But that was the least of my worries at the moment. Now the man leaned in close to RJ and said, "Shoot this cracker in the face. You feel me, RJ?"

The younger man kept his eyes on me. He raised the gun slightly so he could sight more accurately. He mumbled, "Okay, Tight, okay. Give me a second."

I felt the shift in the young man. He was scared of his friend. I would be, too. The man was giving him almost no choice but to pull the trigger. At that point, I knew if RJ didn't shoot, I'd be facing that .45.

The man told RJ, "You own his ass. Now you can take everything from him. No feeling like it in the world." Then the man looked at the Chevy Impala. He craned his head to stare into the interior.

"Hold on, RJ. I think this dude's a cop. He seen us both. You gotta do it now."

Now the crazy guy was using logic. And he wasn't wrong. I'd have been willing to forget about RJ, but I needed to check out his friend "Tight" regarding the homicide a block away.

That wasn't going to happen, though. I swallowed and had a quick thought of each of my children. When you have ten kids, you can't spend a lot of time on each one as your life flashes before your eyes.

RJ was ready. He used his left hand to steady the gun. He started to squeeze the trigger.

CHAPTER 5

AT A MOMENT like that, facing a gun, there's no telling what will go through your head. I was hoping for a miracle. And I said a quick prayer. It wasn't specific or particularly elegant. Just a *Please help me, God.* At least I think that's what I prayed.

Then it happened. A car coming from a side street onto this main road squealed its tires. It wasn't long or really loud. But it was enough. Just enough.

Both men looked over their shoulders to see what had caused the noise. Just a basic reaction, like an instinct. It was a gray Dodge racing away from us.

I took my chance. A movement I had done in training more than a thousand times. I shifted slightly. Reached back quickly with my right hand. Flipped my coat out of the way. Took a firm grip on my Glock semiautomatic pistol. Pressed the release on my holster and slid the pistol out. It felt natural because of all the practice. The idea that a human would be in my sights didn't really come into the equation.

Just as my barrel came to rest, pointing at the robber's chest, I shouted, "Police. Don't move."

I aimed at RJ because he had his pistol out, although I thought the other man was going to be the real problem. But RJ steadied his hands and brought the barrel of his pistol back toward my face. I squeezed the trigger of my own pistol. Once. Twice. I knew I'd hit him center mass.

The young man's arms lowered and the pistol dropped from his hand. It made a loud clank on the hood of my car, then slid down to the asphalt. RJ followed a similar path, staring at me the whole time as he tumbled to the ground.

My natural inclination was to follow the body to the ground with my pistol. I don't know why. It's not like cops are in so many shootings that we get used to them. Each one is traumatic and devastating in its own way.

As soon as RJ hit the asphalt, I realized he posed no more threat. Now I had to deal with Tight, who was already rushing backward, away from me. He fumbled for the pistol in his belt line, and I fired once. Then he spun and sprinted away. I didn't know if I'd hit him or if he'd dropped the pistol. The only thing I could think about was the young man bleeding on the street right in front of me.

I let the crazy man in the fur-trimmed jacket run away.

I dropped to one knee and immediately checked the pulse on the young man I'd been forced to shoot. Blood was already pumping from his chest and filling the indentation at the bottom of his throat. I opened his ratty coat all the way and ripped his Jets T-shirt right down the middle, then used part of the T-shirt to help stop the bleeding.

I quickly reached into my pocket and fumbled for my phone. I hit 911. As soon as the operator came on I almost shouted, "This is Detective Michael Bennett. I am on Third Avenue near 146th Street. I need immediate assistance. I have shots fired, a man down, and require an ambulance ASAP."

I ignored her other questions and went back to working on young RJ. I held the folded T-shirt rag directly on the bullet hole, hoping to stem the bleeding. Blood soaked the cuff of my shirt and speckled my chest. People started coming out of the bodega and some of the apartment buildings.

A young black woman kneeled down to help me. She said, "I'm in nursing school. Let me keep pressure on the wound." She wasn't panicked and kept a very calm tone.

That helped me focus. I kept saying to the young man, "Hang in there, RJ. Help is on the way." About a minute later, I heard the first in a storm of sirens heading our way.

It wasn't until paramedics stepped in and took over the first aid that it really hit me what had happened. I could have been killed. I *should* have been killed. And I had been forced to use my duty weapon. It was the last thing I'd wanted to do. It's the last thing *any* cop wants to do. But I didn't regret it. I couldn't. Not when I hugged my kids tonight.

And now all I could do was stare helplessly as paramedics did everything they could to save this young man's life.

CHAPTER 6

AS MORE PARAMEDICS and squad cars arrived, I simply walked down the street a short distance and plopped onto the curb. I had nothing left. I wasn't even ready to call Mary Catherine. I just stared straight ahead into the empty street. I noticed everything from the rough asphalt patches over potholes to the random Three Musketeers wrapper blowing in the light breeze. It felt as if the city had gone silent.

Even though the paramedics were still busy, I knew RJ was dead. My mind raced, but I couldn't settle on a single thought. I vaguely realized it was some sort of shock settling over me. It's a common occurrence after a police shooting.

It had all happened so fast. Virtually all police shootings do. I'd acted out of instinct. Now I had to let things take their course.

All I knew at the moment was that I couldn't leave the scene. I just wanted to sit here with my thoughts. Silently I prayed, *Dear*

God, have mercy on this young man's soul. I thought about calling my grandfather, Seamus.

Then I heard someone shout, "He did it." It didn't register immediately, then someone else said it. I looked up and over my shoulder to see a small group of people facing me.

A heavyset African American man of about thirty-five pointed at me and shouted, "That cop shot RJ for no reason. He murdered him."

I let him talk. It never did any good to speak up. People had to vent. This neighborhood had fought to shed its reputation from the 1980s. Crime, especially homicides, was down. Cops could only do so much. Neighborhoods and the people in them had to decide to change. And this one had. I could understand some misplaced anger over a shooting.

The vast majority of cops try to do the right thing. That's why they get into the business. A few go overboard. And like anything else, most groups are judged by the actions of a few. It's been like that since the dawn of time.

I recognized that prejudgment was contributing to this crowd's growing fury. They were pissed off. Right now they were pissed off at me. I just took it.

My heart fluttered and my hands shook.

This heavyset guy gathered more followers. He was like a singer energized by the crowd. He turned to face the crowd and yelled, "We're tired of cops treating us like criminals. Now this guy shot RJ for just standing there."

No one was speaking in my defense. Someone had to have seen what happened.

Someone tossed a bottle, which shattered on the sidewalk next to me. A young patrol officer who had been near the paramedics stepped toward the crowd with her hands up like she was trying to calm them down.

An older, lean woman scowled at the officer and said, "Keep your ass over there. This don't concern you."

Another bottle sailed through the air. Then a half eaten McDonald's hamburger smacked me right in the face.

I wiped some gooey cheese from my cheek with my bare hand.

The mob of fifteen or twenty people moved toward me now. I just sat there. Numb. I understood these people's anger. Every interaction with a cop was viewed with suspicion. Some cops' attitudes didn't help, treating everyone like a criminal. Forgetting that most people didn't cause any problems at all.

I cleaned the rest of the hamburger from my face and stood up. I faced the crowd. The young patrol officer and her partner started to move toward me, but I held up my hand to stop them. They would only make things worse.

I mumbled, "Let them vent for a minute. We don't want a riot." I'd been in riots, and they were no fun. This crowd could go either way. There didn't seem to be outside agitators, who could kick demonstrations up a notch to a riot. No one wanted to destroy their own neighborhood.

More garbage flew through the air. A few more steps and the mob would be right on top of me.

CHAPTER 7

I KNEW NOT to say something stupid, like "Let's all just calm down." That had never worked in the history of law enforcement. I couldn't explain that I had done everything I could to avoid shooting RJ. No one wanted to hear that. Not the crowd, not the news media, and certainly not RJ's family.

The crowd was close enough that I could see the heavyset man who was leading them had a cracked front tooth. That was too close for comfort. For the first time it started to sink in that I was in real danger.

Then I heard a voice—a booming, commanding voice. I recognized it immediately. It may not have been God, but it was the best I could hope for right now. It was just a simple "Everyone freeze."

And they did.

My lieutenant, Harry Grissom, stepped out of a black,

unmarked NYPD Suburban. The tall, lean, twenty-six-year veteran of the force looked like an Old West gunfighter, his mustache creeping along the sides of his mouth. He was toying with the NYPD grooming policy, but so far no one had the balls to say anything to him about it.

A gold badge dangled from a chain around his neck. His tan suit had some creases but gave him an air of authority. As if he needed something extra.

He kept marching toward the crowd without any hesitation. As he got closer, he said in a very even voice, "What's the problem here?"

The pudgy leader yelled, "He shot an unarmed man."

Someone in the back of the crowd added, "For no reason."

Other people started to crowd in around Harry to tell him why they were so angry.

And he listened. At least to the people not shouting obscenities. Harry was an old-school pragmatist. He'd been part of the enforcement effort that helped clean up New York City. He didn't need to knock heads. He could talk.

He engaged the heavyset guy. "Who is an actual eyewitness?"

No one answered.

Harry kept a calm tone. "What do you say I give you my card and we talk in a couple of days? That way you can see what we find out. The shooting will be investigated thoroughly. Just give it forty-eight hours. Is that too much to ask?"

The heavyset man had a hard time ignoring such a reasonable request. He tentatively accepted Harry's card.

The crowd wasn't nearly as discerning. That's how it always is. In sports and politics and real life. A rowdy crowd drives the conversation and clouds the issues.

Harry stood firm and gave them a look that had withered many detectives under his command. More police cars arrived, along with a crime-scene van.

The crowd could see things were happening, and they started to lose their initiative.

Harry turned to me without any more thought of the crowd behind him. It was that kind of confidence that had inspired countless cops and defused dozens of confrontations.

He said in a low tone, "You doing all right, Mike?"

"I'm not physically hurt if that's what you mean."

He led me toward his Suburban and simply said, "That'll do for now." It was a complex and touchy subject; he wouldn't be part of the investigative team and, by policy, couldn't ask me any probing questions.

It didn't matter. When I slid into his SUV, I realized he wasn't acting as Harry Grissom, lieutenant with the NYPD. He was just being my friend.

That's what I needed right now.

CHAPTER 8

HARRY DROPPED ME off at my apartment on West End Avenue a little after six. I had done all the procedural shit that overwhelms a cop after a shooting. I talked to a union rep, a Police Benevolent Association attorney, and a psychologist. Finally, I told them I had a tremendous headache and needed to lie down. Really all I needed was my family.

As I walked down the hallway to my apartment, my neighbor, Mr. Underhill, spoke to me for the first time in all the years we'd lived there.

He said, "You doing okay?"

I just shrugged and said, "Yeah, you?"

The older, corpulent man nodded and smiled. Then he disappeared back inside. It was the only conversation I had ever had with the man. It was unnerving.

People wondered how an NYPD detective could afford

such a great apartment on the Upper West Side. If they were bold enough to ask, I usually just said, "Bribes," and left it at that. In reality, the apartment had been left to my late wife, Maeve. She had cared for an elderly man here for years. In that time, her personality and warmth had brought the man from a dour, solitary existence to happiness. He felt such joy being around her that when he passed away he left her the apartment and a trust to help pay the taxes. He had wanted Maeve and her growing family to enjoy it. The apartment was a constant reminder of what a ray of sunshine Maeve had been to everyone she met.

Occasionally, when I was in a weird mood, the apartment could make me sad. The idea that my wonderful wife had meant so much to someone that he had changed our entire family's life was amazing. The fact that she had only gotten to live here a short while was tough to swallow.

The smell of pot roast hit me as soon as I opened the front door. So did two kids. Shawna, my second youngest daughter, and Trent, my youngest son, barreled into me like out-of-control race cars. I didn't mind one bit.

When I dropped to my knees, Shawna gave me a big hug and kissed me on the cheek. "I'm so glad you're home safe, Dad."

Trent chimed in, "Me too."

So much for my hope that I could ease everyone into what had happened to me. And now I understood Mr. Underhill's gross show of emotion. I had known word would leak out. Obviously I'd spoken to Mary Catherine about it. I'd told her not to make a fuss. Have something serious happen to you, then try to tell an Irish woman not to make a fuss. It would be easier to keep the sun in the sky an extra two hours.

Before I could even navigate into the kitchen, Mary Catherine found me and gave me a huge kiss.

"I appreciate the attention, but I'm fine."

Mary Catherine said, "And I thank God for it. But your name has already been on the news. The guy who has the cable access show, Reverend Caldwell, is already in the Bronx saying that you're a murderer walking free."

"I thought you'd learned by now that most people don't have any clue about the facts when they're spouting garbage like that." I half expected Mary Catherine to ask me if it was a good shooting. The only thing I had heard the news got right was that there were two men and a police officer involved.

Shootings were ratings monsters, so every news team covered them from start to finish. They always had the same elements: sobbing family members telling the world that their dead relative had been sweet and would have never hurt a fly. And in New York, no shooting was ever complete without the commentary of the Reverend Franklin Caldwell. The "people's voice."

To distract myself, I wandered back to the corner of the living room where my teenager Eddie had his face in a computer monitor. I needed something normal like this. Foolishly I said, "Need a hand with anything, Eddie?"

He didn't take his eyes off the screen. Another common occurrence. He said, "Thanks, Dad. I think I've got this. I'm writing an algorithm to find documents where references to *The Lord of the Rings* are made. Google just doesn't cut it for me anymore. Do you have any ideas where I should search?"

All I could do at this point was lean down and kiss the teenager on the top of his head. In his case, I'd never be the *smart dad*. The best I could be was a loving dad.

Even though all ten of my kids are adopted, I'm still at a loss to understand where they each got their unique skills. Eddie is a standout, with his phenomenal computer knowledge.

A few minutes later, my grandfather, Seamus, arrived. He was wearing his usual clerical collar, which identified him as a Catholic priest. Even though he'd joined the priesthood very late in life, he loved nothing more than walking around in his tab-collared clergy shirt.

He was the one man who knew not to coddle me. He was also the reason I didn't like being coddled. He said, "Hello, my boy. Will you share a glass of wine with me? Think of it as a way to laugh in the face of death. You can drink and none of it is going to leak out through holes in your stomach or chest."

Then he shocked me by giving me a hug. "Thank God the NYPD trained you well."

We all filed into the dining room. I heard the news come on the TV where Ricky had been watching a cooking show. All I heard was the first line: "The Reverend Franklin Caldwell says he will personally investigate the claims that NYPD detective Michael Bennett shot an unarmed man in cold blood today."

I cringed at the fact the kids had to hear something like that. My grandfather stomped to the TV and shut it off as he threw a quick scowl at Ricky for not turning it off after the show.

We all took our seats at the long table. One chair, as always, was left open for my son Brian. The other nine children, Mary Catherine, my grandfather, and I clasped hands for grace.

As always, Seamus said it. This time it was surprisingly short. "Dear Heavenly Father, all we can say today is thank you."

Silently I added, *Please have mercy on Ronald Timmons Junior's soul.*

CHAPTER 9

ALICE GROFF WAS impressed by New York City. It was everything she'd heard about when growing up in Berlin. Soaring skyscrapers, crowded streets, something to do every minute of the day. And yet she was bored. At least at the moment.

She and her business partner, Janos Titon, had accepted an assignment from a guy named Endrik "Henry" Laar, based in Tallinn, Estonia. He was some kind of cyber genius and had plenty of money. The issue was his God complex. How she hated to hear him go on and on about his ability to break any computer security system. Her grandmother had always told her that men who bragged were hiding their flaws.

If he was so damn smart, why did he have to contract out work? She knew he had a couple of Dutchmen who did dirty work for him. But this job called for a little more subtlety.

They had a list of several New York–based hackers. They

had just found where the first one lived. His name was Tommy Payne and he had gone to some school in Massachusetts known for its technology. All they had to do was convince him to come work for Endrik, who liked to go by the Anglicized version of his name, Henry. If that failed, they'd been told to make sure he didn't talk. That could mean a lot of things. She didn't have time to decipher what Henry actually wanted. She was built for efficiency. That meant if this nerd wasn't willing to work for Henry in Estonia, she'd put a bullet in his head.

Janos said, "Will you recognize him if he walks up the stairs to the apartment?" Janos was from Romania originally and they generally communicated in English. Today was no different.

Alice said, "You've seen the same photo I have. Won't you recognize him, too?"

Janos just shrugged. That was his answer to most things. She was tired of trying to make him more professional. He pretty much did what she told him, and he wasn't afraid of anything. Neither of them were. They both had realized that not many grew old in this kind of profession. That was okay with Alice. She made a lot of money, got to travel, and had no boss leaning over her shoulder. Not bad for a girl who had never known her dad and whose mom had abandoned her as a child. Thank God for Grandma.

Her grandmother was one of the reasons she worked so hard. She made sure the seventy-nine-year-old woman never had money problems. Her grandmother's luxury apartment in Rummelsburg was next to a park and only a block from the Spree River. Alice loved seeing her happy. If that meant having to put up with jerks like Henry and watch boring apartments in New York, that's what Alice would do.

Janos nudged her and said, "That's him walking in now."

Alice looked at the young man with his long, stringy hair in a ponytail. He also had an unfortunate receding hairline. He needed a woman to show him how to groom. That's what she always thought about men with ponytails or man buns.

Janos pulled the Czech-made 9mm and made sure there was a round in the chamber.

Getting a gun in the US wasn't too difficult, but Alice preferred a simple folding knife, or a garrote made from heavy-gauge electrical wire and a couple of plastic handles she could buy at any hardware store.

Janos turned to her and said, "Remember, Henry wants us to get this kid to work for him. No rough stuff unless he completely refuses our generous offer."

Alice smiled. She liked Janos. She felt they made an attractive couple, even though they didn't feel that way about each other. He was the classic lean but muscular, dark-haired Romanian. She felt it was a nice contrast to her curly blond hair. She was the one who could get in anywhere with just an innocent look and a tilt of her head.

Janos, who was a year younger than her at thirty-four, knew her too well. He may have been a wild partier, but he did catch on to patterns. He was interested in the bonus Henry had promised them.

Alice was more interested in efficiency. And maybe having a little fun with at least one of the nerds they were supposed to talk to. Maybe it could be this Tommy Payne.

Just thinking about it gave her a tingle of excitement.

CHAPTER 10

ALICE ASSESSED THE apartment building in the West Village. Washington Square was four blocks east. The famed New York University was also just blocks away. It was a nice building. Too nice for a student. Probably too nice for any young person working in Manhattan. That told her Tommy Payne was probably doing things he wasn't supposed to do with computers.

She couldn't have cared less. She just wanted this to move along quickly. She knocked gently on the freshly painted door. Everything about the building showed it was well maintained. She wasn't sure what rents went for in Greenwich Village, but this was a hell of a lot more than she paid for her grandmother's apartment.

She heard a male voice inside say, "Who is it?"

Alice said, "I have a message for Tommy." She tried to hide her accent and sound as young as possible.

The door didn't budge. Janos stood against the wall so if Tommy opened the door he wouldn't see him.

Tommy called through the door, "A message from who?"

Alice had an inspiration and said, "I'm not sure of her name." That always worked on men. This time was no different. She heard a chain, and then the door cracked open.

As soon as Tommy Payne saw the pretty blond woman in jeans and a colorful blouse, he opened the door wide.

That's when Janos stepped close and shoved the young man into the apartment.

Alice stepped inside. The apartment was dark. There was a distinct smell of old marijuana. Two sixty-inch Sony TVs hung side by side on the main wall. An array of computers and monitors sat on a long table on the opposite wall.

To his credit, Tommy didn't say a word. He lay on the hard-wood floor and looked up at Janos. Normally Alice would chalk that up to sexism, but Janos held the pistol. Anyone would look at the armed person in the room.

Alice tried the nice approach first. She kneeled down next to Tommy and traced her finger along his nose and lips. She smiled and said, "I'm sure you realize that Henry sent us."

Tommy was silent as he nodded his head. His eyes never left the gun in Janos's hand.

She slipped the plane ticket from her back pocket and set it on the coffee table. She leaned in close. "That's an airline ticket to Tallinn, Estonia, by way of Amsterdam. Your flight leaves tomorrow morning. I really think it would be in your best interest to help Henry out."

Now Tommy cut his eyes to Alice. He said, "I, um, I, I—"

Janos kicked him in the leg. "C'mon, you're not in a mariachi band."

"But I, I—"

That was enough for Janos. He shoved the pistol into Tommy's mouth. Alice could hear it crack a tooth on the way in.

The young computer genius's eyes opened so wide Alice thought one might pop out onto the floor. A whimper came from deep in his throat.

This could be messy.

Janos said, "I can't imagine what you do with these giant TVs. If you ever want to watch them again your only answer to us should be yes."

He slowly slid the pistol out of the young man's mouth. Before Tommy could answer, Janos jammed the barrel firmly on the young man's crotch. Janos said, "Maybe I underestimated you. TVs might not be what makes you tick. I saw you looking at Alice's beautiful breasts. I could teach you a lesson and you'd still be able to do whatever you nerds do on a keyboard."

Alice gently pushed the pistol away from the young man's groin. She replaced it with her hand. She wrapped her other arm around Tommy's shoulders and could feel him shaking.

She said in a soft voice in his ear, "Shhhhh, it's all right." Closer to his ear, she whispered, "I think you understand everything now. Isn't that right?"

Tommy just nodded.

Alice said, "That's good." Then she squeezed her hand on Tommy's scrotum. Pulling his loose Dockers tight as she crushed his testicles.

Tommy squealed. His back arched in agony.

Alice kept the same seductive voice as she whispered in his

ear, "That's to make sure you don't get any silly ideas. You'll be on that plane. You'll do what you're told. Or a broken TV set will be all you can pray for. Do you understand me?"

Tommy nodded his head vigorously.

She moved her hand before the urine staining his pants touched her. In the rear pocket of his pants she found his thick leather wallet. She playfully pulled it out, then she reached in her own pocket and pulled out a condom in a purple wrapper. Alice slid the condom into the wallet. She gave Tommy Payne a sweet smile and said, "If you're smart and you go to Estonia for Henry, you might get a chance to use this with me." She kissed him gently on the ear. Then Alice locked eyes with him to make sure he understood. He was too scared to smile or show any excitement.

Alice handed him the wallet and waited while he slid it back into his pocket. His hands were still shaking badly. He was clearly embarrassed about peeing in his pants. Who wouldn't be? Then again, who wouldn't be terrified if someone like Janos had a pistol against their groin?

Alice looked up at Janos and winked. They were a good team. They had made their point.

They might even have some time to sightsee.

CHAPTER 11

I FACED A brief wave of condemnation from the older kids when I banned TV for the night. Like a mutiny on a really lazy pirate ship. It's a fact that people occasionally try to murder police officers, a fact that's often forgotten when people talk about police shootings. It was something I didn't necessarily want my kids to see tonight.

It was bad enough that I was dreading going to bed. I knew what thoughts would be racing through my head as I lay in the dark and stared at the ceiling. I'd showered for twenty minutes and still felt like I could smell gunpowder. I didn't need to hear people comment on an incident they knew nothing about.

After the shower, I lay down on my bed in shorts and a T-shirt just to get a few minutes of quiet time. It was less than a few minutes. My youngest, Chrissy, crawled up on my left side, and Juliana, my oldest, flopped onto the bed on my right side. They both had books. Chrissy's was about kids looking for a treasure. Juliana's was a chemistry textbook.

Neither of them needed me to read. But they did realize I liked having my kids around. They didn't have to talk. They didn't have to work to make me feel better. They just had to be there.

When Maeve and I started adopting children at an alarming rate, I'm not sure I realized they were saving me and not the other way around. I admit, ten adopted kids seems a little over-the-top. But once I lost Brian to the state prison system, I realized ten was just the right number. He was still a hole in my life. One day that would be remedied.

Lying in bed with my two beautiful daughters reinforced my belief about what's important in life. I was never one of those guys who chased money or promotions at work. I didn't think it was important that the Giants won every football game. (Although it wouldn't hurt to win a few more.)

I knew how precious my family was, from the ever-forgiving and patient Mary Catherine to my surly yet supportive grandfather.

I felt myself start to relax with the girls next to me and lost track of time. It seemed like only a few minutes had passed when Mary Catherine walked in and clapped her hands. She said, "Enough of milking your bedtimes. You've got school tomorrow. Chop, chop, let's go."

Juliana didn't even make her usual argument, that she was a senior in high school and didn't really have a bedtime. They both gave me a good-night kiss on the cheek and scurried out of the room.

A few minutes later, Mary Catherine slipped into bed and

shut off the light. Frankly, it was the moment I'd been dreading all day. Awake and quiet in the dark.

Mary Catherine put that fear to rest when she rolled over and snuggled in next to me. All she said was "You doing all right?"

Without conscious thought, I blurted, "You know, we still need to set a date for our wedding. It's tough explaining to my grandfather how a good Catholic girl is living with me without the benefits of marriage."

"What brought that on?"

"I have no idea." Then, after a short silence, I said, "That's not true. I said it because I love you. I just don't know why I said it at this moment. Probably has something to do with the events of the day."

"Seamus and I think it was just God deciding it wasn't your time." Now she was the quiet one for almost a full minute. "Are you going to be in any trouble over this?"

"A cop who pulls the trigger is always in trouble of some kind. But if there were ever enough circumstances to justify a shooting, I think this one had them."

She gave me a squeeze and lifted her head to kiss me on the cheek. Then her lips moved to my mouth. Then I felt her tongue. She whispered something in my ear, but by then I was too far gone.

It turned out my fears were baseless. Mary Catherine made sure she kept my mind on other things.

CHAPTER 12

ALICE GROFF HAD her arm locked with Janos's arm as they gazed into the different shops of Penn Station. They'd looked at a perfume store and sniffed bouquets of flowers. She also made Janos stop near an all-too-American donut shop. She leaned her head on Janos's broad shoulder, to give the impression that they were a couple.

The reason they were shopping was that young Tommy Payne was sitting on a bench not far away, waiting for a train. Janos had been able to figure out that the young man had bought a ticket to some place called Hempstead. Alice wasn't sure where it was, but she knew it wasn't on the way to the airport to catch a flight. Like what she thought Tommy had agreed to. Disappointing.

She broke away from Janos, and he followed her. They casually walked past Tommy, then split up and sat on either side of him. He'd been in a daze, just staring at the floor, until he felt two bodies so close.

The young man was surprised at first, then hung his head when he realized there was no way out of this. He looked like a lost child who had given up.

Alice draped an arm across his shoulders and said, "We gave you a choice. I even gave you some incentive. What are you doing here?"

Tommy seemed to have gained some confidence since their earlier encounter. Maybe it was because they were in public.

He dropped his face into his hands and said, "Look, can't you just say you didn't find me?"

"We don't understand. Why don't you want a good-paying job?"

"You know why. I don't want to go to prison. Henry keeps moving out further and further from his original goals. It was fun to unleash government secrets on WikiLeaks. It made me feel like some kind of god, deciding what people could read about government. It was fun when we shut down Home Depot's credit card system for a day. But then Henry started blackmailing companies to pay him or he'd cut off their internet platforms for days at a time. Shit like that gets you in real trouble."

Janos said, "You don't think ignoring Henry gets you in real trouble?"

Tommy shook his head. "I can't believe you guys spent the whole day watching my apartment, then following me here. I'm not that important to Henry's operation. I'm just a programmer. He knows a dozen guys like me."

Alice laughed and patted him on the shoulder. She said, "Give me your wallet."

Tommy was beaten. At this point, he just casually reached into his pocket and handed it to her.

She opened it and pulled out the condom she had given him earlier. She held it up in front of his face.

Tommy mumbled, "Son of a bitch."

Alice chuckled. She said, "Don't feel bad. Most men fall for it. No one expects a little tracker inside a condom wrapper. They never look to see the thin line of tape holding the wrapper together. When Janos checked his phone forty-five minutes ago we saw you were here and thought we should chat one more time."

Tommy said, "I can't win. If I go to Estonia, I risk getting swept up in a big arrest. Or worse, when Henry is done with me, he'll have me killed and no one will ever hear from me again. He's changed so much from when we started. Now he thinks he's some sort of royalty and can order executions."

Alice didn't say it, but she agreed with Tommy. Henry was an egomaniac. He even tried to conceal his Estonian accent by using a fake English accent when he spoke English. She almost felt sorry for the young programmer. But she wasn't getting paid to have feelings.

She said, "You better come with us."

"Where?"

"I think we've answered all the questions we're going to. You need to understand that life's not fair. Sometimes you have to do things you don't want to. You're like all the other Americans I know. Spoiled. Spoiled and entitled. It's infuriating. You have never known hardship, so you whine about *anything* that happens.

"Europeans are more prepared for adversity. We have to

work together. You Americans are just brats who haven't learned any lessons in life."

She thought Tommy was about to say something, but after being called a whiner, he held his tongue.

He slowly rose to his feet and slouched like an old man as they made their way out to 34th Street. She kept window-shopping so they didn't look like police leading a prisoner.

For his part, Tommy Payne just shuffled along silently.

CHAPTER 13

IT WAS A quiet night, at least for New York. They turned down Seventh Avenue and kept walking. Tommy was still silent.

Janos didn't look like he was paying attention, but Alice knew better. His hand rested on the butt of his pistol and he was aware of every step the young programmer took.

Alice enjoyed the walk. The weather was perfect. She liked seeing the tall buildings. She liked visiting a couple of tourist attractions in every city they visited. In San Francisco, she was disappointed in Fisherman's Wharf. In London, she loved riding the London Eye, especially because the height made Janos nervous.

So far on this trip she had dragged her partner to the Statue of Liberty, St. Patrick's Cathedral, and the Chrysler Building. If they had more time, Rockefeller Center and the Empire State Building were next on her agenda.

At the moment, she had her arm locked through Tommy's so they looked like a couple. Janos was perfectly happy to stroll a few steps behind them in case Tommy did something stupid.

But Alice didn't see the computer genius making too many stupid mistakes. He was, after all, a genius. He was also smart enough to know that working for Henry was a dead end. Alice was only doing it on contract. She didn't think she'd be doing it again.

After they turned again onto a numbered street, Janos rushed ahead of them for a moment and motioned them into a narrow parking lot between a large parking structure and a small Italian restaurant called La something. Many letters were missing from the sign. Tommy showed no reluctance to turn in to the dark lot, where a row of cars were parked on top of each other in a heavy-duty rack.

At the far end of the rack, half a block in from the main street, they stopped and Janos turned Tommy toward him. Janos said, "Dude, why didn't you listen to us?"

Tommy didn't answer.

Janos said, "I did use the word 'dude' properly, didn't I?"

Tommy just nodded.

"You're never going to come around to our way of thinking, are you?" Janos gave him a little smile and patted him on the shoulder to get him to relax.

Tommy shook his head. "No, no, I'll never think working for Henry again is a good idea."

Janos said, "That's too bad. That's too bad, dude." He smiled at his use of the American slang.

Alice knew it was also his signal. She was standing directly behind the computer hacker. He was just an inch or two taller than her, so it was no problem to loop her wire garrote around his throat. It was as clean as she had ever done it, over his head and dropping onto his chest under his throat without a single hitch. It was so fast and smooth that she doubted Tommy even knew what was going on.

She gripped the plastic handles attached to either end of the wire, crossed her hands, and used all of her strength, from her lats through her chest, to tug the wire tight around the young man's throat.

She heard his surprised gasp. Or partial gasp, as the wire cut off his wind.

Janos took a step back. Ever since he had been sprayed with blood when a wire cut a target's carotid artery, the Romanian was always careful to keep his distance. He could be a diva sometimes. He preferred to use a gun.

She couldn't see Tommy's face, but she knew his eyes would've rolled up in his head. His hands flailed at his throat. It was too late. It was *always* too late. Once she had the garrote around someone's throat, they never got away.

He gurgled and Alice knew it was almost done. This was the most exciting part. She kept steady pressure on the garrote.

She had a tinge of regret, because he was cute, in a nerdy kind of way. But they'd already wasted enough time. She hated to be fooled twice by the same person.

She kept the pressure on until his body started to sag. One knee dropped to the filthy asphalt. She took a second to glance in every direction. No one was close by.

He finally stopped moving completely, hanging in the air with his arms dangling almost to the asphalt. His head drooped forward, and a line of spittle mixed with blood dribbled out of his mouth, but Alice did her traditional ten count, just to be sure.

Janos was still in front of her. He nodded, she released the wire, then she pulled it away from Tommy Payne's lifeless body. Janos pushed Tommy next to the restaurant wall, behind the racks of cars. His throat was raw and lacerated, but not ripped open. Alice liked it when things went that way. She wasn't big on a lot of blood.

They walked quickly in the opposite direction they had come from. Janos put an arm around Alice's shoulders to make it look more casual. He said, "You okay?"

She worked her shoulders and said, "Sometimes that's more of a workout than I expect. Did you get the photos?"

Janos let out a laugh and said, "I like how you always think about business. I got the photos and will send them to Henry whenever you want."

Alice said, "Did you figure out the next target on our list?"

"We can start first thing in the morning."

Alice smiled and felt a little more spring in her step.

CHAPTER 14

WHEN YOU'RE USED to getting up early for work every morning, you don't change just because you're on suspension. Like any officer-involved shooting, mine was under investigation, and standard procedure dictated that I could not go in to work. I read that to mean that I could not work at the *office*.

Having gotten out of bed early, I thought I might as well do something useful. I had a couple of ideas. As long as no one found out, I figured I'd be okay.

I heard Chrissy talking in a weird voice and poked my head into her bedroom. She was on a yoga mat, trying to model a downward dog pose for our cat Socky.

I asked, "What cha doing, beautiful?"

She didn't change position. "I was wondering if a cat could learn a dog position. It's really more of a science experiment."

I chuckled and said, "You keep up the good work in the name of science, but be ready to leave in a few minutes."

Jane, one of my high schoolers, struggled with a three-foot-by-two-foot folder and her regular textbooks.

"What's this?"

Jane acted like it wasn't awkward to hold the giant folder. "My portfolio for art class, with Bridget's help. I thought I'd do a retrospective of fashion since the nineties."

I said, "Wow, all the way back to the nineties. How'd you even find photos from back then?"

"Funny, Dad."

I thought it was.

I walked past the small TV in the kitchen with the sound off. I knew what the story was just by the image. The Reverend Franklin Caldwell was standing behind a mound of microphones. I didn't need to turn up the sound to know he was screaming for my head.

I kissed Mary Catherine, who was straightening up the mass of dishes following the feeding frenzy known as breakfast. The kids were scattered around the apartment, getting ready for school.

I said, "I'll go get the van. Tell the kids to meet me out front."

"You don't have to drive them. I can do it today."

"What else do I have to do? Besides, I have a few errands to run later. My city car is at the office. I'm not supposed to drive it on suspension anyway."

She caressed my face with her hand. "Have a cup of coffee and relax. Watch TV for a change."

I looked at the silent screen displaying Reverend Caldwell and decided I wouldn't be following her advice today. "I'll go get the van."

Going down in the elevator, I kept telling myself to make this a normal day. It felt right so far. I usually caught the shift change of the doormen at this time of morning. They were both army vets, regular guys doing a regular job, and I enjoyed hearing their stories. I appreciated their humor and perspectives.

They were standing together out front on the sidewalk when I came through the door. I had surprised them; otherwise one of them would have jumped to open the door. But they greeted me like an old beer buddy.

"Hey, Mike," called the larger of the two men. He was about fifty-five and still hit the gym every day.

The other man, Lou, was a little younger and not nearly in as good shape. Lou held out his hand and said, "I'm glad you're safe."

I said, "Thanks," as I shook his hand. It was always awkward after a shooting. People never knew how to react.

We all chatted for a few moments. Then the taller man, Johnny, said, "Mike, what really happened yesterday?"

"I'm not sure what you mean."

"I don't want to sound like an asshole, but did you really *need* to shoot that kid?"

I briefly considered an answer, then just walked toward the van. What can you say to a question like that? I guess I didn't really *need* to shoot RJ. I could've let him shoot me in the face. Then I wouldn't have to answer stupid questions.

When I got to the van I realized I hadn't answered any stupid questions. I had just walked away.

Son of a gun, is this what maturity felt like?

CHAPTER 15

SOMEHOW ALL THE kids were waiting out front when I pulled up in the van. Johnny, the doorman, couldn't look me in the face when I stopped at the curb. I'd said stupid things before. I knew how he felt. I wasn't going to make it any worse. But I wasn't going to make it any easier, either.

The kids filed in as always: youngest in the back, leading up to the oldest in the most comfortable, forward seats. You see, when you have so many kids, you can't leave things to chance. You buy a big-ass van, like this Ford Super Duty twelve-passenger monster, and then assign seats. It was a microcosm of the country. When you allow for too much choice, it always leads to some form of chaos.

For a change, we weren't racing the 8:45 deadline at Holy Name. Sister Helen, who had been taking over more of the early morning duties, looked shocked to see the van pull up almost six minutes early. A new record!

She even walked over to the van and leaned in the door as the kids scooted past her. "And how are you this morning, Michael?"

"Fine, Sister Helen. And you?"

"Like everyone else around here, thanking God you're safe." She wandered off without another word to me. It may have been the sweetest thing anyone from a Catholic school had said to me since I was six years old.

It gave me a little jolt to get my day started.

I burned up my phone on my ride north. After I stashed the van in a parking lot in Washington Heights, I had my first meeting in a Starbucks. I hate the chain restaurants and coffee-houses. I also hate that I like Starbucks coffee. But I had to go where people were willing to talk to me, and this was where Detective Teresita Hernandez wanted to meet. The eight-year veteran was waiting for me as I stepped through the front door, sitting alone at a two-person high-top in the corner, where no one would hear us.

As I approached, she slid a cup across the small, round table. She smiled as she said, "I remember old goats like you prefer simple black coffee."

I had to laugh. She'd come a long way from a rookie detective in Manhattan North Homicide five years ago.

We caught up for a few minutes. She was working on her master's degree in public administration at City College. Picturing Teresita on a college campus, I laughed at the idea of some young undergrad hitting on her. He'd think he was trying to impress a beautiful coed with long, dark hair, and she'd be deciding whether to break him in half like a pretzel.

Teresita had been my muscle sometimes when she worked

in our squad. No street criminal worth his salt would ever admit that a female had roughed him up. Tough and fearless, she'd left one of the best jobs in the department because she believed she could make more of a difference in the Bronx.

It was probably true. And I respected it.

I said, "Your dad must be glad you're working on a master's degree."

She shrugged. "He wanted me to join him in his accounting firm. But he sees what a difference a good cop can make, so he's supportive. Quietly. Real quietly."

Finally we got around to business when I said, "I don't want to get you in any trouble, Terri. Thanks for meeting me."

She waved me off. "How can I get in trouble when I'm not on duty yet and this isn't an official meeting?" She waited a moment and added, "See? I learned a lot from you in Homicide. Besides, you saved my ass plenty of times."

"To be clear, I'm trying to help on the homicide of the nurse and her daughter. Even though I saw the suspect during my own shooting incident."

"The Bronx is getting stirred up about it. The Reverend Caldwell has been banging the drum pretty hard."

I said, "I can see why he would. A white cop shoots a black resident."

Terri laughed. "The reverend doesn't see black and white. When something like this happens, he only sees green. You can't believe how much money he collects. I heard he also gets a cut of any negotiated settlement."

I moved back to what I was interested in. "You ever heard of a guy with the street name Tight?"

She shrugged, then took a quick look around the room. It

was a police habit, but she was also making sure no one could hear us. "Just from our Homicide guys. They say he's a possible suspect in our nasty double. The report I read said you gave the detectives the name after your shooting. From the description, he sounds like an oxy addict. And crazy. Scary crazy."

"So you don't know him?"

"No. And I haven't been able to find out anything about him. I don't know if it's from fear or that he moves around a lot. He's not clearly visible in the footage of your shooting. He stayed off to the side. Then there's a blurry image as he backed away from you and tried to pull his gun."

That surprised me. "There's video of my shooting?"

"Yeah, but you can't tell anyone. I was only allowed to see it because I'm helping with the mother-daughter homicide. But the footage is pretty clear. The guy you shot, Ronald Timmons Junior, had the drop on you. You showed good tactics. You should teach."

I laughed out loud and said, "No one ever has suggested that before."

Terri said, "Teach tactics, not tact. Or attitude. Or procedures—"

"I get it, I get it."

"Or respect for command. Or…"

I left the Starbucks smiling.

CHAPTER 16

MY NEXT MEETING was a few blocks away. It wasn't at a Starbucks. I saw the man waiting for me in Convent Garden on 151st Street. It was just cool enough that some of the remarkable flowers the place was known for were not blooming, and the wooden gazebo was empty. This should be a quick, casual meeting.

I approached the skinny African American man from the opposite end of the park. He stood in the shadow of a tree in a corner. I wanted to give him a chance to look around and to see me clearly. Maybe I was getting a little paranoid, but informants were not known for their loyalty. And there'd been more and more ambushes of police officers across the country.

His lanky frame leaned against a section of the tall metal fence that surrounded the park. The way he scratched his arm and shuffled back and forth on his feet made me realize he wasn't using. Sometimes that was good and sometimes it was bad; I could never tell how it affected the information provided.

He noticed me. His eyes darted all around the park and the bits of street that could be seen beyond the bushes. He didn't want to be seen talking to me, and I couldn't blame him. No informant wants to be seen talking to a cop. Especially a cop whose face has been plastered all over the news.

He looked nervous, but then again he always did.

I said, "Hey, Flash, you doin' okay?" I had never asked him how he got his street name. I probably didn't want to know. It was my hope he was just a fast runner.

He merely nodded and scratched his neck with both hands. He looked frantic.

I said, "Can't score anywhere?"

He said, "Does it look like I scored? Everyone come down so hard on pain pills, can't find nothin'. H is easier to score. Don't make no sense."

I liked that he was comfortable enough with me to discuss felonies. But if cops only dealt with Boy Scouts as informants, nothing would ever get done. It wasn't the seventies and I wasn't in Narcotics, so I wouldn't let him shoot up even if he had some. It was a tough part of the job that no one ever talked about: dealing with informants meant you were dealing with criminals and drug users.

I said, "Did you find out anything about the guy named Tight?"

"Could be I know him. Skinny as me. A little shorter. Dude's wrapped way too tight. That's how he got his street name." He ran a hand over his close-cropped hair, then scratched it.

He dug in his ear, too. I waited as he inspected whatever had come from his ear.

I said, "Real name?"

He shrugged his narrow shoulders. "Who knows?" His brown eyes took another look around the green space. "I seen him around. He likes the pills just like me. He hit 'em a lot harder than I do. Says it's his medicine."

I didn't think I had to add that technically it *was* medicine. It was just that people like him had ruined a useful tool for people in pain.

I said, "You know anything that could help me find this Tight?"

Flash shook his head.

We stood in an awkward silence until he said, "Ain't you goin' to ask me about the kid you shot? Ronald Timmons Junior?"

"Nope. Separate investigation. I'm just a subject in that one."

"The Reverend Caldwell sees it different. He's got everyone in the Bronx thinking you just kilt that boy. I knew RJ. He wasn't a bad kid."

"He made a bad choice."

"The good reverend says you're a killer."

I thought, *At least I'm not dead.* It was hard for anyone to understand a police shooting. Cops make mistakes. They're human. But they also have to deal with something like fifty thousand assaults a year. How many of those would result in police fatalities if not for training? No one would ever convince the Reverend Caldwell of that line of reasoning.

I walked out of Convent Garden feeling down again.

CHAPTER 17

HARRY GRISSOM WAS curt on the phone. He said he'd pick me up at my apartment in twenty minutes. I told him I needed forty-five to get ready. Really, I needed to race home and act like I hadn't done any unauthorized investigations today.

Harry was his usual gruff self when I slid into the front seat of his Suburban. "No questions. No smart-ass comments. And show some respect."

I had to ask, "Where are we going?"

"What did I just tell you? Enjoy the ride."

"That's what they used to tell inmates on their way to Sing Sing."

"That's a good metaphor. Even if you just made it up."

That didn't make me feel any better as we drove south on West Street. Like a little kid, to make sure I didn't ask stupid questions, I tried to occupy myself. I guessed where we were going. We had passed the building that housed the DEA, which eliminated one choice.

Of course One Police Plaza was the most likely stop. That's where the big brass could really lay into me if they thought it might help their position. The public opinion shift on cops was slow to sweep over the profession. But now that it had, some politically minded managers would do anything to make the department look better. That could mean sacrificing a detective like me. Oh, they'd say it was based on facts and evidence, but I'd know better. And there would be little I could do about it.

This line of thought raised my anxiety. A lot. Now I was nervous.

Then Harry turned east on Chambers Street and I knew we were headed to One Police Plaza. All the thoughts I'd just had seemed to be coming true. Then he surprised me by taking a right on Broadway and pulling into the City Hall complex.

"What's going on, Harry?" I could tell he was considering what he should tell me. "I feel like I'm headed to a firing squad."

We passed through security and Harry pulled into a spot right by City Hall. He turned to me and said, "You're going to be cleared on the shooting. We've got the suspect's pistol and two casings. We have security video from the bodega that shows everything. Forensics all check out. Plus, everyone knows you're not a rookie. But IA and the officials here wanted to make sure everything was done right and covered properly."

I felt like a weight had been lifted off my chest. I wanted to kiss Harry right on the cheek. I didn't care what kind of stubble he had.

I said, "That's great. When can I get back to work? I've got a lot to catch up on." Tight was the main thing on my mind. I had to find the skinny psychopath and get the truth about the murder of the nurse and her daughter. The image of the crime scene was burned into my memory. And Mrs. Evans breaking down and crying at her sons' apartment would never leave my head. It was the best motivation a cop could have.

"Can you run me by the office to get my car?"

"Slow down, Mike. It's a complicated situation. The mayor's office has some concerns about how the public would view a return so quick."

"You mean it's politics."

"You can call it anything you want, but we have a meeting in here right now. You're going to talk to the mayor himself."

"The LFP! No shit."

"If I get the sense you're even thinking of saying the words 'little fat prick,' I will personally throw your kids' cat off the balcony and let you deal with the chaos."

"You'd do that to Socky?"

"After I did it to you."

Normally I'd think that was kind of a funny comment. Coming from Harry Grissom it felt more like a realistic threat.

I recognized a couple of cops in uniform. They all patted me on the back or shoulder. It wasn't the kind of greeting I usually got. But what they were really saying was they were glad I was alive, even if it meant someone else was dead.

We took the stairs to the third floor and turned down a long corridor. We stopped at an office with a sign that said OFFICE OF THE MAYOR, COMMUNICATIONS.

I started to ask Harry why we were here.

He shut me up with just a look.

He knocked once, then opened the door.

There were three people in the large, plush office. A woman stepped up and offered her hand.

"I'm Carol Tedesco, director of communications." She was polished and professional. She looked like she could be TV-ready at any moment.

The thin man in wire-rimmed glasses didn't bother to stand up straight from the table he was leaning on. He just waved and said, "Clark Higson, assistant to the mayor."

Then the other man stepped over to me and offered a pudgy paw. He said, "Alfred Hanna. Nice to meet you."

He wasn't quite as short as I'd thought he would be.

CHAPTER 18

ALFRED HANNA HAD slipped into the mayor's office by the thinnest of margins. Every cop in the city used the term *LFP*, for *little fat prick*, to refer to him. I had even heard *LFP* used on the radio. Since his election, he had managed to piss off virtually all city workers, the Puerto Rican population, Staten Island residents, and even tourists, when he'd referred to a group from Arkansas touring City Hall as "a bunch of rednecks." Nothing anyone else in the city wouldn't have said. But the mayor was held to a higher standard. Barely.

In short, Alfred Hanna was a true New Yorker.

He ran a nervous hand over his slicked-back, dark hair. A long blue tie did little to cover his extended belly. He looked a little like a chipmunk in an Armani suit.

He reached up to put his arm across my shoulders. "We need

to keep this meeting as quiet as possible. That's why we're not in my office. Is that understood?"

Both Harry and I mumbled, "Yes, sir."

He released me and turned to face all of us. He looked at me and said, "I'm very proud of your service to the city. I'm sorry you got put in a position like you did. I know you acted well within policy and did everything you could not to shoot that young man."

I didn't get excited at his little speech. Anyone could tell there was a *but* coming. Harry gave me a really good *command stare* to keep me quiet.

Mayor Hanna continued. "The problem is that the Timmons family is quite popular. The fact that they brought in Reverend Caldwell means they're not going to listen to the results of any investigation. They're also not going to disappear. That means you returning to your regular job would not only look bad for the city, it also could be dangerous for you."

I said, "You don't think a cop's job is dangerous anyway?" I hadn't meant to put the edge in my voice.

"Okay, *more* dangerous than usual. Look, my grandfather on my mother's side was a cop in Queens. I understand the hardships you guys go through."

It surprised me the mayor had a family member who'd been a cop, but it didn't surprise me that he actually thought he knew. Everyone thought they understood the job.

The mayor said, "I don't want to send the wrong message to our city's police officers. I don't want them to step back. I don't advocate less proactive policing. I also don't think you should have to go back to work looking over your shoulder for a retribution attack. Not when we have an alternative."

I said, "So what's this alternate plan you're talking about?"

"Like I said, anything talked about in this room stays here." He turned his bowling-ball head to look at each of us individually. Everyone agreed.

The mayor looked right at me and said, "I've heard that, among your many talents, you know how to find people."

"I've located a few fugitives."

"This is a missing person."

"Why don't you have our Missing Persons Squad look into it?"

"Because it's my daughter."

CHAPTER 19

I READ THE mayor's expression, almost like I would a homicide suspect during an interview. He was uncomfortable. I looked across the office at the only one who might understand what I was seeing.

Harry just shrugged and shifted his eyes to the door in the back of the office.

I said, "Maybe we can speak more freely in private."

The mayor, who was clearly shaken, turned to the door that Harry had pointed out. He motioned for his aides to stay in this office, and I followed his odd gait.

The other room was a small conference room with a table big enough for about six people. A giant portrait of the late former mayor Fiorello La Guardia filled the upper half of one wall. Every mayor wanted to be like La Guardia. Except Ed Koch, who had seemed pretty happy being himself. A window looked down on the parking lot. I could just see the top of Harry's Suburban.

The mayor and I settled into leather chairs at one corner of the table. I gave him a moment to collect himself, then said gently, "Do you want to tell me about your daughter? I thought you only had two young boys."

He took a moment, then said, "Natalie is from my first marriage. It ended in a divorce—a messy, public divorce. Natalie even uses her mother's maiden name of Lunden. It was my fault. Not only the divorce but allowing it to be so public. It cost me an election as an alderman." He took another moment and added, "I've changed. More than anyone can believe, especially my ex-wife and daughter. I read that you have daughters yourself."

"Six."

"Good lord."

"And four boys."

"Oh, my God. I haven't heard of a Catholic family like that since I was a kid. Back then every neighborhood had two or three families with eight-plus kids. How do you manage?"

"First of all, I am Catholic, but all my kids are adopted. And second, I don't manage anything. We're a family. We all work together. Kinda the way it's supposed to be with the city. Everyone works for the greater good."

"If only. No matter how we come down on a decision, there's always about half the population that's pissed off. I like the idea in principle, but in reality you have a unique family."

"You have no idea."

"I envy you, Detective. You know what's important and appreciate it. I learned that lesson a little late in life. Now I just hope it's not too late." He took a moment to wipe his eyes with an embroidered handkerchief. "Let me show you my Natalie."

He held up his phone. A photo of a smiling brunette in a cap and gown filled the screen. A tall woman, who I assumed was her mother, held an arm around her shoulders, and the mayor stood off at a distance, smiling.

He said, "This was her high school graduation. She was on her way to MIT a few months later. She was a computer prodigy. Even as a child, she learned to change the code on programs to fit her needs. She's amazing."

I thought of Eddie. Would I be able to afford MIT? Would he get a scholarship? I had a number of kids to get through college. I hoped I could figure out a way.

The mayor continued. "Natalie went off the rails a little bit. Her grades dropped. She was more interested in pushing the envelope than learning the basics of computer science. She started to party more. She and I grew more distant. She got bounced out of MIT. A few months ago she enrolled in City College, but it didn't last."

I listened and all I heard was an anguished father. I didn't hear the politician I saw on TV regularly. I didn't see the man cops grumbled about every single day.

The mayor wiped his eyes again with his bare thumb, then said, "Now she's twenty-one. No one has heard from her in three weeks. Her mother's frantic. Frantic enough to ask *me* for help. Some of her friends say she fell in with some hackers. I don't know, but I'm scared."

Now I was in familiar territory, talking to a frightened parent. I could deal with this. I understood this. I said, "It'll be okay, Mr. Mayor. We'll find her."

His eyes were rimmed red when he looked up. His voice was much softer. He said, "Really? You think so?"

"Yes." I really did.

The mayor sniffled. He said, "I might be able to help you, Detective."

"How so?" This was always treacherous. People who thought they could help you also thought they could crush you if things didn't go the way they wanted.

"If you find my daughter, I might be able to help you with your son Brian. I know about his unfortunate situation. I could make some calls, see what happens." He looked at me as if he expected me to say something. Then he added, "Just one father helping another."

CHAPTER 20

IT TOOK A little time to get everything together. I rode with Harry to pick up my car. On the way, he had one of his little talks with me. He called them "talks"; the squad called them "lectures." Either way, we had learned it was stupid to ignore Harry's advice.

He said, "You need to stay under the radar. It doesn't help anyone if they know you're already back on the job. You had a tough break. You had to shoot that kid. I know the feeling. Things will get better. Eventually smart people look past the crazy public outcries and examine the evidence and investigations. The mayor has just given you a shortcut to get back on the street. Don't blow it."

Who could refute such deep wisdom as "Don't blow it"?

When I walked into the office, Terri Hernandez sat at the once-empty desk next to mine.

I said, "What are you doing slumming down here?"

"Temporary duty assignment. Supposed to fill in for some old geezer who was on suspension. I guess that didn't last long."

"I've gone from suspension into exile."

"What happened?"

"Moved to a missing persons case. Low-key, low profile, and low probability of excitement."

"So you're cleared in the shooting?"

"Not officially."

"Who are you looking for?"

"Not supposed to talk about it."

"Even to me? You used to tell me everything."

"Wish I could, but I made a promise."

"You and your promises. One day you'll promise someone too much and it'll get you in hot water."

"That was probably today."

Terri smiled. "I believe in you. Hell, even my dad asks about you."

I smiled. "How's Ramon?"

"Irascible as ever."

"He's a smart man. Listen to him. What's he always say, 'Marry rich and as many times as needed'?"

"Actually, he likes to say, 'Marry a rich old man. Repeat if necessary.' That's coming from a man who's been married thirty-eight years."

"Some guys are lucky."

Not long after grabbing a few things from the office and trading jabs with Terri Hernandez, I was in the neighborhood of Natalie Lunden's apartment near NYU. This was a younger neighborhood with an interesting vibe. The students from NYU mixed with young professionals and the occasional stockbroker from the financial district. The area was loaded with mom-and-pop restaurants and that made me realize I hadn't eaten. I don't know if it was the relief of being back at work, but I was suddenly famished.

I swung a few blocks out of my way to the Burger & Barrel. It was a little nicer and more expensive than my usual lunch places. But, I reasoned, it was well after lunch; if I didn't have some protein immediately, I might faint. Sometimes I'm dramatic even to myself.

The sports bar sat right on Houston Street and looked a little touristy but was known by the locals for its burgers. I wouldn't call it a cop hangout, but cops liked eating there. Service was decent and the burgers outstanding.

One of the TVs above the bar had the news on instead of ESPN. I didn't pay much attention until the camera cut away to a shot outside some city administration buildings. I saw the Reverend Caldwell speaking into a microphone like he was addressing a crowd of thousands. It took even me a moment to realize it was simply a one-on-one interview with a local reporter. All I heard him say was "And now a murderer is walking free among us. Are the streets really safe?"

The older African American man behind the counter walked past the TV and absently switched it to Fox Sports 1. I didn't even mind the negative story about the Giants' offensive woes. Anything was better than hearing the tubby reverend call me names in public.

In my notepad, I looked at the list of several names the mayor had come up with of Natalie's friends. A kid named Tom Payne, a woman named Chang, and a couple of other names. All of them supposedly computer people.

I wolfed down my burger and even considered adding a beer to my tab. I stuck to a Coke and gathered my notes together.

I caught the attention of the bartender. He was older than I'd thought. Maybe in his early seventies. But he looked good. Like an in-shape grandpa.

I said, "Can I grab my bill?"

He shook his head. "You don't get a bill. Thank you for your service."

Holy cow, did I need to hear something like that about now. I laid a ten-dollar tip on the bar. I was a little choked up and couldn't speak. That surprised me.

The bartender said, "This too shall pass. That's what they told me when I came back from Vietnam. No one gave a damn about me. I remember walking through East Harlem in my uniform and someone threw a tomato at me. Another woman called me a baby killer. But they all came around. It may have taken twenty-five years, but people finally understood that we were just doing our duty. You'll see. The same attitude will come around about cops. In the meantime, stay safe."

I had to shake the man's hand before I headed over to Natalie Lunden's apartment.

CHAPTER 21

I USED THE key the mayor had given me to slip into Natalie's apartment. I took a run-through quickly to make sure no one was home. It would be embarrassing to discover her asleep in her bed. Stranger things have happened. Kids are called in missing all the time who end up being exactly where they're supposed to be.

I had a case when I was in the Bronx of a missing three-year-old. The call came in at about four in the afternoon. The mom was frantic. She was also suspicious of her boyfriend. I made a cursory check of the apartment, then went looking for the boyfriend.

I found him in a sports bar near Yankee Stadium. He had an attitude that was infuriating. He said, "Why you bothering me about that brat? He's Valerie's problem, not mine."

I thought he was lying. I asked him where the boy might go or what interested him. The man ignored me, watching a Yankees–Red Sox game on TV.

No way I wanted to waste time. Every minute counted with a missing child. I wanted to threaten him or scare him in some way. He'd spent a year in Rikers, awaiting trial on a robbery, and been arrested half a dozen times over the years. I couldn't threaten much that would scare him.

Then I had another idea. I'd let others threaten him. I took the remote from the bar and changed all the TVs at the same time to HGTV. The reaction was understandably outrage.

I said in a loud voice, "I'll turn the game back on as soon as this man answers my questions about a missing boy. A three-year-old. So you need to decide if it's easier to take the remote from me or make him talk." I noticed all the eyes in the place fall on the boyfriend.

Someone said, "Why won't you help someone looking for a missing kid?" That was the nicest thing said.

Quickly, the boyfriend realized the danger he was in and jumped up to tell me that his girlfriend's sister always took the boy without telling anyone. She felt like the boy was more hers than her sister's.

Twenty minutes later, I was back at the apartment, asking about the mom's sister, Crystal Fuches. According to the mom, Crystal was, let's just say, *untrustworthy*. They clearly didn't get along.

I found Crystal Fuches two blocks away. She was nothing like her sister had made her out to be. She was a bank teller who was concerned about her nephew. She took him some afternoons to give him a healthy meal and read to him. I was impressed.

She said, "I'm surprised my sister and her no-good boyfriend even noticed he was missing."

"To be fair, only your sister missed him. She seems nice. Just in a difficult situation."

"A situation she constantly puts herself in."

"Have you seen your nephew?"

"Of course. I put him to bed an hour ago. My sister never looked up from her phone."

When I rushed back to the apartment and checked the boy's room, he was snoring, bundled in his blankets.

That's why I always check every room in an apartment more than once during an investigation.

Natalie's apartment looked fine. A little messy, but it was a typical twenty-one-year-old's apartment. Except that she had no roommates. That was unusual down here where an apartment like this regularly went for more than four thousand dollars a month.

The quick background I had done on Natalie and her mother hadn't shown any large incomes. I knew the mayor was proud of coming "from the people." He lived on the mayor's two-hundred-thousand-dollar salary. That sounded like a lot of money, but in New York, even when you were living for free in Gracie Mansion, it didn't get you that far.

There was no super in the building, so I called the leasing office. I explained to the property manager who I was and that I was looking for a missing person. The woman on the phone sounded helpful, and I found the office a few blocks away.

The woman who met me at the office, Renee Schobert, was about my age and very well put together, in a professional dress with a colorful scarf. Her sandy hair draped down her right shoulder.

Renee ushered me into her office, crammed with file cabinets. She said, "I pulled out Natalie's file after you called. There's nothing out of order or unusual. Except her deposit and six full months of rent were paid at the same time."

I said, "So you don't know her personally? Didn't ever visit the apartment?"

She shook her head, then slid the open file across to me. She said, "The entire amount was wired here from Danske Bank in Tallinn, Estonia."

I glanced at the wire transfer and wrote down the information on the bank. The address was Narva Maantee 11, 15015 Tallinn, Estonia. I wasn't sure what this meant, but I knew it was important. It was one of those gut feelings cops on TV always seem to have. They only came to me occasionally. It took me years to recognize them and longer to trust those kinds of feelings.

Just as I was finishing my notes, Renee Schobert looked closely at me and said, "Oh, my God, you're the cop who's been on TV. The one who shot that kid in the Bronx."

I nodded, hoping to get out of there quickly.

She said, "How could you shoot an unarmed boy like that?"

I could've explained to her what happened. I could've told her not to listen to some of the things she hears on TV. But I had a job to do. And I thanked God that I had something to keep me occupied. That way I didn't focus on the exact question she had asked.

I thanked her and slipped out of the office quickly.

CHAPTER 22

I WAS GLAD to be home just as it was getting dark. I decided to play down anything I was doing, officially or otherwise. Mary Catherine still felt I needed a break, and, yeah, I was too chickenshit to tell her I was back at work full-time.

Hiding exactly what I was doing at work didn't turn out to be a problem. Mary Catherine met me in the hallway as soon as I walked in. The way she hugged me, I knew something was up.

I stepped back to look her in the eyes and said, "Tell me what's wrong." After you've lost a wife to cancer and you've dealt with the problems of ten kids, you rarely have time for people to beat around the bush. Not that Mary Catherine ever did.

She came right to the point, as usual. "Some of the younger kids are upset. They were teased at school. Excuse my French, but that asshole, the Reverend Caldwell, stuck a microphone in Jane's face and asked her if you felt any guilt at all."

That hurt. Any parent will tell you they would take any amount of abuse so their kids wouldn't have to.

I said, "Is Jane upset? What did she say?"

Then Mary Catherine let a smile slide across her beautiful face. "She used a few words that we don't allow in this house and the nuns at Holy Name would usually frown upon. Only in this case, Sister Sheilah backed her up. She looked at the reverend and said, 'Let's see you use that quote on TV, you jackass.'"

I couldn't help but laugh.

Mary Catherine said, "It was quite the scandal at school today. Things have quieted down now."

Trent saw me and rushed over to give me a hug. He looked up at me with that sweet face and said, "Michael Sedecki and some of his friends said you were a racist."

"That seems like an odd thing to say to you."

"I pointed out to them that I'm black and I have a black sister, a Korean sister, and a Hispanic sister. They said it didn't matter. Then they said I was com-compli..."

Mary Catherine offered, "Complicit?"

Trent said, "Yeah. Exactly. What's that mean, anyway?"

I said, "It means the kids were just being stupid." I kissed him on his head and hugged him. Nothing I had seen as a cop had ever affected me like the smallest injury to my children. Physically or emotionally.

When Trent hustled away to do his homework, I said to Mary Catherine, "Now, what exactly happened with the Reverend Caldwell?"

"Sister Sheilah dealt with him."

I laughed out loud. No one had ever crossed Sheilah twice. At least not by choice.

Mary Catherine snuggled in close to me and wrapped her arms around my midsection. "This will be like a vacation. I can have you all to myself tomorrow."

I said, "I, ummm…"

She stepped back to look at me.

I blurted, "I'll be back at work full-time tomorrow." I held my breath.

Mary Catherine didn't say a word. That was worse than anything else she could say or do. I was in real trouble.

CHAPTER 23

I WAS STUCK. I knew better than to chase after Mary Catherine immediately. She needed to calm down. Not that I would ever say that aloud. She once told me she felt it was in her DNA to blow up, then take a short time to calm down. This was a textbook example of one of those times.

I ducked into the dining room, where Eddie, Ricky, Trent, and the twins, Fiona and Bridget, were all in various stages of homework. The long dining room table served multiple purposes. With ten kids, any house or apartment would feel like one of those tiny houses on TV.

A big rule in our house: homework was to be done before dinner unless there were extenuating circumstances. That included basketball practices, dance lessons, and after-school meetings. But not TV or playing on a cell phone.

This was a rare night, with none of those things occurring. All the kids greeted me with smiles and waves. I was rarely much help with their very specific homework assignments, but I was great for moral support.

I sat on the couch and knew better than to turn on the news. I gazed out the wide windows to catch a glimpse of the Hudson River.

Chrissy hopped onto the couch next to me. She didn't say anything. Just smiled and started reading a book, about a young girl who volunteered after 9/11. I liked to see her read non-fiction books occasionally.

I could tell when she was really concentrating and when she was faking it. When concentrating, her brow furrowed. She could really focus. When she was faking it, her eyes darted around the room and she finished a page every six minutes.

I said, "What's wrong, pumpkin?"

"I don't feel like doing my reading for today. I keep trying, but I just can't get excited about it."

"Do you like the book?"

"Oh, yeah. It's really good. I just don't like the way people have been talking about you. I don't understand why people are mad at you."

I sighed. "Neither do I."

There was a long pause, then Chrissy said, "Are you sorry you shot that man?"

I draped an arm across her shoulders and pulled her tight. Kids really do know the right questions to ask. I'd been struggling with the shooting. Reliving it over and over again. Dreaming about it. And my little girl had crystallized one of the main issues: I regretted the shooting, but I couldn't apologize for wanting to live.

I said quietly, "I am sorry. I'm sorry I had no choice. I had to shoot that man if I wanted to have chats like this with a girl like you. Sometimes in life things like this happen. Then you have another choice. You can let it bother you the rest of your life and affect how you act. Or you can appreciate the extra time you have. Every time I look in your face, or one of your brothers' or sisters' faces, I thank God that I'm alive."

She gave me a quick hug. As she was about to scoot off the couch, Mary Catherine reappeared.

She said, "Room for one more?"

Chrissy immediately squealed, "Yes," and scooted in next to me so Mary Catherine would sandwich her between us.

Mary Catherine looked at me like she needed permission to join us.

I said, "I'm thinking."

Mary Catherine dropped the pitch of her voice and said, "Don't think too long."

"Okay. Maybe you can join us this once."

I suspected the errant elbow I caught in the face as she slipped past me to sit next to Chrissy was no accident.

CHAPTER 24

CHRISSY DOZED OFF on the couch next to me, and Mary Catherine moved so she could snuggle up close. Now *I* was the middle of the sandwich.

Mary Catherine dropped her head on my shoulder and said, "I'm sorry I blew up, Michael."

I lifted my head and stared at her.

She said, "What? What's wrong?"

"I almost thought I heard you apologize. I'm worried you might've suffered a head injury. Or perhaps we'll have to call my grandfather to complete an exorcism. This doesn't sound like my Mary Catherine."

She punched me in the arm. Hard enough to hurt, but not hard enough for me to whine about it. She said, "I'm serious. I'm sorry I lost control. I also think we should talk about it."

"About going back to work? You knew it was going to happen."

"Not this fast. You've been through something traumatic. We all have. Don't you think you need some time to recover?"

I thought about how much to tell her. Then I said, "It's not exactly like I'm back on the street. At least it's not my usual assignment. I'm working a missing persons case."

"Really? I thought you only worked homicides."

I explained to her my meeting with the mayor. Not in great detail. I remembered the admonition to keep things quiet. But I couldn't just lie to my fiancée.

When I was finished, Mary Catherine said, "What's he like, the mayor?"

I shrugged. "He's a politician. But he's not quite that dick everyone makes him out to be. Talking to him, I had the sense that he was a concerned father. I understood that."

"Everyone has their good and bad."

"Is that an Irish saying?"

"No, *Reader's Digest.*" Mary Catherine looked at me with those big, beautiful eyes and said, "Could you have refused?"

"I could have, but..."

"But what?"

I could hear in her voice she was getting annoyed again. I blurted out, "It might help Brian." I told her what the mayor had said about making some phone calls.

"Is that right? Is it right to use a person's position, like the mayor's, to help your family? Can he even make a promise like that?"

I said, "He didn't *promise* anything."

Mary Catherine said, "But is it right to use his position like that?"

"No, probably not. Do you want me to refuse?"

"No way. I want Brian back. I miss him."

I said, "Exactly." Everyone is an idealist, until the issue affects them. I knew I was going to do what I had to do.

CHAPTER 25

ALICE GROFF AND Janos Titon had to move on to someone else after they eliminated Tommy Payne from their list. The next nerd they started looking for was named Jennifer Chang. Alice had one photograph of her. She was a really cute twenty-four-year-old Asian woman from Los Angeles.

They didn't have a lot on her other than a couple of possible addresses and the fact that she lived with another computer genius named Oscar Gonzales. Alice smiled at a line Henry had written in his notes about her. He pointed out the fact that her relationship with Oscar was platonic. That immediately told Alice that Henry was interested in Jennifer for more than her computer skills. At the end of the notes, Henry had added that she was not to be hurt, no matter what.

Alice also smiled at the idea of someone telling her how to do her job. She hurt people. That's what she got paid for. She wouldn't let something like an infatuation interfere with her job. If the cute Ms. Chang didn't want to get hurt, she should do as they say. Henry needed to think with his head more. He also shouldn't show vulnerabilities like that.

Henry wasn't like a drug lord or a Russian gangster. He wasn't so ruthless that he would track people down for a slight to his honor. But he was relying more and more on the two crazy Dutchmen he used as muscle. They were always eager to show how tough they were.

Alice had no desire to tangle with them.

Janos looked at the notes and said, "So all we do is ask Jennifer to come back with us. Nothing more."

"Are you certain? It doesn't help Henry's business reputation if we let this girl walk."

"What are you saying? Kill her even if we don't have to? That's no business, that's just weird." Janos turned to stare at Alice. A smile crept over his face. "Or is there something else? Are you jealous of young Jennifer? Is that why you want to put a bullet in her?"

Alice was silent for a while. Finally she said, "Not jealous in a romantic way. Henry prizes these computer people but barely acknowledges our contributions to his business."

"He recognizes us with cash. I'll take that any day. So let's not hurt this girl. Please tell me you're smart enough to know not to harm a purple-dyed hair on Jennifer Chang's pretty head."

Alice frowned but managed to avoid an overt promise, and they went about their business.

One of the addresses they had was a brownstone in Queens. They were dressed professionally today and expected this to be a simple visit. Janos was even wearing a tie he'd bought from a place called Daffy's, not far from Times Square.

They found the apartment door on the first floor but got no answer. Janos slipped a credit card out of his pocket.

Alice said, "What are you going to do with that?"

"I saw this on TV. I'm going to jiggle the lock open."

"What TV show?"

"I saw it at home. It's an American show. *The Rockford Files*."

Alice shook her head, knowing it would never work.

After a short and furious bout of wiggling the card, Janos got frustrated and used his shoulder to smash in the door. The flimsy doorframe snapped on the inside, and they found themselves staring at an empty apartment. Not just that no one was home; there was no furniture or clothing.

Alice mumbled, "Damn."

On their way out of the building, a young man was now sitting on the stairs, navigating a Samsung tablet. He looked up and smiled. "Are you guys looking for Oscar?"

Alice kept Janos from saying something stupid. She immediately said, "Why? You know where he is?"

"Are you from Columbia or Fordham?"

This time Janos spoke. "Columbia. Do you know where Oscar moved?"

"Yeah. He and Jennifer found a place near Midtown. It's above a warehouse that holds caskets and funeral parlor accessories. Like a wholesaler." He gave them directions.

Alice stood behind the young man as he spoke with Janos. She started to calculate the odds of leaving a witness like this behind. If something happened and an investigator was thorough enough, this young man might be able to provide a description of them. That went against her professional ethics. Never leave viable witnesses.

She slowly slipped her right hand into her purse and felt the handles of her garrote. The young man was oblivious as he engaged Janos.

Alice tried to assess if she really needed to eliminate a witness or just thought she might enjoy it. If she was honest with herself, she didn't mind feeling people struggle under the power of her arms and shoulders focused on the wire of the garrote.

To be on the safe side, she pulled it from her purse. Both hands ready to go.

Janos had all the information he needed. He thanked the young man and took a few steps down the stairs to the street.

Alice was still in a perfect position to act.

Then the young man said, "I've applied to Columbia. Do you think you guys could help me?"

Before Alice could do anything, he jumped right into his pitch. It covered his academic career since middle school. He had two years of college and was hoping to get in and finish at Columbia.

The young man brushed hair out of his eyes as he finished up. "I have enough financial aid lined up, along with money from my parents. I'm not a computer genius like Oscar or Jennifer, but I have really good grades and I'm interested in business." He sounded proud of himself as he finished his list of accomplishments, from being in the marching band in high school to having straight As at SUNY Brookhaven.

Alice held up her homemade garrote. Then she caught Janos waving her off. Her partner said to the young man, "You seem like a good kid. But you need to aim lower." Janos gave him a thumbs-up and added, "Hang in there."

Alice decided the conversation was too bizarre for the young man to ever think they would be involved in crime. She slipped the garrote back into her purse and hurried down the stairs to catch up with Janos.

Janos had a wide grin on his face and said, "Did you hear my good American accent? That kid totally believed I worked for Columbia University."

Occasionally Alice really enjoyed working with her goofy partner.

CHAPTER 26

IT FELT GOOD to be back on the job. And having a different assignment helped make it interesting. If you don't get something out of your job other than money, what's the point? One of the things I love about police work is that you never know what might happen. I live my life in a constant state of surprise and excitement. Not a bad way to spend your time.

Over the years, I'd explored the idea of applying to the FBI or pursuing promotions within the NYPD. But days like this always convinced me that being a detective was the best possible position. Not just any kind of detective, but an NYPD detective. To roam over this great city and meet interesting people made me excited to start work almost every day.

I had a list of names the mayor had given me. They were acquaintances or friends of Natalie's. I had spoken to the mayor's ex-wife, who now lived north of Albany. She knew more about her daughter's day-to-day life and friends but offered nothing of great importance. At least nothing that looked important at the moment. I'd seen divorce ruin families. I got the idea that the divorce was only part of this dynamic, though the mayor himself had taken the blame.

The mayor's ex-wife had started to worry about her daughter a while ago. She felt the rising fear of a parent. She didn't care what I did or who I was as long as I found her daughter.

I spoke to a bright young woman named Allie Andrus, who was a senior at NYU. She had been friends with Natalie since middle school. I thought I'd get some real insights, but all she said was that they had drifted apart. Now Natalie hung out with a group of computer hackers. Allie used the phrase "cyber-punks." That sounded a little dismissive to me.

I spoke to two other friends on the phone and then landed on the name Thomas Payne.

When I ran the name through NYPD computer indexes, I was shocked to learn he was the victim of a homicide. His body had been found a few blocks from Penn Station.

That changed everything. It could be a coincidence. But if you believe in coincidence, you probably shouldn't be a cop.

I immediately got on the horn and reached Detective Ed Arris. He gave me directions to Payne's apartment and said he'd meet me in a few minutes.

Ed and I went back a few years. He was six foot four but had more bulk than me. Some of it had to do with his football career. He'd played at Hofstra about the same time as their best-known NFL player, Wayne Chrebet.

He shook my hand, then enveloped me in a bear hug. "Good to see you, Mike. We've all been worried about you."

I waved off the sentiment, but it touched me. I had to change the subject, quick.

I said, "How do you like Manhattan South?"

"You know how it is. I'd been up in the Bronx a while. NYPD likes to spread out their black detectives. This is a pretty easy gig compared to the Bronx. I figure I'll pull the plug in the next ten years anyway."

I noticed how well kept the building was as we walked to the front door of the apartment. There was no doorman, but the electronic security was outstanding. Four different cameras caught the front of the building. An expensive awning covered the sidewalk leading to the entrance.

Ed said they had no leads. Just a body that had been strangled with a ligature. In this case, he thought it was some kind of wire.

Ed said, "Screwed up the victim's neck pretty bad. Deep laceration, but it didn't sever any arteries. The poor kid choked to death. He was dead at least twelve hours before someone from a restaurant next door noticed the body jammed up against a wall behind a row of parked cars. The kid's family is devastated."

Every homicide detective knew the feeling, talking to a family who had just lost someone. Death notifications were one of the worst parts of the job.

Ed fumbled with the keys, then we ducked under some yellow crime-scene tape across the doorway.

As soon as we stepped into the apartment and I saw the two TVs and all of the computer equipment, I knew this was related to the missing Natalie Lunden.

CHAPTER 27

IT'S ALWAYS A surreal experience to be in the apartment of a dead person. Their life is told in the belongings they left behind. Secrets are held in correspondence and emails. Even their TV viewing habits might be looked at. Anything that could give a detective a hint of what led to the homicide.

Cops like to say a good homicide detective is born, not made. The gift has more to do with the determination to keep looking at things until they make sense. With all the new forms of communication, from instant messaging to email, investigations have changed dramatically. More opportunities to catch a killer also means much more information to pore over. Cases, at least more complicated cases, take longer.

I believe experience is what makes a good detective. Varied experience, not the same one over and over. Experience is a tricky thing. You never realize how important it is until you gain it. The ultimate catch-22.

This was a very nice two-bedroom apartment most professionals would kill to live in. Somehow a twenty-four-year-old computer whiz had found a way to pay for it.

Ed proceeded to brief me as we walked through the apartment. He said, "We found an airline ticket to Estonia."

Immediately I thought about the wire from Danske Bank in Estonia that paid for Natalie Lunden's apartment. Things were starting to pop.

Ed continued, "The victim had a Long Island Rail ticket to Hempstead in his pocket."

"A fairly big town. I think it's the biggest in Nassau County. He have relatives there?"

Ed said, "I spoke to his parents, who live in Hicksville. They weren't expecting him. Of course, they're in shock. The only thing they could think of was that his grandmother has a house in Hempstead she lets him use. I looked up the address. Good place to lie low. It would be hard to connect it to him."

I said, "You think he had a change of heart about the trip to Estonia. Maybe he was running."

Ed finished my thought. "And whoever he was running from caught him. It's possible. We have some grainy surveillance photographs that show him leaving Penn Station with a couple. A well-dressed white woman and man in their thirties. Not enough to make an exact ID. But the surveillance cameras downstairs show what may be the same couple visiting the building earlier that evening. Excellent images, but not a single match in our system, and they may have been visiting someone other than Payne. This one really has us stumped."

"No drug connections?" That was usually the first and most likely reason for a homicide in New York.

"No, nothing. He'd been in school until eighteen months ago."

"His parents pay for this apartment?"

"Nope."

"Interesting."

"And confusing. I can't find what the kid did for money, but he was doing okay."

"I'd say so."

I had told him I was looking for a witness. Technically, it was true. I had been waiting for the next question.

Ed said, "What's the connection between the witness you're looking for and Payne? Can the witness help me on this homicide?"

"Truthfully, I don't know. But if I ever find her, it will be one of my first questions."

"What kind of case is she a witness to?"

"Ed, this is gonna sound weird coming from me, but I can't talk about it." It was embarrassing to tell one of my brother cops something like that. The FBI did that kind of shit all the time. That's why none of the local cops worked with them much. I didn't like saying it to a fellow detective.

But he took it in stride and we continued exchanging a little information and looking through the apartment again.

Finally I said, "Okay, Ed, I've seen enough. Will you keep me in the loop?"

"Sure, no problem. Will you do the same?"

"As soon as I'm authorized, you'll hear the whole story. For now, I have to shift my focus to another witness."

"Down here in Manhattan South? I have a lot of contacts."

"I think I need to go to Columbia first. Last I heard she was registered there."

Ed said, "I seem to recall you having a little trouble at Columbia not that long ago. Will they let you on campus? They're not known to help the police much."

"I have a few contacts. I need to find this girl. I'll see what I can pick up on her and if she knows anything about your victim."

"Is this witness's name a secret, too?"

"No, not really. Her name is Jennifer Chang. She's a computer genius, too. That's why I think it might all be related."

Ed laughed and said, "If you don't know it by now, everything's related in police work."

CHAPTER 28

I HADN'T BEEN to Columbia University in some time. During my last visit, looking into rumors of a teenage hit man, I'd found the student studying at Columbia's Butler Library. The young man was bright and eloquent. He was also an armed psychopath, which became clear when he pulled a pistol on me while we were chatting. We're credited with the only running gunfight in history inside a Columbia library.

Thinking about that shooting, and my most recent shooting, left me feeling a little dejected. It really did seem like people were much more open to using violence to get away from the police. It made me scared for the generations of cops to come.

A security guard at the campus was a retired NYPD sergeant. It was clear on the phone he didn't want anyone to see him talking to a current NYPD detective, but he did a search of the university's records and found that Jennifer Chang was an enrolled student.

There was no way to tell if she was attending her classes, but he knew some of the university's IT people. That's where I was headed, north of the main campus. I should've picked up on his tone and chuckle. He said, "Jason is a little different."

"How so?"

"Let's just say he lives in his own world. Play by his rules, and he could be a big help."

I found the offices not far from the Hudson in a four-story brick-and-glass building that looked more like a large warehouse than a hub of technology. I entered the front door, and the first thing I saw was a page of copy paper with the word *Infrastructure* scribbled on it with a ballpoint pen. An arrow pointed down. I took the narrow staircase next to the sign.

It felt a little like a horror movie. The underground floor was poorly lit and there was no one around. Literally. I had not seen one person since I entered the building. I found another sign just like the first one with an arrow pointing to the end of the hallway.

My shoes echoed off the concrete floor, which looked just as cold as the colorless walls. A stale odor assaulted my nose.

Finally I found a door with one more matching sign that said *Infrastructure.*

I knocked and heard someone shout from inside.

I opened the door and saw a man, about thirty, with long red hair tied in a ponytail. He looked up and said, "Are you Bennett?"

I nodded.

"Todd in Security told me you'd be coming. He said you

were trustworthy and on a noble quest. I respect anyone on a noble quest."

It took me a moment to realize this guy had played one too many Dungeons and Dragons games.

He said, "My name is Jason. Jason A. Manafort. But Todd said you wouldn't put my name in any reports. Can I trust your word of honor, sir?"

"No one will ever know I was here or that you spoke to me."

"And your quest? Is it really noble?"

"I'm looking for a missing girl, and Jennifer Chang might know where to find her. I just want to make sure she's safe." I waited while Jason considered this. He wasn't taking our encounter lightly. I wasn't sure if that was good or bad.

Then Jason patted the seat next to him and turned to his computer monitor. He said, "I did a little background. I needed to meet you and make sure you were worthy of receiving this information."

I watched as he brought up Jennifer Chang's registration information. I copied down an address in Midtown. It looked like more of a warehouse area. Some of the warehouses had apartments above them. I also looked at Jennifer's official school ID photo. Like most college students, she looked too young to be in school, but that was just a product of me getting older.

She was cute and had purple streaks running through her hair. She had been born in California and appeared to be of Asian descent. Nothing in her file was useful for my investigation, other than the address, which I intended to visit as soon as I was done with the Royal Handler of Information.

I talked with Jason for a few more minutes and asked if there was anything else he thought might help me.

He said, "Do you know what a MAC address is?"

I recalled Eddie telling me about a computer's unique address, the string of two-digit numbers and characters. All I said to Jason was "Of course I do."

He brought up a different screen on his computer. He said, "I found her ID on the Wi-Fi in Butler Library. I even checked security video to make sure it was her. Anyway, when she signed on, this is the address that came up."

I looked at the screen and copied down the twelve digits. I didn't know how to use it myself, but I thought I could find someone who did.

I also didn't know how to thank Jason. He was stepping outside the normal protocol for Columbia employees to speak to the police. I dug in my sport coat pocket and found a challenge coin from Manhattan North Homicide. Most police units make their own coins, mementos that some people collect. This one showed a crime scene on one side and our unit's logo on the other side.

Jason stared at it in his hand for a moment and said, "I'm honored that you would entrust me with a symbol of your quest."

I said, "Thanks for the help." It seemed shallow in the face of his sincerity, but I didn't have time for a big show of emotion. I had to check Jennifer Chang's apartment.

CHAPTER 29

ALICE GROFF AND Janos Titon had followed the directions from the kid outside Jennifer Chang's old apartment. His directions had been right on the money, and his description had been fairly precise. The apartment was on the floors above a warehouse that dealt with caskets and funeral accessories.

They'd waited until the warehouse closed and it was dusk. Now they marched up two flights of wooden stairs, their footsteps echoing in the warehouse below them. They could hear the echo through the vents and a couple of windows that looked down into the warehouse.

Alice nudged Janos and nodded toward a series of extremely subtle security cameras. They were all directed at the door.

Janos muttered, "Computer geeks. They're the same in America as they are in Estonia."

They were still dressed professionally, so Alice wasn't worried about what they would look like on security cameras. She knocked on the door.

Clearly whoever was inside had been watching the cameras and waiting. The door opened a crack with two heavy security chains on it. A tall, skinny man, with remarkably thick glasses, peered out at them. He spoke with a Hispanic accent as he said, "Who are you? What are you doing here?"

Alice had a little speech prepared about being from Columbia University and looking for Jennifer Chang. She was going to say they had come about a financial aid grant. Vague and non-threatening. The best kind of story.

Before she could say anything, Janos wedged his foot into the open doorway and had the barrel of his Czech pistol under the thin ridge of bone the man thought of as his chin.

Janos said, "It doesn't matter who we are. You're going to open this door or I'm going to open your face. Your choice."

The man was stunned. He stammered, "How, how, can, can I undo the chains with the door open?"

Janos said, "Give me your hand." He waited while the man stuck his hand between the doorjamb and the open door. Then he took a firm grip of the man's index finger and put the barrel of the pistol against his hand. He said, "You can close the door as far as your fingers. That should be enough for you to undo the locks."

A few seconds later, Alice casually followed Janos through the open door.

The man was wearing blue tiger-striped silk boxer shorts and a T-shirt that said I'M A HACKER, BUT I DIDN'T SCREW UP DEMOCRACY. He trembled like a frightened Chihuahua.

Alice said, "Are you Oscar?"

He nodded nervously. His long curls swayed in the air. Sweat beaded on his gaunt face.

"Where's Jennifer?"

He paused for a moment and said, "I don't know any Jennifer."

Janos whacked him on the side of the head with his gun. He stood over the fallen computer nerd and looked down at him. "The next time I use the gun, it won't be to hit you."

Alice kept a very calm tone. "Tell us where Jennifer is right now and you can go about your business. I promise we're not going to hurt her."

Oscar rubbed the side of his head, then looked at the blood on his fingers. "I haven't seen her in a couple of days. We're just roommates. She lives her life and I live mine."

Janos said, "It's going to be a lot tougher to live your life if we don't find out where Jennifer Chang is right now." He carefully placed the barrel of the gun on Oscar's forehead. He let that sink in for a moment.

Oscar's eyes looked up at the gun and Janos standing behind it.

Alice truly didn't know what Janos was going to do. From a professional cost-benefit analysis, it didn't matter. If Oscar wouldn't tell them where Jennifer was, his death meant little to her.

Oscar still didn't say a word.

Janos pulled the hammer of the pistol back.

Oscar swallowed hard and his whole body started to shake.

CHAPTER 30

ALICE WATCHED SILENTLY as Janos kept the gun to the computer geek's head. Frankly, she'd seen her partner do something similar so many times it barely rated her interest. Once, while collecting a debt for a Marseille loan shark, she had watched Janos torture a man until he revealed the target's location. If she could sit through fingers being severed, watching this thin man beg for his life wasn't a big deal.

Janos very calmly said, "Tell us where we can find Jennifer. Then we'll be out of your hair. She won't even be upset you told us. We have a job offer for her."

Oscar continued to tremble. But Alice saw something else. He was making a calculation. He was justifying telling them where the girl was.

Alice gestured to catch Janos's attention. She motioned for him to wait.

He just stood there with the pistol in his hand.

After more than thirty seconds, Oscar blubbered, "Okay, okay. I'll talk to you. Just please, please take the gun away."

Janos looked at Alice. She nodded and he lowered the gun. They both had to help the terrified man off the floor. They hefted him from under his arms, and she was surprised a skinny computer nerd could feel so heavy.

They tossed him into his rolling chair in front of a gigantic computer monitor. The screen was broken up into eight squares. Each square corresponded to a camera. She recognized the one at the front door and a second one in the hallway.

One of them showed a shower. She caught a glimpse of someone walking past the camera.

Alice said to Oscar, "Where are all your cameras located?"

He gave her a sly smile. The kind only computer-literate people give to people with less experience.

She cut her eyes to Janos. He immediately placed the barrel of the gun to Oscar's temple. That straightened out his attitude.

He spoke quickly. "They cover all sorts of places. Security here in the building. I have one in the warehouse and at the front door just so I know what's going on. The one in the shower is for my boyfriend, Hector."

Alice said, "Why does Hector get special attention?"

"I make sure he showers alone. And I like to watch him shower."

"Does he know about the camera?"

"No one knows about any of my cameras. As long as I let the landlord leave the door to the warehouse unlocked so the workers can eat on the roof occasionally, he doesn't care what I do."

Now Janos said, "Let's get back to Jennifer Chang. Where can we find her?"

"There's a coffeehouse. It's up closer to Columbia. I think it's on La Salle, a block east of Broadway. It's called Brew. It's a place a lot of programmers meet. Good Wi-Fi, good coffee. No one asks any questions."

Alice asked, "How often does she go there?"

"Almost every day. Probably more often than she comes here. She's got a guy she likes to see up that way. It's nothing serious." Oscar swiveled in the chair so he was only looking at Alice. It was like he was trying to blot out the reality that a Romanian holding a gun stood next to him.

Oscar regained a little of his confidence and said, "Is the job offer you have for Jennifer from a guy in Estonia named Henry?"

Alice hesitated. Finally she said, "What if it is?"

"She won't be interested. At all. She told me all about the operation. She said Henry was starting to go crazy. He kept using them for bigger and bigger jobs. She didn't want to be around when things went bad."

Alice shrugged and said, "We still have to make the offer."

That's when she caught sight of someone on the security camera. He was tall and wearing a blue sport coat. He looked like a cop. She glared at Oscar and said, "Who's that?"

Oscar turned and looked at the monitor. He hit a couple of buttons on his keyboard and other cameras picked up the feed. Now Alice and Janos could see the man from several different angles.

Oscar said, "I don't know him, but this is the only place he could be coming."

Alice put a finger to her lips to make sure he stayed quiet.

Janos placed the barrel of the gun to his head to be doubly sure.

CHAPTER 31

I FOUND THE building listed as Jennifer Chang's residence on her Columbia University registration form. It was about where I thought it would be, south of Midtown. I was still skeptical about the address until I saw a residential door next to the administration offices for the warehouse. The offices were closed for the evening, but the residential door was open. I stepped into the dark entryway, then headed up the wood stairs. This was no-frills. There were wide glass windows that looked into the warehouse from the second floor. Years ago, the apartments here must've been some kind of offices. The housing shortage in Manhattan made crazy spaces into apartments.

It was the kind of building I used to show the kids when they were younger. The most interesting field trip we went on was at Ricky's request, after we saw a documentary about how bean sprouts used in Chinese food are mostly grown in New York City. The bean sprouts' seeds were just dumped in a big metal container that looked like a dumpster. Then watered. And a week or two later, you had full-grown bean sprouts. The other kids couldn't believe I wanted them to spend their afternoon inside a dark, damp warehouse. You know what they say: you can't please all the people all the time.

This building was just as interesting in its own way. I stopped to stare through one of the windows and saw that the warehouse was some sort of distribution point for caskets. I saw different manufacturers, Thacker and Astral. They all were stacked along a path to a loading dock, where a semi was already backed in. The door was open and the trailer was mostly loaded.

The place also reminded me of a girl I'd dated when I was in college. She lived above a mom-and-pop funeral home across the street from Van Cortlandt Park in the Bronx. I had to walk through the embalming area to get to the stairs to her apartment. I'd say the relationship "died," but in reality, she killed it. She decided a finance major from NYU was a better prospect than a philosophy major from Manhattan College. Probably a smart move.

I walked along the hallway, looking for the door to Jennifer Chang's apartment. It was a well-sealed door and very little light came from underneath. But a door was ajar across the hallway. I opened it fully and looked in for a minute. It was silent and empty inside.

I had nothing to lose, so I knocked on Jennifer Chang's door. A good solid knock. Not a police knock. Not a boyfriend tap.

And I waited. It wasn't as if I had a warrant. I just wanted to ask her a couple of questions about her missing friend. So I tried the doorknob. No cop alive wouldn't test a door to see if it was open. It was natural curiosity.

Then I wondered if I should jimmy the lock. Who knows what I might find inside? An address book? No, I guess not. Everyone stores their numbers in a phone now.

I knocked again.

CHAPTER 32

ALICE WATCHED THE computer monitor carefully. She'd decided the tall man in the sport coat was definitely a cop. He had a handsome face and broad shoulders. She'd also decided she wouldn't mind him putting handcuffs on her just for a night.

She watched him wander around the hallway for a moment. Then he gave a solid knock on the door.

She looked at Oscar and reinforced the command to keep silent, running her finger in a slashing motion across her throat. There was no way Oscar would realize that was literally what she'd do if he spoke.

She motioned toward the door with her head. Janos quickly and quietly moved across the floor. He stood to the side of the door and held his pistol out about head height. Then he edged around to the center of the door and started placing the barrel at different locations, kept looking at the computer monitor to see if he could line up the shot through the door.

Oscar motioned Alice closer to him and whispered, "The door is reinforced with extra metal and a thick plastic material in the middle."

Alice asked softly, "Why? To make this like a bomb shelter? Does it have to do with the warehouse?"

Oscar said, "I think it has to do with noise and vibration from the warehouse. But the door is solid and thick."

Alice made a hissing sound to get Janos's attention. She shook her head for him not to shoot, but he didn't turn around.

She was too late. Janos was already squeezing the trigger.

Alice quickly glanced at the computer monitor and saw that his gun was lined up just about with the cop's face.

CHAPTER 33

I PAUSED RIGHT in the middle of the door. For a fleeting moment, I thought I'd seen a shadow from under the door. Just something that moved very close to the doorframe.

Then I heard a faint tapping sound. Not in any rhythm. Just like someone was moving something around on the metal door.

I tried the knob again. This time with a little pressure on the door. It was solid and secure. Probably best that it was. The last thing I wanted to do was terrify a witness I needed to talk to. If Jennifer was home, I didn't want to just barge in.

I looked back at the warehouse. I stepped over to a window and wondered if it would be worth waiting here. How long would she be out? What if she didn't live here at all? These are the same kind of questions I ask during every surveillance.

It was definitely easier before I had kids. Especially when Maeve had worked evenings at the hospital. I'd stay out on surveillance all night to catch a witness. The alternative was going home to an empty apartment.

Now it was the opposite. Now I had to manage ten lives, even if one of them was at a prison upstate. I also wanted to talk to my grandfather. Often he came up with the best advice, without even knowing anything about police work.

I stepped back to the door and knocked one more time. I wasn't going to get an answer. I knew it.

On a cop's instinct, I moved from the door to the side of it. Just in case someone crazy on the other side did something stupid.

Thirty seconds later, I started back down the hallway. I took the stairs quickly, then hesitated as I stepped out onto the side-walk. I wondered why they didn't have better security. Maybe they locked the door at night.

I'd come back tomorrow and see if I could find her.

CHAPTER 34

ALICE WATCHED AS Janos looked over his shoulder at her. He released his finger from the trigger but left the gun trained on the door. Then Alice motioned him away from the door altogether.

They watched the computer monitor to see what the cop was doing. He looked through the windows into the warehouse, waited, knocked again, then started to walk away.

Oscar showed her how to view the cameras he'd set up all around the building. It was impressive. She watched the cop hurry down the stairs, then step out the front door. From there, the camera on the outside of the building caught him pausing next to the door.

Alice smiled and said, "Very impressive system, Oscar. I hope you don't waste your talents working for a corporation or the government. You could do very well on the wrong side of the law."

They all laughed. Oscar was smiling now. He thought the danger had passed. He wanted to be part of their little group.

Alice realized this was not going to happen. He was a witness who could identify them. And she was starting to wonder if it was even worth it to ask Jennifer Chang to come back to Estonia. She'd just say no. It was a waste of time. Maybe eliminating Jennifer would be easier for everyone. And more fun.

No matter what happened, Oscar knew too much.

Janos had the same thought. He smiled and said, "Oscar, will you give us a quick tour of the warehouse before we leave? I think it's cool how your apartment is above it. Did you say there was a door to the warehouse up here?"

Oscar nodded and said, "They're supposed to lock it every evening, but they almost never do. No one from the building wants to go look at coffins."

Janos allowed Oscar to slip on some jeans and loafers for the tour. Once they were down in the warehouse, Janos kept walking at a fast pace to the loading dock where the truck was backed in.

Oscar caught up to Janos with Alice directly behind him. The truck was three-quarters full with pallets of caskets. There were four stacked on each pallet. A huge spool of plastic wrap on rollers was in the truck. It looked like quitting time had come just as they were about to wind the plastic around the four caskets already in place on the truck.

Alice said, "Is this truck safe just sitting here?"

Oscar nodded. "The big sliding door is shut in front of the truck. The trucks usually leave right at eight o'clock in the morning." He glanced at the shipping document on the casket directly in front of him. "Looks like these are going to a place in Lincoln, Nebraska."

Janos lifted the lid of a casket. He rubbed his hand along the inside and said, "That's nice. Silk." He gestured to Oscar.

Oscar put a hand inside the casket and said, "Nice padding, too."

Casually Janos pulled the gun from his rear waistband. In a single, smooth motion, he moved it from behind his back and put a bullet into Oscar's chest. The gunshot echoed in the giant warehouse, booming off the walls.

Oscar stood absolutely motionless. No expression on his face other than a little surprise. The dark stain blossomed on his T-shirt. It spread out and seeped downward. Oscar made one raspy attempt to suck in some air. Then he made a little gurgling sound.

Before Oscar could even flop onto the ground, Janos caught him with his left arm and redirected his weight. He slipped the computer programmer into the casket with hardly a noise.

Oscar was still breathing for a moment inside the casket. A rough rasp that didn't seem to give him much air. The bullet must have just nicked his heart. Blood was really spreading across his crazy hacker shirt. You couldn't even read the word *democracy* through the dark stain.

Blood bubbled up onto Oscar's lips and suddenly it felt like he understood exactly what was happening. Somehow, through the shock, it had dawned on him that he was inside the casket.

Alice stepped closer. The shot had come so fast that she had been as surprised as Oscar. The noise had barely bothered her as it dispersed across the room. She took a quick look at the floor of the truck to make sure no blood had dripped down.

She also looked in the casket and caught the last couple of twitches from Oscar. It was the cleanest shooting she'd ever seen.

Even *she* hadn't expected it. She was a little disappointed she hadn't gotten to use her garrote.

On the bright side, it was one more loose end handled. Tomorrow they would go to Brew and see if they could find Jennifer.

The more Alice thought about it, the more she wanted to use her garrote on Jennifer. She didn't care what Henry thought. Maybe it would teach him to show her some respect.

Besides, it would take away the sting of not being able to use it on Oscar.

Janos carefully closed the casket. Then he took the plastic wrap and ran it around the sides of the four caskets just like on the other pallets.

He looked at Alice as he said, "No one will remember if they wrapped the caskets yet or not. This way, it will be days, maybe weeks, before anyone finds Oscar. By then we'll be back in Europe collecting a fat paycheck from that asshole Henry."

Alice liked the sound of that.

CHAPTER 35

IT WAS DARK by the time I got home. But it felt good to shed the stress of the day as I walked through the front door. The place was its usual beehive of activity. I said hello to Mary Catherine and the older kids, who were doing their homework at the dining room table, and it sounded like Ricky was working in the kitchen. No doubt my little chef was making us some kind of Cajun delight. Whatever Emeril Legasse said, Ricky made happen.

Neither Mary Catherine nor I had the guts to tell Ricky we weren't particularly big fans of spicy Cajun food. But he had a passion, and I intended to support him. Even if it cost me the lining of my stomach as I got older.

I ran over in my head the visit I'd made to Jennifer Chang's apartment. Something about it still felt odd to me.

Indescribable. Just a weird tingling on the back of my neck. Was she trying to avoid me? If that was the case, she wouldn't have gone back to the apartment above the casket warehouse.

Fiona, Chrissy, Bridget, and Shawna were all huddled around the coffee table in the living room. I walked into the room to a chorus of "Hi, Dad" in unison.

I clapped my hands together as I approached and said, "What have you girls got cooking over here?"

Shawna smiled and said, "Monopoly, and I already have houses on three properties. I also own all four railroads."

I caressed the cheek of my beautiful daughter. We had no information about her biological parents. When she first came to us, I had assumed both her parents were black. But now, as she got older and her hair fell down in long curls, I suspected she could be half Hispanic. Every one of my kids was as different as could be; even the twins, Fiona and Bridget, had entirely different personalities. It just made our lives that much more interesting and exciting.

I made my way to the computer in the corner of the living room. As usual, Eddie had commandeered it, and we were far enough away from everyone else that no one would hear our conversation.

I tried to sound casual. "What's going on, buddy?"

"Usual."

"You follow some of the hackers online, right? I mean, staying up with the trends."

"I guess."

Computer prodigy or not, he was still a teenager. No conversation was that easy. I said, "You talked to me a couple times about networks and some of the different programs you use. If I had the MAC address of a computer, is there any way to pin down where it shows up on Wi-Fi?"

Eddie hesitated. I could see him working the question over in his mind.

I said, "This is unofficial, not Dad asking. If you can do it, I really need to find someone. You won't get in trouble, no matter what sketchy websites you have to visit for this."

Eddie said, "There are different programs out there. Or, I should say, networks that keep track of that kind of stuff. I'm sure there's someone at the police department who knows how to do it."

"Let's say I was just trying to keep my distance from the office. And that time was a little bit of an issue. If I gave you the MAC address, do you think you could find some leads for me? No questions asked about how you do it."

The kids knew that when I told them they wouldn't get in trouble, nothing would happen. Once you start hedging on promises, it's a slippery slope. The kids won't trust you and can't come to you with real problems. Eddie knew this.

He smiled and said, "This could be a good little test."

I gave him the twelve digits my odd contact from Columbia University had provided, the MAC address for Jennifer Chang's computer.

Eddie said, "I might need a while to find this. I have a couple of websites I can look at."

"It won't show a name or anything that gets out on the internet, will it?"

He just gave me a little condescending laugh. I mostly deserved it.

I watched him for a few seconds, then turned to head into the kitchen. Before I made it five steps, Eddie said, "Got it."

He spent another minute or two finding more information. He looked up at me and said, "It looks like this computer regularly signs on to a Wi-Fi network run by a coffeehouse kinda near Columbia. The place's name is Brew."

CHAPTER 36

I DROVE A little north from our apartment to the area around Broadway and 123rd, to a short street called La Salle. I had a feeling deep inside me that things were not nearly as they appeared. This case was turning weird fast. The fact that one of the witnesses I needed to find, Tommy Payne, had been murdered made it more immediate.

Whatever had happened to Natalie Lunden, I no longer thought she was just a spoiled kid acting out. I'll admit, like any human being, I'd approached this with a little bit of an attitude. Maybe it was because of my feelings for the mayor. Maybe it was experience. I'd thought after digging around for a day or two I might find Natalie hiding at a friend's apartment. Just another kid who basically ran away from home.

Now, the more I looked into it, the more concerned I became. I'd had some guys from the NYPD Intelligence Bureau see if they could find out anything about her or her friends. So far, it looked like she hung out with mostly computer people, and it looked like some of them didn't follow the rules. That worried me even more.

I had to start considering the possibility that she'd been kidnapped. But there had been no ransom demand or any other contact with her parents. That was weird if it was a true kidnapping.

I wondered if it had something to do with the mayor's un-popularity. But the fact that he'd approached the police about his daughter made me believe he would've told us about a threat.

Add in the element of computers and programs like the one Eddie had used to find this coffeehouse, and my mind had started to swim. I don't consider myself an old guy, but I was beginning to feel like one. Technology had left me behind. Sure, I could text and send an email. But when Eddie started talking to me about the things he did on the computer, it was like he was speaking another language.

I drove past the coffeehouse. It was so average it could've been used on *Seinfeld*. Just a simple square storefront with the word *Brew* scrawled in an odd font against a plain background. Wide glass windows on either side of the front door showed a brisk business.

As I looked at the cars parked in the area and the people walking along the sidewalk, I realized I wasn't exactly sure what immediate threat I was looking for. Maybe a couple of big mobbed-up guys in suits. Perhaps some skinny kid in a T-shirt with an odd computer saying on it.

For a cop who knows the city and understands his job, it was disconcerting to be at such a loss.

The other thing that had been nagging me was the Tommy Payne murder. That meant someone else might be looking for Natalie Lunden. Or for Jennifer Chang. Maybe that seemingly typical thirty-something couple who visited Payne's building the night of his death. I needed to be alert.

I dumped the car in a lot a few blocks away and started heading toward the coffeehouse. The entire way, I kept looking for anything out of the ordinary. Then it hit me. Was I jumpy from the shooting? Was Mary Catherine right? Should I have taken more time off?

It was tough to wonder if I was as good a public servant as I thought.

Today I wore a light windbreaker just to cover the Glock on my hip. I felt like I blended in, that no one would necessarily assume I was a cop. I noticed a patrol car parked at the end of the block. I was suddenly questioning my skills, but I hoped I wouldn't need assistance.

After all, I was just looking for a twenty-four-year-old female computer nerd. How rough could it get?

CHAPTER 37

ALICE AND JANOS took a cab uptown. Alice had insisted the driver let them off near City College. She didn't want anyone to connect them to the coffeehouse Oscar had told them about. They had been so careful up to this point; they'd even eliminated two potential witnesses and destroyed the surveillance videos at Oscar's apartment. Alice didn't want to screw things up now by stupidly letting a cabdriver know exactly where they were going.

Once they were on foot and walking south toward La Salle Street, Alice started to plan things more carefully. There was no one around to hear them talk, but still, Alice wished they spoke a common language other than English. Janos had picked up very little Dutch or French, even with all the time they had spent in those countries. Alice couldn't say much in Janos's language. She had worked with him for three full years and hadn't picked up ten words of Romanian. She didn't tell Janos, but she felt like it was useless to learn a foreign language that so few people spoke.

Now, walking the streets of New York, they spoke the same language as most of the people around them as Alice finished her reasons for why they should just kill Jennifer Chang and move on.

Janos shook his head and matched her quiet tone. "I'm not used to being the rational one. What do you have against this girl? We were told to make her a job offer and not to hurt her. We may not like Henry, but he is our employer. At least for a little while longer."

Alice said, "It's a waste of time to look for this girl. We already know she's not going to accept the job offer. And it's too hard to try to force her to come back with us. All she'd have to do is let out one loud yelp on a plane and we'd both be facing armed TSA agents. She knows what we know. Henry's turned into some kind of a monster. I even sent him a text the other day telling him this was our last job for him."

"What did he say?"

"He's a condescending prick. He just texted me back and said, 'We'll see.' I don't even know what that means."

Janos said, "Why do you want to kill this girl?"

Alice took a moment to answer. "We make the offer and if she accepts, great. If not, she's just another witness who can identify us. She has to go."

Janos shrugged. That was his universal sign that he somewhat agreed. Or at least it made some sort of sense to him.

From Broadway they turned east, onto La Salle Street. They could see Brew across the street and up a block.

Just as she always did, Alice checked her purse to make sure she was ready. The homemade garrote in her hand and a knife she'd bought at a hardware store made her feel more secure and confident.

She noticed that Janos reached back to feel the butt of his pistol. He always kept it in his belt line in the small of his back. That way he could wear untucked shirts and the pistol would be hidden, and also available to Alice in an emergency.

Like that time in Tallinn, when a drug gang had been trying to pressure Henry, and Alice and Janos were sent to talk to them. Immediately it had been clear there was going to be more than talk. While the three drug dealers were looking at Janos, Alice was able to draw the gun from Janos's back.

Five shots later and Henry had no more problems. He'd given them a huge bonus. That was back when he was still sane.

Alice missed that Henry. He had been a good boss then.

CHAPTER 38

I STEPPED IN the front door of the coffeehouse. I don't know what I had expected would happen. Maybe I thought I was like a sheriff in the Old West, that everything might come to a standstill when I walked through the front door. Then I sprang back to reality. I was in one of thousands of coffeehouses in New York City. No one noted my arrival.

I took a moment to scan the whole room. There was a counter and about twenty small tables. On the opposite end of the counter was a take-out service with its own door to perhaps an alley in back. That was smart.

The counter was nearly full. Most everyone in the place was young. About ten of them looked like my idea of a stereotypical hacker: raggedy clothes, long hair, and expensive computers.

Two men at the counter turned and looked me over. They

looked like tourists. Definitely not Americans. Their red Zappos and the Kappa logos on their jackets told me that.

No one else in Brew stuck out to me. Everyone had their nose buried in a tablet or computer. There was almost no conversation. This was unlike the Starbucks I occasionally frequented near the office. (But I still wouldn't walk into our squad bay with a Starbucks cup.)

Then I saw her. Almost in the middle of the room. Jennifer Chang was difficult to miss, even prettier in person than in the photograph from Columbia. She still had the purple streaks in her hair, but she had the hair tied in a simple ponytail. She had bright eyes that were currently focusing on an iPad in her hands. The diamond stud earrings told me she might have done some of the same lucrative work that paid the high rents Thomas Payne and Natalie both afforded.

I considered different ways to approach her. Sometimes you didn't have to use *shock and awe*. She had no record. She probably had never dealt with the police before. She'd have no idea how to act or what to say.

She was only a handful of years older than Juliana. That always seemed to me to be a good approach: treat younger people like you'd want your kids treated. I needed information, not an arrest.

I worked my way through the busy coffeehouse, careful not to knock anyone's computer off the table. I wasted no time once I was in front of Jennifer Chang's table. I slid out the chair and sat down across from her.

Her dark eyes looked over the top of her stylish tortoiseshell glasses, then did a quick scan around the room to see if anyone had noticed me sitting down with her. She didn't look frightened.

Her eyes drifted back to her iPad for a moment.

I kept quiet. Now I was curious as to what she might say.

She set the iPad on the tiny table in front of us, pushed her glasses up her nose, and said, "I don't see any reason why I should talk to the police."

She'd turned the tables on me. Dammit. Now I was the one who was surprised.

"What makes you think I'm the police?"

"Aside from the way you stepped in here and surveyed the whole room? Then how you stepped right up to me and sat down without invitation? I'm sorry, in New York that screams 'Police.'"

"Aren't you curious why I'm here to talk to you?"

"I know why. So the only thing I can say to you now is, I want to talk to my attorney."

CHAPTER 39

ALICE GROFF SKIDDED to a stop when she looked through one of the windows of Brew. The only thing she could focus on inside the coffeehouse was the pretty and vivacious Jennifer Chang chatting with the cop they'd seen at her apartment the night before. No matter how she did the calculations, this did not turn out well for her and Janos. Jennifer talking to the police. And too many witnesses to act right now.

Janos nearly ran into her when she stopped short.

"What is it?"

"The tall cop from last night. The one who tried to get into Oscar's apartment. He's in there talking to Jennifer."

"No shit. That's a puzzler."

Alice was losing her patience. "And what do you propose we do about this puzzler?"

"What *can* we do about it? As I see it, we have two choices.

We can lay back out of sight and try to get to Jennifer later." He stopped talking as he looked over Alice's shoulder at the coffeehouse.

Alice prodded him. "Or?"

"Or we deal with both of them at the same time. You wanted to eliminate Jennifer anyway. Why don't we see if they leave together? I have my pistol. We can surprise them and just keep moving quickly. We can also tell Henry we were trying to keep Jennifer from talking to the police about him."

Alice considered the plan. It was surprisingly satisfying, considering Janos had come up with it. The plan also had the benefit of being simple and direct.

Janos had a tendency to make elaborate plans and then not stick with them. Once, in London, they had set up a job where Alice would pick up a target, act like she was ordering an Uber, and Janos would pick them both up. After driving the victim to a construction site, Alice intended to garrote him.

All went well until Janos made a pass down the crowded street and saw the man standing on a corner. He ran the man down and kept going. Janos did not understand why Alice was so angry. He said, "I saved us hours. No one can pin the stolen car on me. We're still getting paid. What's the problem?"

Alice didn't want to admit it at the time, but she had been excited to use her garrote. Janos had stolen the opportunity. She didn't want that to happen this time. Not with Jennifer Chang.

Alice stepped away from the window so no one from inside would notice them. She pulled Janos into the empty, recessed doorway of an apartment building next door. She pulled him in close so if anyone noticed them they would think she was being affectionate.

Alice said, "We can't screw this up. We need to get in there to see how well they know each other. Maybe this is the first time he's been able to talk to her. I'd also like to hear what she's telling him."

Janos said, "Then I can blast them when they come out?"

"We might have to be a little more subtle. Maybe figure a way to lure them into an alley."

"So you can use that horrible garrote?"

"You mean the *silent* garrote?"

"Something tells me the cop would be hard to handle. Even for you."

"I have less interest in him. Let's see if Jennifer leaves with him or alone. That will dictate how we proceed."

"Listen to how well we can communicate in English now. We fit right in here."

Alice had to smile at her partner's sincerity. He really didn't think they spoke with accents. She reached up and caressed his face. The Romanian could be charming and sweet.

Janos had a broad grin. He was displaying the deficiencies in Romanian dentistry. His two front teeth were straight and white. But after that there was almost no pattern to the way his teeth grew, all of them at different angles. It was only now that she realized this was why he smiled with his lips closed most of the time.

Alice said, "What are you grinning about?"

"You can be nice. But right now you don't want to be subtle. You want to be able to use that garrote on that girl."

There was no time to play games. "So what if I do? Are you with me on this plan?"

Janos nodded.

"Neither of them have ever seen us. We can walk right into that coffeehouse, sit down right next to them, and they will never know who we are."

"Until we kill them."

Alice nodded. "Until we kill them."

CHAPTER 40

I'LL ADMIT TO being a little surprised that Jennifer Chang made me for a cop so quickly and that she wasn't going to say anything.

She leveled another glare at me and said, "When do I get to speak to my attorney?"

"You're not under arrest. I just want to talk to you."

She immediately started to pack up her iPad and slip it into her purse.

I leaned back in the chair and let her think I didn't care. Finally I said, "Are you going back to your apartment above the casket warehouse?" That one caught her by surprise. Now she knew I was serious. I had to keep going. "I'm not looking to cause you any grief. I'm just looking for a missing girl. That's it. I swear to God."

"Why should I believe you?"

"Because I'm a good Catholic. My grandfather is even a priest." I waited. That one usually killed with a slightly older group. I had no idea how millennials viewed Catholicism. They sure didn't care much about cops one way or the other.

"What's the name of the girl you're looking for?"

"Natalie Lunden. I just want to make sure she's safe."

"So you're really not looking to arrest anyone?"

"I didn't say that. If Natalie is being held somewhere against her will, then whoever took her has to pay the price. As well versed as you are in criminal procedure, you probably understand the street law as well."

She settled back into her chair. "I haven't seen Natalie in almost a month."

"No one has. Her mother's frantic." I didn't know if Jennifer knew who Natalie's father was.

Jennifer looked around the room quickly. She was suddenly jumpy.

"What's wrong?"

"Another one of my friends is missing. He's not answering his phone or anything."

"What's his name?"

"Tommy Payne."

She didn't know her friend was dead. I wasn't sure this was the right time to tell her, but I couldn't build any kind of trust by starting out with a lie.

"I'm afraid your friend Tommy is dead."

She looked stricken. She choked back some tears and managed to ask me a couple of questions. Just simple ones. The kind a family member of a murder victim usually asks. "How?"

"When?" "Are there any suspects?" I answered all of them quickly, and she seemed to handle it reasonably well.

I gave her some time to gather her thoughts. She pulled a tissue from her designer purse and blew her nose. She sniffled for a little while until she was ready to talk. Then she leaned in across the table and said in a very clear and determined voice, "Is there anything I can do to help you catch whoever killed Tommy?"

"I'm not the detective on the homicide. I'm just looking for Natalie. But I can think of something that will help both me and the homicide detective."

"What's that?"

"Tell me about Estonia."

CHAPTER 41

I PULLED OUT a small notebook and settled in to hear Jennifer Chang's story. Like most people about to talk to the police, she paused for a moment. She looked around the room as if she was conducting countersurveillance.

She said, "If Natalie's in Estonia, she's with a hacker named Henry."

"Henry."

"His real name is Endrik. Endrik Laar. Henry's just the Anglicized version of his name he prefers. I'm pretty sure he's from Estonia originally. He's there now, at any rate."

"Who is he? What's he look like?"

Jennifer thought about it for a moment. These computer people didn't just spout off. They considered questions and the best way to answer. Finally she said, "I guess Henry is about thirty. He's a little on the short side. Not even five eight. He used to be as skinny as a rail, but now he's muscular. I mean absolutely ripped. Part of it is because he trains with some former Olympian from Germany. Part of it is steroids. I think that's what changed his personality. He used to be the typical funny, nice, young computer guy. But he's changed."

"How so?"

"It started with his moods. As he brought in more and more money, it was like he realized how much power he had. Then he hired people specifically as enforcers. They were the ones who kept all the programmers from talking to the police. I think it's worked pretty well. To my knowledge, he's never been arrested."

"Why would Natalie be with Henry? Are they an item?"

"That's a complicated question. Henry had relationships with all three of the female programmers during the time I worked with him, here in New York. A girl from Latvia named Svetlana. Natalie. And me." She stared at me to see if I was shocked or would offer any judgment.

I said, "I remember what it's like to be young. I don't care about any consensual relationship. But I am trying to get a handle on if Natalie was forcibly taken or ran away to be with her boyfriend."

Jennifer said, "It's hard to say. Natalie was into Henry for a while. When we first started working with him, we thought we were doing something special. Exposing secrets. Forcing businesses to admit when they were cheating people. But pretty quickly Henry figured out the real money was in essentially blackmailing retailers. He'd knock out their website for an hour, then tell them to pay some outrageous sum or he'd knock out the website for three days."

"But he couldn't knock it out permanently."

Jennifer gave me a flat stare. "Amazon does more than six hundred million dollars in sales a day. Do you think if some hacker who proved he could knock them offline asked for five million dollars to leave them alone they wouldn't go for it? Henry does it all the time. And by setting up his bank accounts in money havens like Belize, Switzerland, and the Cayman Islands, it makes it impossible to find him."

I put down the pad and crossed my legs. "What is Natalie like?"

"Nice girl. Very close with her mother. When you told me her mom hadn't heard from her I knew something was wrong."

"Is she a hacker, too? Does she enjoy cracking systems?"

"We *all* enjoy breaking security systems. She is more into creating the algorithms than actually cracking the systems. She never seemed to care about money, either."

"Do you think she's in trouble?"

Jennifer didn't have to think about this one. She looked me right in the eye and said, "Yes."

CHAPTER 42

ALICE AND JANOS stepped through the door of Brew. They didn't try to hide or be subtle. No one knew them. Their rough plan involved waiting until Jennifer and the cop left and then somehow luring them to a secluded area. Eliminate both of them. Then flee.

What the plan lacked in details it made up for in boldness.

Alice said to Janos, "You shoot the cop. Don't hesitate once we get them outside. He doesn't look like someone you want to screw with. I'll deal with Jennifer."

Now, as she stood by the front door of the coffeehouse, she took a moment to appreciate Jennifer completely. It wasn't just that she was pretty and stylish. This girl was dead-on smart. Alice would see what all those brains did for her with a wire around her throat.

She and the cop looked like they were talking pleasantly. The tiny tables left little room for anything but a cup of coffee.

She thought about Henry, too. He shared the same superior attitude as Jennifer. Alice wondered how he'd react once he heard that Jennifer was dead. She had a story to cover herself and Janos. She liked the idea of that Estonian asshole mourning over his lost Asian love.

Alice let her eyes scan the rest of the coffeehouse. It seemed like a lot of students. The place was wedged between City College and Columbia University. There was no shortage of smart young people to frequent a hipster coffeehouse like this.

She noticed everyone had a computer. Most people didn't appear to be casually browsing Facebook, either. They had their noses buried in screens and were tapping away at keyboards.

Oscar had been right. This place was a hangout for hackers.

Alice looked at the line to order next to the counter. She wouldn't mind a cup of tea.

She glanced down the counter until her eyes fell on two men. They were both grinning at her.

At almost the same time she saw them, Alice heard Janos exclaim, "Oh, shit."

It was the two crazy Dutchmen who worked for Henry. Her text to Henry must've had more of an effect than she thought.

Then she saw both men slip off their stools. A moment later, she saw the guns in their hands.

CHAPTER 43

AS I DIGESTED Jennifer's words, I looked up, and again I noticed the two men at the counter, the ones dressed like Europeans. One was tall with his blond hair tight and neat. Both of them were in decent shape, if dressed a little oddly.

I'd noted that their eyes had followed me as I walked in. Now I noticed they were smiling at a couple who'd just stepped in the front door.

Something wasn't right about it. I couldn't put my finger on it immediately. The shorter of the two men, a guy about thirty-five with long, stringy hair, put his hand behind his back. It was a common movement and normally wouldn't draw notice. But I was on alert. And, to me, it was the definition of a *furtive movement*.

I took a moment to inspect the couple who had just entered. A man and a woman dressed in dark, casual clothes. There was nothing unusual about them, except for the fact that an unknown couple had entered Thomas Payne's building the night he was killed. And been with him in the train station. I kicked myself for not requesting a copy of the surveillance footage from Ed Arris.

Once the two of them noticed the men at the bar there was a distinct, silent confrontation.

Then the men at the counter drew guns.

I acted completely out of instinct, as if one of my own children were sitting at the table with me. I dove out of my seat, scooping up Jennifer Chang on the way. We landed hard on the polished floor and slid a few feet into another table.

I would've heard the cursing and comments of the people we had bumped into except the screams of the people near the counter drowned them out.

I didn't have to look up to see what was happening. This wasn't the eighties. New Yorkers were not used to guns coming out inside coffeehouses. A wave of panic swept over the small place.

The screams were completely masked by the sound of the first gunshots.

CHAPTER 44

IN THAT SECOND before Alice could react, but after she'd seen the Dutchmen, Christoph and Ollie, she froze. It wasn't fear. It was shock. And confusion. There was no reason for those two psychopaths to be here. Unless Henry had decided to cancel their contracts permanently.

Alice heard Janos mumble, "What the hell?" She felt him move as he reached for his gun. In an instant, her plan fell apart. She had relied on her plans for almost a decade. Her strength in this business was that she was a planner. Most of the people working for criminals like Henry gave little thought to their jobs. Point them in the right direction and they killed someone.

Now she wondered if plans were worth it. Christoph and Ollie never planned anything, and now they had the drop on her and Janos.

Christoph had some kind of 9mm pistol. Ollie had a machine

pistol. It looked like an old-style MAC-10. It was funny what raced through her mind in this moment of shock. Of course, it was Ollie who didn't hesitate.

He flicked his head to move his stringy hair out of his eyes, something Alice had seen him do a thousand times. It gave Janos a moment to step from behind Alice and bring his own pistol into play.

As the two men maneuvered to get off their first shot, Alice heard the wave of terror in the coffeehouse. It started with the cop sweeping Jennifer off her seat and onto the floor. Then people started screaming almost immediately. The distressed reactions began at the counter and seemed to work around the room in a counterclockwise motion.

Her ears were already stinging from the screams when Ollie and Janos fired, almost simultaneously. The sound of Janos's pistol next to her ear was painful. It was probably the closest she'd ever been to a gun going off without any warning.

Suddenly it was as if her head had been plunged underwater. Sounds were muffled and garbled. But she could feel each shot. The concussions jolted her.

Janos's pistol had a deeper, solid report. Ollie's machine pistol had a higher pitch that sounded like a typewriter. A typewriter that never ran out of bullets. At least it felt like that to Alice. It probably felt like that to anyone who'd ever been shot at.

Dishes crashed to the floor. There was a mad dash for the take-out door at the end of the counter.

Alice felt the limitations of her knife and garrote when everyone else had a gun. For the first time she noticed a small sign above the register that said GUN-FREE ZONE. NO FIREARMS ALLOWED IN THIS BUSINESS.

A barista in a white T-shirt staggered away from the two Dutch killers. A red splotch spread across his upper chest.

At least one of Janos's bullets flew wide. Alice dove to one side, looking for cover. A couple of overturned tables near the door were her only chance.

Everything was happening way too fast.

CHAPTER 45

MY HEAD WAS swimming. That's the feeling I got when I heard gunshots. At least that's what I told myself. More likely it was just fear. But a detective with the NYPD couldn't generally admit to being afraid of anything.

At the moment, I wasn't afraid—I was terrified. I was lying on top of Jennifer Chang. She probably still wasn't certain what was going on. I'm sure she wasn't happy about a large man lying on top of her, but I thought that would be the best way of keeping her from being harmed.

Like many gunfights, this one had started with a couple of shots traded back and forth. The difference was that *unlike* most gunfights, the trickle of shots had turned into a flood. From three different guns.

Now everyone around us was panicking. They started to

shove and run, knocking over chairs and tables as they rushed for the exit at the other side of the room.

I lifted my head, then scooted in front of Jennifer and peeked over our table. All I could focus on was the guy with long hair holding the trigger of a MAC-10. I couldn't believe the number of rounds being spewed out from the small machine pistol.

One of the staff members, a young man with long hair held in a man bun, took a round right in the chest. He kept walking in a daze, then tumbled onto the floor just past the counter. A female patron lay a few feet from him. The gaping hole in her face leaked blood onto the shiny flooring.

A huge stack of dishes tumbled off a table somewhere. The crashing sound competed with the gunfire. It added to the hysteria. This was exactly what gunfighters counted on. They wanted chaos all around them so it would be harder to identify them later. Eyewitness testimony was notoriously shaky and, contrary to what most people would think, not the best evidence to convict someone.

I pulled my Glock but was hesitant to fire. I didn't want to attract gunfire back to me with so many civilians huddled close by. That included Jennifer Chang, who was now on her knees and sobbing.

I risked looking at the main door. The woman had edged over to kneel behind a pileup of overturned tables by the door.

The man she had come in with crouched with his right arm extended. He was actually trying to aim during the exchange of gunfire. It had to be tough, with bullets whizzing past him from a machine gun and another pistol.

Then the man by the door went down. I think it was two shots from the pistol shooter at the counter. The rounds caught him just below the neck, in his upper chest. Both impacts stag-gered him. He shuffled back until he bumped into the frame of the door.

The glass in the door, which had already been penetrated by a couple of bullets, shattered as soon as he bumped it.

As the man stood there a moment, three rounds from the machine pistol struck him. All three rounds caught him at just about the center mass of his chest. He dropped the pistol, then tumbled out the door that now had no glass in it. His feet dangled over the bottom of the door and his body lay on the sidewalk.

The long-haired man with the machine pistol slipped another magazine through the grip of the gun.

Just then, Jennifer stood up and tried to make it to the door.

CHAPTER 46

ALICE HAD JUST found a little safety behind the tables when she turned back to Janos. Janos was hit. He backed away a few steps until he bumped into the door. The glass in the door just fell out of the frame and tinkled onto the ground.

Everything seemed to freeze. The shooting stopped. Alice could hear only the screams. The two Dutchmen stared at Janos.

Then Ollie fired a stream of bullets into Janos's chest.

Her friend and partner collapsed through the door. His legs extended across the bottom of the doorframe. His dropped pistol spun on the floor until it was a few feet from Alice. She looked up at the grinning killers, then scanned the room. She couldn't see where the cop and Jennifer Chang had ended up.

This was it. She and Janos used to joke that it didn't matter if they saved money or took serious risks because they knew they would die young. There was no one in this line of work who didn't die prematurely.

She made a calculation quickly in her head, whether she had enough money in the bank to take care of her grandmother for the rest of her life. Not that there was anything Alice could do about it now.

She made up her mind.

She lunged out from behind the tables and grabbed Janos's pistol with her right hand. As she was slipping back behind cover, both of the Dutchmen opened fire again, splintering the tables easily.

A sharp pain radiated up her arm. It was what she imagined someone having a heart attack might feel. She looked down at her left forearm. Blood leaked out of a wound almost at her elbow. Her first bullet wound. Now she was pissed.

She spun to the opposite end of the tables. The movement surprised the Dutch killers. They had been expecting her to pop out from the side closest to them. She could see the surprise on their faces as she fired three quick shots.

Both men started to dive out of the line of fire. She lost sight of them completely.

Then she saw something else. Jennifer Chang was up and running for the other door. It was too perfect. Everything lined up. Her bright blouse was like a target with her purple-streaked ponytail swaying against it.

She knew she didn't have much time. Alice lined up the shot carefully. Then fired one time. She felt a wave of satisfaction as the computer programmer flew off her feet and slid into a wall.

Alice moved away from the tables with the pistol up. Now she was looking for Christoph and Ollie.

A shadow from outside fell across her face. She risked a quick peek over her shoulder. It was the last clear view she would ever have.

Ollie had slipped out the door and had his machine pistol pointed at her from outside.

He showed no emotion as he squeezed the trigger.

Alice heard the first few shots, then everything went black.

CHAPTER 47

HARRY GRISSOM MET me at the Columbia University Medical Center. Jennifer Chang was in surgery. I didn't know what else to do but wait right here.

Harry was wearing a suit and looked like a lawyer from Wyoming. He shook his head as he approached me in the back of the waiting room. There was no one else in the dull, clean room. I sat at the edge of the only couch. I'd been staring at the seven empty metal chairs spaced along the opposite wall. A TV, hung high on the wall, played CNN, but I hadn't been listening.

Harry shook his head and said, "Jesus, what happened?"

I shrugged. Just like I'd told an investigating detective, "I have no idea what happened. I didn't recognize any of the shooters. I didn't see where anyone went. And the one person I was trying to keep safe ended up shot in the back."

I looked up at my lieutenant and said, "What's it like at the coffeehouse?"

Harry said, "We've got the dead couple who were part of the shoot-out and two dead civilians. We have four more with serious wounds."

I cringed. People buying coffee shouldn't have to worry about being blasted by a gun. This was crazy. I looked at Harry and said, "It has to be related to the mayor's daughter. The woman aimed at Jennifer as she ran away."

Harry said, "And she had a homemade garrote in her purse."

"Like the one used to kill Tommy Payne near Penn Station?"

"I've already called Ed Arris. We think it's the murder weapon."

"Harry, this shit has gone from doing a favor for the mayor to a full-blown conspiracy. We have to do something. We have to find Natalie Lunden. She's in real danger."

Harry put his hand on my shoulder. "You need to get some rest. That's all you need to worry about right now. Spend a little time with that beautiful family. Someone will call you as soon as there's news on Jennifer Chang."

Reluctantly I agreed with my friend. I waited until Harry left, then I waited a while longer. I checked with the nurse one more time.

I had to fight the feeling that Harry had lost faith in me. I felt like I'd let people down. Especially Jennifer Chang. I wondered if anyone would even keep me up-to-date on the shooting. Technically I wasn't suspended. But cops rarely like to be seen talking to a detective sent home for any reason.

I was sure rumors about me would spread quickly. They'd

revolve around some imagined confrontation I had with management. No one would believe that my friend of almost twenty years had suggested I go home and see my family. Instead, I would go home after I was sure Jennifer Chang was out of danger.

CHAPTER 48

I WALKED THROUGH the front door of my apartment completely drained. It's easy to imagine that a homicide detective always feels drained when arriving home. That's not accurate. I usually get a bolt of energy anticipating seeing my kids and Mary Catherine. I love coming home to my family.

Tonight it was different. I had absolutely no energy and I couldn't focus. I wondered if the cumulative effect of the shootings had finally caught up to me.

I had lingered at the hospital until I found out Jennifer Chang had made it through surgery and was in recovery. A young surgeon named Susan Jones had come out to talk to me, even though she knew I wasn't family and wasn't the detective on the case involving Jennifer.

She was in her scrubs with more than a few blood smears and other stains. Her hair poking out from under a surgical cap was limp with sweat, and wide perspiration stains had seeped from under her arms. No one could ever tell me that surgeons weren't athletes on some level. To stand and concentrate for so many hours without a break takes real determination and stamina.

Dr. Jones motioned me to sit down on a couch. I think it was more about her getting off her feet than delivering bad news to me. She said, "I'm very impressed you waited here for her. I heard you tried to shield her from the gunfire. That's brave, even for a cop."

"Is Jennifer going to recover?"

"She lost a lot of blood. The bullet entered about four inches from her spine but worked its way through her torso. Her stomach was perforated and her left lung collapsed. She'll be in the ICU for days, maybe weeks."

I sagged in my seat.

The doctor touched my arm and said, "You've done all you can. There won't be an update for some time. Please go home and get some rest. I don't even know you and I have to say, you look terrible. Please forgive me."

She gave me a weak smile and then was gone.

I'm not even sure how I made it back to the apartment. I was on automatic pilot.

Now I stood in the doorway and still couldn't shake all of my fears about Natalie Lunden. Whoever she was involved with meant business. I believed she was in Estonia. In fact, I knew it. But I had no idea if she was there by consent or if she'd been forced to go.

This was troubling on a number of levels. Having my oldest daughter, Juliana, greet me at the door only emphasized my fears. How would I feel if Juliana disappeared like Natalie? I'd be calling in all the favors I could. I was starting to understand the mayor a little better.

I made my rounds in the apartment, greeting each kid individually. I could tell that Mary Catherine was still worried about me. Sometimes I wondered if she and Harry Grissom secretly traded phone calls about my mental state and general health.

Eventually I found myself next to the computer with Eddie. After I caught up on his daily life, school, and basketball, I got to the point. "Eddie, I'm having a little trouble comprehending some kids who are drawn to working with a certain hacker in Estonia. I know the money is pretty good, but is there something else?"

Eddie's face positively lit up. "Dad, you have no idea. It's the closest a kid like me will come to having a superpower. Just because I understand computers and most people really don't. Once I found out I understood what hackers were talking about, it was easy. I follow a couple of forums online and read some blogs by hackers. It doesn't surprise me the hacker is based in Estonia."

"Why's that?"

"Estonia is considered the most wired republic in Europe. The government views access to the internet as a human right. They spent a fortune on infrastructure to attract high-tech companies."

"Most kids your age don't even know where Estonia is. I'm very impressed."

"We studied it in history class. How, after World War II, the Soviet Union essentially took control of Latvia, Lithuania, and Estonia. That makes their rise as a computer power all the more impressive."

I sat for a moment, thinking about Holy Name. I knew it was a good school. I've sent all my kids there. But I didn't remember learning anything like that when I was in school. Of course, my interest in history didn't come on until I was in college.

Then Eddie explained to me the draw of young people to crack security systems at different companies or government facilities. It was the cyberpunk's version of climbing Mount Everest. Basically, they did it because it was there.

I settled back in my chair and said, "Eddie, would you mind showing me some of the forums and blogs that you read?"

By the smile on my son's face you would've thought I'd given him a Jet Ski. He loved this kind of stuff.

CHAPTER 49

AT EIGHT O'CLOCK, we all gathered around the speak-erphone on the breakfast nook counter. I'd bought the phone at Best Buy specifically for these nights. Sure, it was a little crowded with twelve people trying to get close enough to both hear the speaker and be heard when they spoke.

This was our weekly call from Brian. It was the one night no one ever argued about what we were going to do. No one wanted to miss even a moment of talking to their brother.

Mary Catherine and my grandfather, Seamus, always sat in two straight-backed chairs closest to the phone.

At one minute after eight, the phone rang and Seamus hit the button within a second. He looked like a gambler in Las Vegas asking for another card.

We settled down to a near silence. After Brian said hello and told us how everything was going, everyone got to say hello and one other thing. It took about ten minutes to work through the whole family.

I was touched to see how excited the kids were to talk to their brother. It meant I'd done something right raising them. Ten kids in a family was difficult enough. If some of them didn't get along, it could be brutal. I found it was easy enough to keep everyone happy if they were busy. Sports, clubs, family playdates—it all added up. And right now I appreciated that arithmetic.

Trent told Brian about basketball and sports. Chrissy told him about our cat, Socky, who now was producing solid poop after a week of diarrhea. I never tried to edit what my kids were going to say.

Finally I got to ask some questions that were important to me. "How do you like Fishkill Correctional?"

"Compared to Gowanda, it's great. I'm taking a bunch of classes. I already told you I earned my GED. Now I'm working on getting certified as an air-conditioning repair mechanic. They have the population separated by security risk so I'm in with a bunch of younger, nonviolent offenders."

I thought I might cry. Here was my oldest son. Along with his sister, Juliana, my first treasure. A year ago I was afraid he'd thrown away his whole life because he made some poor choices. Now he was making good choices. More important, he hadn't given up on his life. He'd just made a detour or two. He had some goals, and I was so proud of him I couldn't speak for a moment. Luckily, plenty of other people were there to fill in.

Seamus said, "What are you doing for fun?"

"This place gives us full TV privileges at night. As long as we follow the rules and don't have any marks against us, we can watch whatever we want. I've been reading a lot, too."

Jane, our resident super reader, was quick to ask, "Who do you like to read?"

Brian didn't hesitate. "Elmore Leonard, and a newer author named Mark Greaney. Can't get enough of either of them."

Now I was at a loss for words. I'd never known Brian to read for pleasure. And he sounded excited about his studies.

Brian said, "This place is so much better than Gowanda I can't believe it. But I still miss home. I miss all of you. If I get home, I promise to keep reading, and I'll get a job. I swear."

I was quick to say, "Buddy, you don't have to make any promises. We want you home as much as you want to come home."

Eddie said, "I'm trying to teach Dad about computers and hacking."

Brian laughed like we were playing a prank on him. Then he said, "Really? I'm impressed, Dad. You won't be sorry you picked up a new skill. We even have computers available to us here. One guy from Schenectady got arrested again for stealing credit card numbers using the computer from our class."

Mary Catherine took a moment to tell Brian all the meals she would cook for him as soon as he got home.

The call ended after our allotted twenty minutes and we had been forced into quick good-byes. If anything, it made me consider the mayor's offer of help more seriously.

CHAPTER 50

DETECTIVES AT THE NYPD have an unusual relationship with one of their own units, known as Intel. The Intelligence Bureau has a mysterious aura about it. Generally the unit recruits the best and brightest from all the NYPD divisions to provide command staff with intelligence about growing crime trends and potential catastrophes.

Since the 9/11 terror attacks, the unit has grown and wields more influence. One thing most people don't realize about it is that it has offices outside New York, too. In fact, the NYPD has offices outside the US. Some of those offices are in Europe and the Middle East. It's hard to imagine an NYPD officer roaming the streets of Madrid, but in the new millennium, that's a reality.

I learned a long time ago that Intel is an incredible resource for a detective. The staff are smart and helpful, and don't care about claiming credit for a case. That cuts down on turf wars.

I'd given all I had on Natalie Lunden and the cases surrounding her to my friend in Intel, Lieutenant Tony Martindale. I gave up telling him what to do with information years ago. He'd talk to sources and other agencies, especially with connections overseas, and somehow he always worked magic with everything I gave him.

Once, when I had nothing on a homicide except a partial fingerprint, Lieutenant Martindale had a source in the Guatemalan military who matched the print to one of their former soldiers. As a result, I made the arrest and also helped Narcotics bust up one of the bigger drug-running groups in the city. The former sergeant in the Guatemalan army confessed to the homicide and would be in Sing Sing until the middle of the century.

Yet the only ones who claimed any credit were Narcotics detectives. Tony Martindale never opened his mouth once, even though he was the one who had cracked the case for everyone.

That's why I trusted him with everything I knew, or suspected, about the hacking ring run by the mysterious "Henry" in Estonia.

The day after the Brew shoot-out, I was in the lieutenant's private office in a corner of the Intel unit. The office suited him. There were journals on combating terrorism, the newest firearms, police tactics, public administration, and even one on photography. This guy was like a computer. He read everything and didn't care one way or the other if people utilized him.

I sat in an uncomfortable metal chair as the lieutenant rolled around behind his desk on his ancient Office Depot discount chair. He was giving someone crime statistics over the phone while checking his email and answering a text. And this was a slow day for Lieutenant Tony Martindale.

Finally he hung up the phone, looked at me, and said, "I'm sorry, Mike. As you can imagine, it's crazy around here. But I have the information you asked about."

I knew not to do anything except smile and nod. I didn't want to risk sending him off on another tangent that might take five or ten minutes. He waited for a comment, then picked up a folder from a pile on his desk like he knew exactly which one to reach for.

He leaned back in the black chair and said, "You might've stumbled onto something big. This guy you asked about, Endrik Laar, has about ten aliases. He has three official IDs issued in Estonia and Latvia, but none of the three IDs has the same photo. None of the investigators I spoke with over the phone are even sure if they have an accurate description of him."

"What are they tracking him for?"

"Cybercrime. The son of a bitch has a decent blackmail business going. The big corporations are terrified of hackers like him. And the young programmers flock to him. They know they can make a lot more money with him than they can at a legitimate job."

I asked, "Anyone have any idea about US nationals working for him? Specifically the name I gave you, Natalie Lunden?"

The lieutenant gave me a grin. "I assume you know who her father is."

"I can neither confirm nor deny that I know the identity of Natalie Lunden's father."

Lieutenant Martindale let out a hearty laugh. "Spoken like an Intel detective. If you ever get tired of chasing down murderers, we'll always have a place for you here."

I didn't want to tell him that showing up at One Police Plaza every day would cause me too much stress. I'd probably end up with some rash or other disgusting reaction.

The lieutenant said, "I've done a favor or two for the LFP."

"How'd it work out?"

"Just did my job. He seemed okay in a pudgy politician kind of way." He waited for me to either laugh or agree.

Instead, I said, "We can still keep this conversation between us, right?"

"Intel is known for its discretion. Now, here's a list of potential addresses and associates of Mr. Laar." As he handed me the papers bound in a small folder, Lieutenant Martindale gave me a sideways glance. "You're not thinking of going to Estonia, are you?"

"Why?"

"We don't have an office there. Would be difficult to give you much support."

"So I'd be on my own?"

"I didn't say that. I just said it would be *difficult* to help you. The NYPD never leaves a man behind. We'd make sure you had what you needed."

"What about the Estonian police? Would they help if I needed it?"

"Who knows? They deal with the US Embassy and the FBI Legat who covers all the Baltics. It'd take a while to get official approval for your trip through the FBI."

"Then let's forget our brothers and sisters who work for the federal government. Is that okay?"

Martindale laughed again. "I rarely think of them here in New York. You're good to go as far as I'm concerned."

I always appreciated my visits to the NYPD Intel Bureau.

CHAPTER 51

IT'S SURPRISINGLY EASY for an NYPD detective to get an audience with the mayor of New York when you have information about his daughter. Within thirty minutes of my call to his assistant, I was in Mayor Alfred Hanna's main office in City Hall.

If I had ever questioned the mayor's concern for his daughter, I now realized it was genuine. Although overweight and out of shape, the mayor was always known for dressing well; the *New York Post* had even branded him "the dapper dumbass." Today, image seemed to be the last thing on his mind. He looked like he hadn't slept in three days.

The mayor already had a synopsis of the shoot-out at Brew. He knew it was related to his daughter. That only made him more anxious. We sat on a black leather couch. I noticed a photo collage on the wall, images of his daughter from toddlerhood to her graduation from high school. There were other collages of his sons, but this one struck a chord. I wouldn't look any better than him if one of my kids was missing.

I didn't know how else to say it, so I got right to the point. "Mayor, everything I've learned points to your daughter being in Tallinn, Estonia. I need to take a trip there to run down more leads. I'm afraid that if your daughter was there of her own free will she would've been in touch with her mother. Just a phone call. Something. That's why I need to travel."

The news about his daughter bothered the mayor. For a moment, I thought he might cry. Then he looked up at me and said, "I can't authorize travel like that. That kind of expense to find my daughter would cause the press to eviscerate me. There's already been enough coverage of my divorce. That's what drove the wedge between Natalie and me in the first place."

From a public employee's perspective, I understood what he was saying. From a father's perspective, I was baffled. I would use everything in my power to find one of my kids. To hell with the media or anyone else.

The mayor stared silently out the window for a few moments. Then he turned to face me again. The couch felt like a giant beanbag chair forcing us to sit close to each other.

The mayor said, "I know what you're thinking, Detective. You think all I care about is my political position. That's not correct."

Now I heard the weariness in his voice. He was beyond exhausted and just wanted to find his daughter.

The mayor continued. "I'm in a catch-22. I can't authorize excessive city funds for a public employee to find my daughter. And I can't use my own money to pay a public employee. I want to find my daughter, but I've also sworn to uphold laws and stick to a code of ethics. You guys at the PD and the people at the fire department may hate my policies about pay raises, but I made them in the best interest of the city. And now I can't send you to find my daughter because it's not in the best interest of the city. In fact, it goes against every position I ran on. Favoritism, funneling resources to the wealthy areas, and corruption within the city government itself."

As he talked, his voice got stronger and he almost sounded like he was on the stump. But I understood what he was saying. I was even a little surprised by what he was saying. He was trying to do the right thing, no matter how hard it was. I had to respect that. I also had to tell him what I intended to do.

I said, "Mr. Mayor, I'm going to go look for Natalie on my own. No one needs to know. Not the media, not your constituents, not even your aides."

Now the mayor stared at me. His mouth dropped open in surprise. All he could manage to say was "Why?"

"Because I'm a father, and I have daughters."

CHAPTER 52

I BRACED FOR a brisk discussion, or what some people might call an argument, when I finally got Mary Catherine alone that night. I explained everything that had happened and finished with "That's why I feel like I have to go to Estonia. That girl may be in real trouble, and no one's going to do anything about it."

I almost felt like closing my eyes and shying away as I waited for a torrent of Irish anger. Sometimes she used insults I had to look up or ask my grandfather to translate to judge how angry she was.

Mary Catherine was constantly concerned about me at work. She understood my sense of duty and the fact that I loved my job, and she maintained that she fell in love with me after I was already a cop. She understood it was part of me. That didn't mean she kept quiet about her concerns.

This time she surprised me. As we stood on our balcony, listening to the gentle sounds of the city, she leaned across and kissed me on the cheek. Then she slid in close and locked arms with me. She didn't say a word.

After a full minute, I had to ask. "Do you have a problem with me traveling to Estonia?"

"Will I miss you? Yes. Will I worry about you? Yes. Do I understand why you feel you have to go? Once again, I'd have to say yes. Michael, you're nothing if not predictable when it comes to doing the right thing."

I gave Mary Catherine a sideways glance. "You're being re-markably reasonable about this. Am I walking into a trap?"

"I know how precious your daughters are to you. I just worry for your safety. You can't fix everyone's problems."

"No, but I might be able to fix this one."

"Can you count on anyone for help over there? The FBI? Anyone?"

This could've been an opportunity to ease her fears and tell her there was nothing to worry about. But that flew in the face of my policy of being open and honest with the woman I intended to spend the rest of my life with. "No, I'll just be a tourist."

Mary Catherine said, "A tourist who might have to tangle with a gang."

"A gang of computer geeks." Okay, so I was misleading her a little bit.

My grandfather wandered out onto the balcony to join us. I had filled him in earlier on what I planned to do.

Seamus said, "I've made a few calls. You'll have some help from the clergy if you should need it."

"Great, I could use some tough, elderly backup. Maybe they

173

can help me put these boys on the right track and convince them to forget about crime."

Seamus didn't even bother with his usual scowl.

Mary Catherine said, "I didn't realize the Roman Catholic community was so big in Estonia."

Seamus said, "It's growing all the time. But in this case, I spoke to one of my friends in the Orthodox Church. He understands your situation and is prepared to help. Marty Zlatic is the rector of St. Laszlo's in Tallinn." He handed me a sheet of paper with a confusing phone number.

I stared at my grandfather and said, "You never fail to surprise me. I thought you only conned other Catholic priests."

The old man smiled. "I have friends across all denominations. You need only ask and I can find someone to help. We all talk."

That seemed to satisfy some of Mary Catherine's concerns. At least for the moment.

CHAPTER 53

AS WE STOOD near the TSA line in JFK, I wondered what the European tourists arriving thought of my horde of kids, fiancée, and grandfather all huddled around me. They probably viewed the scene and thought I must be on my way to a combat zone.

Chrissy was crying. I was not sure why. Even Trent was a little clingy. He stood right next to me with his arm around my waist.

Eddie handed me a sheet of paper. He said, "Just some computer terms that might keep you from looking stupid."

I appreciated his faith in me. I glanced at the sheet and the first term I saw was *laptop*. How tech illiterate did he think I was?

Shawna motioned to me to lean down. She pulled me closer and whispered in my ear, "I love you, Dad. I'll think about you every minute you're away."

It was the sweetest thing a little girl could say to her father. It choked me up for a moment while I said good-bye to everyone else.

I gave each one an individual hug and kiss. Then I found I needed a giant hug with everyone crammed together. We must've looked like a rugby scrum.

This whole weird case had crystallized for me just how much my family meant to me. It sounded sappy to say they were my whole world. But they really were.

As we held a hug for a few seconds, I felt the missing Brian like a physical pain. It made me think about a verse from Matthew. I could just get it roughly right in my head. "If a shepherd cares for one hundred sheep and one wanders off, will he not leave the other ninety-nine to look for that one?"

Now that verse made more sense than ever before.

Mary Catherine sobbed as I gave everyone a last, giant squeeze, and she slipped in as the others started to break the hug. She wrapped her arms around my neck and pulled me in for a long kiss. I could taste her salty tears running down her cheeks. I prayed I could slip away without bawling like a little kid myself.

She broke the kiss, then whispered in my ear, "I love you so much that I know you'll come back to me safe. If you love me the same way, make sure that happens."

That was the best challenge I'd ever been given.

Seamus was indispensable as he helped break up the crowd around me and held them for a moment as I backed away.

A TSA agent who had witnessed our extended good-bye gave me a flat stare as I turned around. I thought I was about to get a touching comment about how beautiful my family was or some earnest words of encouragement. Instead he cleared his throat and said, "Get in that line," pointing to a winding line of people at the far end of the security area.

About ten minutes after our good-bye, as I stood in line, waiting to take off my shoes and walk through a security scanner, I got a text.

It was from Mary Catherine.

All it said was I love you.

Now I started to tear up. That was all the encouragement I needed.

CHAPTER 54

AFTER A REASONABLE layover in Frankfurt that gave me time for a quick bite, my Lufthansa flight to Tallinn went quickly, and we landed at the Lennart Meri Airport fairly late in the evening, local time. I would've liked to see the place during the day for a better look at the giant panels on the roof. I wasn't sure if they were decorative or solar, but either way, they were impressive.

It was a pleasant-looking, bustling terminal. Even at this hour, the place had decent traffic around the kiosks for Nordica, the national airline of Estonia.

Almost as soon as I started heading through the main terminal, I noticed two men following me. One was about six feet tall and lean. He was younger and clean-cut. His partner was pudgy and a little sloppier. He looked like a guy who bowled in Cleveland on Wednesday nights.

The shorter man had to take two steps for every one his partner took. His comb-over took a hit as he tried to move quickly.

If I was in New York, I would've known exactly where to stop and lay a trap. I'd also have a gun. Here, all I could do was move a little faster.

I took a corner.

They followed.

I took another corner.

Same result.

I could see the wide, automatic doors that led outside almost a hundred yards in front of me. I'd never make it without these two catching me, so I made a quick left turn into a hallway that led to bathrooms and some kind of maintenance area. It was the best chance I had to surprise them.

I slipped in next to a support column. If they looked down the hallway, they wouldn't see anything. I wasn't sure of my plan beyond that. I quickly scanned the area to see if there was anything I could use as a weapon.

It reminded me of a time when I'd been surprised by two would-be muggers in Philadelphia, when a two-foot-long piece of metal rebar I picked up from the ground in front of a construction site slid nicely up the sleeve of my jacket. The two muggers, who had been following me for three blocks, never even noticed me stop. When they caught up to me in front of the convention center near Chinatown, I was ready for a confrontation. Like all bullies, muggers count on fear and intimidation, so when I realized all they had was a knife between them, I let the rebar slip into my hand. It had taken only one swing through the air to frighten both of the men into a sprint toward North Broad Street.

But in this hallway, I saw nothing remotely helpful. Now all I could do was ball my hands into fists.

CHAPTER 55

I FELT LIKE I was behind the column for hours, until I heard the men talking in low tones. I couldn't even tell what language they were speaking. Then one of them started to walk down the hallway toward me.

It was the taller of the two men. Good. If I took him out, the second man appeared easier to deal with. The tall one walked right past the post, focused on the men's room door down the hall. Apparently he was pretty sure that's where I had gone.

As soon as he was past me, I rushed him like a defensive end. I could hear him lose his breath as I caught him by surprise and knocked him about four feet through the air. He landed on the polished floor and slid another two feet into the wall.

I had no time to admire my handiwork, though I did have a moment of satisfaction. Any time you knock down someone bigger and younger than you, it's a point of pride.

I was going to kick him in the head to make sure he was out of the fight when the other man appeared almost right next to me. I had my right fist prepared to aim for his chin. Or should I say chins. He was sweating, and his black hair fell in every direction, like he'd just stepped out of the shower.

Before I could take any action, he said one of the few things that would freeze me in place.

"Detective Michael Bennett, we're FBI. Stand down."

Anyone could say that. But a seasoned cop knew when he heard another seasoned cop speak. Plus, we were in Estonia and this guy was speaking English with a Boston accent.

I kept my posture with my fist cocked.

The shorter, pudgy man eased around me to check on his friend, who was coming up onto his hands and knees. He helped him up, and they both faced me.

The shorter man said, "Put your goddamn fist down. We're adults. We're also Americans in a foreign country. Don't embarrass us."

I said, "How'd you know I'd be here?"

"Are you kidding me? You think there are no former NYPD detectives with the Bureau? You think they don't know what's going on with your useless Intelligence unit? I had to hump it up here from our official office in Riga, Latvia. You know how far that is?"

I didn't know what to say, so I shrugged and said, "Pretty far."

The FBI agent mumbled, "Asshole." Then he looked at me and said, "You bet your ass it's pretty far. Maybe not by US standards. But driving a shitty road three hundred kilometers is no picnic. And I had plenty to do in Riga. I hardly ever come up to Estonia."

I thought it best to play along. "So you must have a pretty big area of responsibility. All of the Baltics and what else?"

"Don't get me started. Three of us do the work of two entire squads. And you know why?"

"No, why?"

"Because it's our job. We actually *have* jurisdiction here and work closely with the national police. As far as we're concerned, you're just a tourist who's here to cause problems. Which is why we took the time to haul ass up here and meet you right at the gate."

"That was very thoughtful of you. I don't generally get that kind of service from the FBI in New York. Although they often deliver a similar speech about jurisdiction. Do they teach you that at Quantico? I'm sorry, I don't even know your name." I smiled and stuck out my hand, knowing that would annoy these FBI agents more than anything.

The tubby guy groaned in frustration. Finally he shook my hand. "My name's Bill Fiore. This kid who can't take a body blow is Matt Miller. We know you're here on a case. But we'd like to know exactly what you're doing four thousand miles from home."

"At the moment, I'm knocking around a couple of FBI agents. Tomorrow, I thought I might do some sightseeing."

Fiore said, "Do you think we're idiots?"

"Is that a rhetorical question?"

"Smart guy, huh? I got news for you, Mr. Big Shot Detective, you're not welcome in Estonia. Your ass is coming with us until we can load you on a plane back to the States." He took a moment to run a hand through his hair and flop it back into place over his spreading bald spot. He was about forty and, on closer inspection, looked like he used to be in reasonable shape. Maybe the food in Europe agreed with him.

I gathered my thoughts. "I really don't see what legal authority you have to send back a tourist. I'm not here on official business."

"Bullshit. You NYPD guys think you can do anything and go anywhere because of your Intel unit. But we have legal authority to be here. You don't. That's why you're getting on a plane tomorrow and heading back to New York, before you cause any problems."

The younger guy, Miller, grabbed me by the upper arm like I was a suspect being led away in cuffs. I had to admit he had a serious grip.

Fiore fell in on the other side of me as they started marching me toward the main exit.

CHAPTER 56

IT FELT LIKE I was being marched to prison. Had my mission failed so quickly and completely? Maybe someone in the Intel unit disagreed with me going to Estonia to look for the mayor's daughter and had tipped off the FBI. Maybe it was someone in the mayor's office itself. Either way, my heart sank. I walked along silently. I didn't see what I could do at the moment. I couldn't even ask to speak to someone at our embassy. It was my own government detaining me.

I wasn't about to hurt another US cop, no matter how much he annoyed me. All I could do was walk along. I was trying to resign myself to the situation.

A younger man in a FILA jacket walked past and bumped into Bill Fiore. Then he turned around and started shouting at the FBI agent in what I was sure was French. And he sounded pissed off.

To my surprise, Fiore answered him in French. And he sounded like every other annoyed Bostonian I had ever heard. Except he was speaking French.

Their voices echoed a little in this less busy section of the airport. A young woman closing up her newsstand for the evening looked on silently.

Fiore faced the man and stepped toward him. The tubby FBI agent had no fear, that was for sure.

Then someone else came from the side and bumped into the younger FBI agent, Miller. He bumped into him hard enough to knock him off his feet. Apparently this guy had a hard time staying upright.

I wondered if I would have to help my captors in some sort of confrontation. Then a pair of strong hands grabbed me from behind and started leading me toward the front door.

A voice from behind me said in English, "Just keep walking. Don't do anything stupid."

Not doing something stupid was always my goal. I had found that I was not always able to accomplish that goal. For the moment, I moved along with my new captors. But I was looking for an angle. Something that would help me if I fought or if I ran.

I couldn't believe it, but suddenly I was worried about the two FBI agents' safety. I had no idea who these new guys were, but I didn't want them to hurt any cops.

Outside, a beat-up red Fiat skidded to a stop right in front of us. I didn't like the looks of this at all. If I got in that thing, there was no telling where I would end up. Or, more important, who I might end up meeting. I had to do something.

I started to turn and look back into the terminal. A strong

forearm kept my head from turning and shoved me forward. That was one plan out the window.

Where were the uniformed cops in this airport? If something like this happened in JFK, there'd be a dozen cops pouncing on us right now. Here, about to be shoved into a car headed to God knows where, I had to think of something else fast.

CHAPTER 57

AS SOON AS I was shoved into the back seat of the Fiat, I swung my elbow back. I had no idea where I would catch the person behind me, but I was hoping it'd be the face. My plan got hazy after that.

The man behind me blocked my elbow. Hard. His forearms felt like steel. Then he surprised me.

The man called out, "Whoa, hold on, Ace. I'm on the job."

I froze at the combination of a Brooklyn accent and the code for a plainclothes NYPD officer. "I'm on the job" goes back decades. The origin is unclear, but it means "I'm a cop." So I listened.

The Fiat sputtered away from the curb. The airport building faded from the side-view.

I glanced out the rear window to see if the FBI agents were following. It looked like we were in the clear, although I had no idea what the FBI would drive in Estonia. In New York, if they weren't in a Crown Vic or a Taurus, they were in some weird seized vehicle, like a Land Rover or Cadillac.

I sat back in the seat. The man next to me settled down, too, giving me space like a zookeeper would with an agitated animal.

He said, "That's better." He stuck out his hand. "I'm Barry Davis, NYPD." He grinned as if he'd just told a joke.

I took his hand and assessed him. He was a powerfully built man, about forty-five, with a crew cut that had gone gray.

I realized my hand was on my elbow where I had tried to strike Davis. It still throbbed a little, but I wasn't going to admit it. I controlled my breathing, then pushed my hair back into place. I was stalling as I accepted my new surroundings and companions.

I said, "The driver doesn't speak?"

Davis smiled. "He'd rather not be identified, seeing as how we're way out of our home base doing a favor for Lieutenant Martindale."

"That's a good partner."

"The best. And he doesn't want to know why the FBI tried to detain you. You know, plausible deniability and all that shit. We figured they were more worried about their jurisdiction. They hate the NYPD."

I asked, "Where are you assigned?"

"Paris."

"No shit. And you came all the way up here to help me?"

"NYPD never leaves a detective behind." He handed me a folded newspaper. "Or unarmed."

I opened the paper to see a black Beretta 9mm inside. I pulled the slide back a few centimeters to check if a round was in the chamber. It was loaded and ready to go.

Davis smiled and said, "In case of emergency." Then he handed me a card with just a phone number. "Any problems you can't handle, call that number. I'll be in Bonn on an unrelated issue. We're off the books. No official engagement at all. But that doesn't mean you're alone."

"Thanks. Did Martindale tell you what I was up to?"

"Nope. And I don't want to know. Remember, we'll deny everything if you cause a bunch of shit here."

I was impressed by Martindale's tight lips. "I won't do anything that reflects poorly on us."

Davis laughed. "Me? I was never here. How can it reflect poorly on me?"

I smiled. "I meant I won't embarrass the NYPD."

"Still not an issue I'm worried about. Cops have got enough to worry about. All I care about is that you get home safely."

"Thanks. That's my main concern, too."

We pulled up to a four-story hotel on the edge of the city.

Davis said, "You're all set up here. Good luck." He handed me my small carry-on bag, which I thought had been lost in the scuffles.

Then they were gone.

CHAPTER 58

CHRISTOPH VISSER AND Ollie Van Netta were happy to be back in Amsterdam. Here the pot was better, they knew plenty of girls, and Christoph was able to stop by his mother's apartment.

His mom was always happy to see her engineer. At least, that's what he told her he did for a living. A traveling engineer. His fake diploma from Erasmus University in Rotterdam hung on the wall of her living room, along with photos of his late father.

Christoph enjoyed playing the role of dutiful and respectable son. He liked seeing his mother happy and proud, and when he visited home, he did everything his mother expected of him. He even attended mass at Christmas and Easter.

Christoph knew this deception would work because for twenty-five years his father had worked as a collector for a loan shark. Christoph's mother had believed her husband's lie, that he was an accountant for a private equity firm.

The gullible tend to be the happiest.

No matter what he told his mother, Christoph wanted to take care of her. She was the only one in his whole life who cared what happened to him. She was the only one he didn't want to disappoint.

When he killed someone when he was young, Christoph realized it didn't bother him. That wasn't to say he enjoyed killing; he didn't. He did it to make money. Money he planned to use on a nice house for his mother. And a wild apartment for himself.

He had, on occasion, *appreciated* killing someone. Like those asses Janos and Alice. He and Ollie had made good money for that one, but it had been fun, too. It had been satisfying.

He found Ollie at his favorite coffeehouse on the edge of the tourist district in Amsterdam. He usually went to a place on Handboogstraat called Dampkring. Tonight, he was in a smaller place, down the street, that didn't mind when Ollie dozed off in a booth, as long as he spent plenty of money and didn't cause problems.

They both had been careful to keep their profession a secret. Since they had met Endrik Laar, who liked to be called Henry, their fortunes had seen a serious upturn. They didn't have to seek out work. Henry paid well. And they liked their small, shared apartment in Tallinn, Estonia.

In Amsterdam, Christoph maintained his own apartment. He brought home too many women to make sharing an apartment reasonable. It also gave him a sense that he was on vacation whenever he came to his hometown.

Ollie lived with his father, who operated a bed-and-breakfast in the suburb of Haarlem. His father didn't know and didn't care what Ollie did for a living. That worked out great for Ollie. Aside from occasionally taking out the garbage or checking in a guest, Ollie did little to help his father.

Christoph took a moment to shake his partner out of his hash-induced daze. The thirty-eight-year-old blinked his eyes a dozen times and sat up straight, as if he'd just heard a fire alarm. He brushed his brown, greasy hair from his eyes and tucked the long strands behind his ears. He looked surprised to see Christoph.

"Hello, my brother. What brings you to Nirvana?"

Christoph said, "You need to straighten up. Henry has a job for us."

"Where?"

"I'll give you a hint. Our Nordica flight leaves in two hours."

"Shit. Back to Estonia?"

Christoph said, "It shouldn't be too bad. Henry is going to give us a bonus for going to New York to kill Janos and Alice."

"Those assholes had it coming." He scratched his head, then looked at Christoph and asked, "Why do you think Alice shot the Asian chick in the back?"

"I guess she was just a bitch. We'll never know. And Henry is pissed."

Ollie said, "He's been quick to use us lately. He's cutting into our party time. I wonder what he wants done now."

Christoph said, "He said something about a cop from New York."

CHAPTER 59

THE NEXT MORNING, I was up and moving early. Early by Tallinn, Estonia, time—it was the middle of the night in New York, and I got a text telling me to call home no matter the time. I made a quick call to let Mary Catherine know I was safe. Somehow I neglected to tell her about my excitement at the airport. Just that I was staying in a lovely city with a beautiful Old Town district on a hill not far away.

Her sleepy voice made me homesick. She said, "You promise to be careful?"

"Sure, but what could go wrong? I'm in a country with a low crime rate looking for a missing girl who hangs out with computer geeks. I think I'll manage."

She let out that warm Irish laugh and said, "I love you."

"I love you, too."

Then it was back to reality.

The breakfast in the main room of the hotel included three different kinds of fish. I'm not used to salted smelt for breakfast, but they weren't bad.

Then I hit the streets with a vengeance. Not like I might in New York. There, I knew every street corner, most hustlers, and a lot of cops. Here, it was just me, hoping I didn't do anything to be noticed.

I had several addresses I wanted to check out from Tony Martindale's Intelligence Bureau resources. The folder he'd handed me on Henry hadn't provided much information, but this turd looked to be bad news from the description they'd acquired through different informants.

Usually a criminal was known to be either tough or smart. This guy appeared to be both. But he had no actual criminal history. No arrests at all. That was the sign of the worst kind of criminal: one who was smart enough to work the system or avoid detection altogether.

The brief from Intel said he'd attacked the computer system of Aldi grocery stores in Germany. He had crippled all of their systems, then demanded ten million euros to let them operate again.

The only thing that had stopped him was a bank screwup. Somehow the account he had been using in Russia at the time was viewable by the police. That saved the German company a fortune.

In addition to several other cyberattacks, Henry was listed as responsible for three separate murders, two in Estonia and one in Russia. I thought, *And at least one in New York*. That didn't count the dead at the coffeehouse.

The more I found out about this "Henry," the more I looked forward to finally meeting him.

I walked along Pühavaimu, on the edge of the Old Town district. The medieval city walls rose right from the sidewalk, and a plaque advised me that Old Town was a UNESCO World Heritage Site. It explained that the first wall went up around the capital in the year 1265 during the reign of Margaret Sambiria, thus it is named Margaret Wall.

The streets were filled with tourists, and among them I heard a number of American accents. My cabdriver had told me Estonians greatly preferred to hear English to Russian if someone wasn't going to speak Estonian. Cruise ships docked at the main port and shuttled busloads of tourists to Old Town to see Toompea Castle as well as farther east to see the Kadriorg Palace. At the moment, I was dodging those crowds.

At least two cruise ships were in the port, which I could tell by the different groups. Some had blue bags with the Princess Cruises logo on them. Others had Norwegian tags on their shirts. Each group shuffled along like the *Peanuts* gang, all closed in and cramped, trying to hear their guide.

I took in the city as I looked for the first address on my list, which turned out to be a warehouse. I could tell by the windows and how clean the interior was that it'd been used recently. That fell in with what I knew about cybercriminals. They tended to move from location to location. I inspected the warehouse, hoping to find some clue as to where the operation had moved.

I was surprised to find the front door unlocked. I walked in carefully, taking a few photos with my phone as I went. At the far end of an empty loading bay, a man in some kind of a janitor's uniform pushed a wide broom.

When he noticed me, he smiled and waved. He said something in Estonian.

I held up my hands and said, "I'm sorry, I don't speak Estonian."

The man, who looked to be about fifty with short gray hair, perked up and said, "English?"

I nodded, and he walked over to me.

"I like to speak English. Where you from?"

"New York."

"New York, America?"

"That's the one." I also gave him a quick thumbs-up.

The man was small and a little hunched over. He patted me on the arm in a friendly gesture. "I'm Gunnar."

I took a chance and said, "Gunnar, do you know where the company that was here moved?"

He gave me a confused stare, then smiled. "Computer company?"

I nodded.

"They have new building. On Tartu Maantee near Toit's City."

"What's Toit's City?"

"Nice café. You eat. You like."

I had to smile. That was perfect. I thanked the man and eased away from him as he tried to practice more English on me.

I stepped outside into the bright sunshine of the Estonian morning. As my eyes adjusted, a man in a suit approached me. I could tell by the way he was walking that he was looking specifically for me. The hairs on the back of my neck stood up.

I felt for the pistol stuck in my waistband. Now I really appreciated the efforts of the NYPD last night at the airport. I had almost refused the offer of the gun. Now I was glad I had it.

The man stopped ten paces in front of me and immediately held up some kind of government ID. The way he did it, and the look of the ID, left no question that he was in law enforcement. It was almost a universal method of identification.

He spoke English with only a slight accent. He said, "Mr. Bennett, I need to speak with you."

I was made.

CHAPTER 60

THE COP SEEMED a little casual as he approached me. Maybe he wasn't used to the same threats American cops faced every day. And like many criminals in the United States, I was armed.

I didn't want to be searched and have the pistol discovered. But there was no way I was going to hurt a cop, either. He knew me. By name. That was disconcerting. It was a little surreal to be on the other end of a police stop. The fact that I was in a foreign country only made it more uncomfortable.

He was about my age and fit. Maybe six feet tall. His eyes scanned me from head to toe. Then he said, "Why are you here?"

"You mean, here on the street?" I hated when someone tried to double-talk me in New York. Now I was on the other side of the conversation, and frankly, it was kind of fun. I saw the frustration on the cop's face. I could tell he was wondering if maybe his English wasn't as good as he thought.

Then he said firmly, "What are you doing in Estonia?"

Not being a hardened street criminal, I stammered but didn't come up with a smart-ass answer. Finally I spat out, "Sightseeing." I had to wonder if this guy was legit. Was he on Henry's payroll? I became more apprehensive the longer he just stared at me.

Then he pulled a phone from his pocket.

I didn't know what to do, so I just stood there. I didn't want to make any threatening moves. I certainly wasn't prepared to run.

The cop spoke English on the phone. He said, "Yes, it's definitely Bennett." He listened to someone speak for a moment, then replied, "We'll wait right here."

I had a sinking feeling in my stomach.

I had never heard anything specifically about Estonian cops being corrupt. Certainly not like I'd heard about Russian police or the police in Mexico. I had to make a decision. Was this something I could risk? Not just for my safety but for Natalie Lunden's? If Henry was as powerful and rich as I'd heard, he could buy a couple of cops. Or at least outfit someone to look like a cop.

I needed to do something. I just wasn't sure what.

CHAPTER 61

I LOOKED THE cop in the eye. He wasn't concerned or frightened in the least, and he wasn't going to back down. I considered running. Then I thought it through. The idea of hiding from the police while searching for a missing girl seemed foolish.

A green Peugeot turned the corner and headed for us. I looked up and down the cobblestone street. There weren't as many tourists now. Where were the crowds when you needed them?

The car came up to the curb right next to me. A window rolled down and the driver called out, "Get in the car, Detective." That made my cheek twitch. This was getting worse by the moment.

Then I leaned down and looked through the open window. Sitting behind the steering wheel was the tubby FBI agent, Bill Fiore. He didn't look particularly happy to see me. After the way the NYPD had snatched me away from him at the airport, I understood his frustration.

He said, "What are you waiting for? A better invitation? Trust me, I'm doing you a favor."

I glanced over at the cop who'd approached me. He was waiting to see how I responded.

I said through the open window, "Forgive me if I don't trust the word of an FBI agent telling me he's doing me a favor. And as a New Yorker, your Boston accent makes it sound even less plausible."

"Always with the wisecracks. Shut up and get in the car." He waited for a moment and added, "Now."

I nodded to the Estonian cop and slipped into the front seat of the Peugeot.

As we pulled away, Fiore said, "The Estonian cops couldn't care less what US law enforcement is doing in their country. As long as we don't cause problems. And that's the only reason you're here, Detective Bennett. To cause problems."

"And how would you know that, Special Agent Fiore?"

"Because I'm not a dumbass. You think I don't know who helped you escape at the airport?"

"Maybe you're not as stupid as you look."

Fiore chuckled. "I could say the same about you."

I said, "So we're fighting a turf war four thousand miles from home?"

"It's not a turf war. You have no jurisdiction. And now your ass is going home."

I said, "You don't even know exactly why I'm here. I'm looking for a missing girl."

"I know, I know. Spoiled rich girl whose father could fire you."

"It's not like that. He hasn't threatened me or offered me anything. You don't understand. She's fallen in with a group of cybercriminals. She could be in danger."

He pulled the car roughly to the curb and turned to me. His voice ticked up in volume. "No, *you* don't understand. She's *with* that group. She's helping them. They've caused all kinds of shit and made enemies on both sides of the law. Even the goddamn yakuza thinks they've been disrespected. A Colombian cartel wants them to pay tribute. And don't get me started on the Russians. Who knows what those dickwads will do."

"She may be a kidnap victim. I might even have a location. A warehouse over on Tartu Maantee, across from a café named Toit's City."

"Doesn't matter. Too dangerous. We can't have a shoot-out in Tallinn. It's not the South Side of Chicago. I intend to get you to the airport and sit with you until your flight at 2100 local time. You'll be back in New York tomorrow. As I understand it, you're a pretty decent homicide dick. Go back to solving murders."

I gave him a sideways glance as an idea popped into my head. "You had to be some kind of real cop before the FBI." The *real cop* dig was inadvertent. Every big-city detective knows the FBI hates that. It just came naturally.

Fiore was used to it. He proudly said, "Brookline, Mass. How could you tell?"

"The 'homicide dick' comment. Only an old-school cop would use a term like that."

He nodded his agreement.

"I can't believe a cop would let a missing girl go without any investigation. You've been with the Feebs too long."

"Suck it, Mr. NYPD. I'm just following orders."

"So were the guards at Auschwitz."

"That's a low blow."

I sighed and looked down at my lap. Then I set the trap. "I guess you know all about me."

"More than I care to."

"So you know my grandfather is a Catholic priest."

"It's about the only thing redeeming I've heard about you."

"He asked me to pick up research documents while I'm here. They can't be mailed or shipped. They're at a Russian Orthodox Church named St. Laszlo's. Do you know it?"

"Sure. It's not a main tourist attraction like Alexander Nevsky, up on the hill, but I've passed it a million times."

"If I leave the country quietly, will you just let me pick up the envelope first? At least I'll accomplish one thing on this trip." I felt a little guilty pulling the Catholic card, but Fiore relented.

"As long as it only takes a minute."

CHAPTER 62

CHRISTOPH AND OLLIE had wasted no time once their Nordica flight landed early in the morning. Henry had someone meet them at the airport who provided a car and a couple of Czech pistols, but Christoph still had to run by their apartment and pick up his favorite knife. He never knew when he might need it.

Ollie had slept only a couple of hours, but he seemed alert and ready to go. Christoph often marveled at his partner's ability to bounce back after a hard night of partying. Although he'd seen that hash had less of an effect on Ollie than heroin.

They were lucky to catch the American cop just as he walked out of his hotel. They followed the cab and waited for the right moment to strike. Henry had instructed them to capture the detective and bring him back to their current headquarters. As a last resort, they were authorized to shoot him.

From the very beginning, Ollie mocked the American cop. He laughed at the way the cop stood in front of the hotel, waiting for a cab. He was tall and handsome and looked like a statue. Ollie stuck his hand in his shirt like Napoleon and posed. He said, "Why is an American detective here? Maybe he can scare criminals into surrendering in New York, but does he realize he has no pull here?"

Christoph laughed. He didn't know why the American detective was here or what his interest in Henry was. All he knew was that his boss wanted the cop brought to him and that Henry paid well. For someone who made his living beating and killing people, it was a pretty simple task.

They were both shocked to see the cop go directly to the warehouse where Henry used to have an operation. This guy was well connected and informed.

Ollie said, "Let's grab him as soon as he comes out of the warehouse. We can slip him into the back seat without anyone noticing."

"What if he gives us a fight?"

"Henry said we could shoot him. You stand by with your pistol in case he gives me any shit."

Christoph shrugged. His partner's plan was simple and direct. He liked it.

The hitch came when they noticed an Estonian policeman they recognized approach the entrance to the warehouse.

Ollie said, "What's that uptight prick doing here?"

"Probably the same thing as us."

"Too bad Henry couldn't get him on the payroll."

Christoph said, "You think Henry would appreciate it if we blasted both of them right now?"

The decision was moot when a green Peugeot pulled up and the detective got inside.

Ollie said, "What should we do? Probably stay with him for a while, huh?"

Christoph had to agree.

CHAPTER 63

I CALLED MY grandfather.

Fiore made me put the phone on speaker so he could hear everything we said. It was a pretty smart move. Too bad I had confidence that my grandfather was craftier than any FBI agent ever born.

He answered his personal residence phone immediately. He had a slight scratch in his throat and I knew I had woken him from a sound sleep.

I said, "Hey, Grandpa, it's Michael calling from Estonia." Me calling him "Grandpa" would've immediately alerted him that something was up. I could tell by the pause he was trying to figure it out.

He said, "What time is it there, Michael? Because it's god-awful early here. Everything all right?"

"Sorry. I forgot you're seven hours behind us in New York."

"How's the trip so far?"

I could tell he was stalling as he figured out what was going on. He had to hear that we were on speakerphone. I wasn't going to make the obvious move and tell him. That might tip off the FBI agent that we were planning something.

"Everything's good. I'm coming home early."

"Why's that?"

"The FBI is forcing me to go home. In fact, an agent is driving me to the airport right now. Can you call your friend at St. Laszlo's and tell him I'll pick up that reference material you needed?"

Seamus played it perfectly. All he said was "You bet, boyo."

I thanked him and hung up. I looked over at Bill Fiore and said, "Satisfied?"

He nodded.

"I won't tell an elderly priest that a good Catholic boy from Brookline, Massachusetts, didn't trust him. And that you made me talk to him on speaker."

Fiore visibly softened for a moment. "I know you're not a bad guy. My guess is you're over here for all the right reasons. But the FBI has to maintain a relationship with all the countries that allow us to operate within their borders. I can't have every hotshot cop in the US coming over here, thinking they can do whatever they want."

"How many cops want to come to Estonia?"

"You have no idea how much cybercrime originates from here. Teenagers with access to high-speed internet are figuring out schemes to bilk old people out of money in the US. Every swinging dick in this country has a computer."

"Sounds like it's a good idea for me to leave."

"Finally you're making some sense."

CHAPTER 64

THANK GOD ST. LASZLO'S was on the way to the hotel, where I still needed to pick up my carry-on bag. It was hard enough to convince the FBI agent to bring me to the church, let alone to let me get my bag before we headed to the airport.

The church was certainly not as grand as the Alexander Nevsky Cathedral on the hill in Old Town; it looked more like a suburban church in Baltimore. But it was still clearly Orthodox, with the three horizontal bars on the cross, the bottom bar at an angle and much smaller than the middle bar.

There were no tourists here. Only a few cars were in the parking lot alongside the church, probably the staff vehicles and something for the priest to drive.

We parked on the street directly in front, where a walkway lined with budding bushes led to the main entrance.

I opened the door, and Fiore opened the driver's door. He

just looked at me and said, "You think I'm going to let you just walk away? I'm with you until I see your smiling face walk down the Jetway to your plane."

This could get tricky. I considered how far I'd be willing to go to escape the FBI's custody.

A priest in his clerical cassock stepped out the front door and waved to me. He was nothing like I had expected. I don't know why I had assumed a friend of my grandfather's would also be an elderly man, but this priest was in his early fifties with slightly graying hair. He looked to be in pretty good shape and had clear, blue eyes.

He hurried down the steps and along the walkway, extending his hand. "You have got to be Seamus's grandson, Michael. I would see the resemblance anywhere."

I wasn't sure if that was a compliment. But I shook his hand and thanked him. I said, "This is my"—I paused for a moment, then finished—"friend, Bill Fiore."

The priest said, "I'm Martin Zlatic, but everyone calls me Marty." His accent was almost unnoticeable.

We chatted for a minute about some of the work my grand-father had done and his interest in history. I guess we went on too long because the FBI agent said, "I hate to break this up, but can we grab your grandfather's envelope and get going?"

Marty said, "I'm so sorry. Yes, of course. Follow me, please."

If my grandfather had called and tipped Marty off, he was one of the best actors I had ever met.

He took a moment to show us the altar, mentioning that his congregation stood during mass, which explained why there were no pews. I thought about some of the sermons I'd sat through in my childhood—that was a long time to stand.

I knew the clock was ticking. Whatever this priest had in store for me, I hoped he did it soon. Fiore was getting more impatient by the second and could call this whole thing off. I tried to signal Father Marty with a look, communicating that we were up against a deadline.

He led us past the altar into the back corridors. They felt like a maze. I noticed Marty subtly picking up his pace as Bill Fiore started to drift farther back from me. It was right then that I realized this priest wasn't fooling around. He knew exactly what he was doing. And he was exactly the kind of friend I'd expect my grandfather to have.

We took one corner, then another, and I swear we were headed back to the altar, but instead we just kept walking.

I heard Fiore call out, "Hey, wait up." He took a wrong turn and I heard some language that shouldn't be used in a church. Then a more urgent, "Where'd you guys go?"

Suddenly and without warning, Father Marty pressed what looked like a solid wall and shoved me into an opening. I slipped inside just as I heard Fiore yell, "Bennett, you better not leave this church." I thought I heard the FBI agent running as Marty followed me inside the dark, narrow corridor and set the panel back in place.

He said, "There's no time to lose. Come with me." He squeezed past me and nearly jogged down the remarkably constricted hallway.

We took a flight of stairs down. I had to hunch over to make it through the next hallway. Then we descended a long staircase that disappeared into the dark.

My heart was racing as I wondered what I could accomplish while trying to avoid the FBI. It seemed like it took a full minute, but it probably wasn't nearly that long before Marty opened the last door. The sun hit me right in the face. I looked around and didn't recognize anything.

Marty pointed up the hill and I saw that we'd traveled through some sort of basement and out a back door. We might've been as far as three blocks away from where Bill Fiore had parked his car, if you considered the elevation. It was the cleanest getaway I'd ever made.

Marty smiled and said, "Old Russian Orthodox churches are full of surprises. I'm glad we could use them to help you on your mission."

"My grandfather told you why I'm here?"

"To save a girl who's missing."

"I can't tell you how much I appreciate this."

The priest frowned and said, "I can delay the FBI agent a few more minutes still. Find this girl."

CHAPTER 65

AFTER HIDING OUT in a tourist welcome center for a while, I hailed a taxi and told him exactly what Gunnar, the janitor, had told me. Twenty minutes later, I saw Toit's City café and a series of office buildings and warehouses across the street. This had to be the place.

I was literally like the dog who'd chased a car and caught it. Now what to do with it? I was standing there, looking at a likely location for the infamous Endrik "Henry" Laar, and only then did I realize I needed backup. Damn. Good luck and a little help from a priest had put me in a position to find Natalie, but I didn't think it was smart to barge in. I did have a gun, but only sixteen rounds of 9mm ammo, and there was no telling what was inside the warehouse.

I stepped into the café. A few minutes later, I was seated with a cup of coffee for my own version of surveillance. I had no vehicle, no official authority, and no backup. Suddenly my brilliant plan looked like a six-year-old's idea.

I pulled out a paper napkin and made a few notes on it. If nothing else, once the FBI caught up to me, I could give it to them. But I wasn't ready to surrender just yet.

I kept watching the windows of the building across the street. There was definitely someone inside. So far, I had counted only two men. One matched the general description of Henry. Well under six feet, around thirty, neatly groomed, and wearing a blue T-shirt with some sort of emblem on it. The other man was older and heavier. If there were just two men, I might have a decent chance if I got inside.

I wondered if that was my attempt to build confidence. But I had no chance of finding Natalie if I didn't at least go into this warehouse. I did, for about thirty seconds, consider how it might screw up Fiore's operation if there was a large-scale investigation into the cybercrime organization.

I'd seen these conflicts of interest a dozen times, like when the FBI arrested someone on a minor fraud charge who the NYPD had under surveillance for a major RICO charge. Even within the NYPD, different units would step on one another's feet; more than one homicide surveillance I had conducted had been interrupted when the Narcotics unit made a quick bust.

But I decided I had to take the chance. *Sorry, Fiore.*

CHAPTER 66

CHRISTOPH ALWAYS WOKE before his roommate and business partner, Ollie. Even if they were just taking a midday nap. Christoph wondered what would happen if he weren't around. Would Ollie sleep twenty hours a day, like a house cat?

Often Christoph used the time to work out or run, to counter the effects of all the partying they did. Not today. He woke from his little nap with a brutal headache. He needed something to take the edge off and started to look through the apartment.

Christoph was astounded when he opened the medicine cabinet, looking for aspirin. The cabinet was a stoner's dream. There were at least twenty ounces of pot organized by different strains. Even the strains were divided between *indica* and *sativa* so Ollie would know what would relax him and what would give him energy.

Ollie also had at least six eight-balls of heroin. They all looked to be from the same batch of Brown Sugar.

And on the bottom shelf, Ollie had bottles and bottles of pills.

Christoph smiled. Ollie was nothing like he appeared. He was organized and deliberate, even if he looked like he perpetually just woke up.

Their apartment in Tallinn was nothing special, a two-bedroom with a nice living room. Someone from Henry's operation had managed to hack into the neighbors' Wi-Fi and entertainment package so they could stream movies while they were high and watch Blauw-Wit Amsterdam football. The apartment, in Maakri, wasn't far from either the Olympic Park or Grand Prix Rävala casino, with easy access to bars.

They'd stayed on the American cop after his discussion with the Estonian national policeman, following him with another man in the green Peugeot. They called the plates in to Henry's people; the tag came back as from some holding company in Latvia. They wondered how to get a better fix on who could be driving the cop around.

Then the weirdest thing happened. They followed the Peugeot to St. Laszlo's Church in Sikupilli. Bennett and the driver got out and greeted a priest who came out the main door. After a ten-minute wait, Christoph and Ollie saw the driver rush back out of the church, followed by the priest. The driver was clearly furious and jumped into the car. Where was the cop? Had Bennett escaped from this man? The way the man was dressed and acting made it seem like he was some kind of government official.

They had no way to figure out where Bennett had disappeared. They weren't about to question a priest. Instead, they decided it was time to eat. And then they had come to the apartment. Christoph knew they'd find a way to follow the cop again later.

A text came in from Henry saying he'd need them shortly. With no aspirin in sight, Christoph downed some Vicodin instead. They had to show up to demonstrate to their boss that they were reliable. Even if sometimes they weren't.

Christoph took a few minutes to gather his stuff. The pistol that had been provided, some extra cash, and a four-inch combat knife he always left at the apartment when they went back to Amsterdam. He liked the feel of a knife in his hand. He also liked the effect it had on people when he questioned them.

Now that he was ready, Christoph knocked on Ollie's bedroom door. "C'mon, Ollie. We've got to earn our pay."

A minute later, Ollie stepped out of his bedroom dressed in the same clothes he'd worn the day before: an AC/DC concert T-shirt with a hole in it and off-brand blue jeans.

Christoph said, "Why don't you ever try to dress a little better? At least wear clean clothes."

Ollie looked placidly at his partner. "It's my image. I have to sell it. No one expects a sloppy, fat guy like me to be a killer. You, you look like a professional. Tall, handsome. You scare people. I'm an asset when I look like this."

Christoph saw his point. He said, "Henry's expecting us. I'm sure he wants us to do something with the cop."

Ollie said, "I think the American is too risky. He doesn't look like any kind of pushover. Henry hasn't offered any bonus for this job, either."

"Are you saying we should pass on the job?"

"I'm saying, as professionals, we need to evaluate the assignment, not just agree to everything Henry says. If you haven't noticed, he's become a little unhinged. He's into feuds and grudges. He may not be our best choice of employer going forward."

"Do you want to tell him that now?"

Ollie shook his head. "Let's see how much trouble the American is first. If we even pick up on his trail again. We need to think about ourselves and our future."

Christoph realized how much he'd underestimated his partner.

CHAPTER 67

I CROSSED THE street in front of the little café. There was no real traffic. Not by New York standards, anyway. A tiny Fiat, a Mini Cooper, and some odd eastern European car whizzed by. They made me feel like a giant.

The building I was walking to was more of an office than a warehouse. It was modern and stood three stories high. The windows were on the small side, making me think it was an older building. No doubt it was solid.

Inside the tiny lobby, I checked the directory. The only business officially listed was a web designer on the top floor. The five other nameplates were blank.

A ground-floor door to the left of the directory was ajar. I looked through the opening but couldn't see much, so I tentatively touched it and pushed it open. I was trying not to give away my element of surprise, all I had in this situation.

The wide room was about fifty feet long with high ceilings. A catwalk ran around the edges of the room with a few office doors spaced along it. The space looked like it'd been a small factory floor where a boss could walk around and watch the workers below.

The place was empty except for a few desks and tables. I didn't see anyone around. I slipped all the way inside. When I had stepped about twenty paces from the door, I heard a voice.

"Hello, Mr. Bennett. I've been expecting you." The speaker had a slight accent. It almost sounded Russian, with a hint of Scandinavian.

A man stepped onto the catwalk. It was the same man I'd seen from the café, still in his blue T-shirt and casual slacks. "I thought you'd have been here sooner."

I said, "You must be Endrik Laar."

"Please, call me Henry."

I wasn't sure what I had expected. The file description had just said white and male. Jennifer Chang had mentioned he was about thirty, on the short side, and a workout buff, but I guess I hadn't thought of all the variables.

He was shorter than I'd imagined. Maybe five six. He was definitely ripped. The veins in his arms told me he was serious about weights. His whole look screamed steroids. Add in the agitated pacing and I could see why people were afraid of him. Maybe he really was as smart as I'd heard. A mix of smart and crazy was rarely good.

I kept my composure when two men stepped through the doorway near me. They kept walking until they were positioned on either side of me, about a dozen feet away. They didn't know I had a gun, and I thought I'd save that surprise. Maybe it would teach Henry something as well.

Then a man stepped through a doorway across the room from me. It was the janitor from the last warehouse, Gunnar. That surprised me.

Henry smiled and said, "I didn't want to take any chances. We thought it would be easier for you to come to us than for us to find you. Gunnar was kind enough to wait for you at our last location and tell you where to go. But then you didn't show up here right away."

The gray-haired "janitor" smiled and said, "And by the way, mate, my English is pretty good. I was raised in North Hampton."

Son of a bitch, Henry had already made me feel stupid.

This was not the first impression I had wanted to make.

CHAPTER 68

STARING UP AT the master cybercriminal standing on the catwalk, my mind raced. Even with the surprises Henry was throwing at me, I tried not to show what I was thinking. It was time to get some answers. I decided to treat our conversation like any other interview: start with easy questions, then move on to the hard ones. Simple.

I said, "How'd you know I was in Estonia?"

Henry gave me a laugh that sounded fake. Practiced. "We break corporate security systems. Did you really think we couldn't clone the mayor's phone and hack his email? I've known everything you were going to do. I even know the nasty name the NYPD calls the mayor. And, by the way, so does he. Shame on you. LFP indeed." He wagged his finger at me.

I no longer thought of the mayor as a *little fat prick*. Now I realized there were too many people fitting that description.

Take out the *fat* and Henry was at the top of the list at the moment.

I said, "I'm impressed you could hack the mayor of New York's phone without being detected. It's really quite clever." I chose my words carefully. To Henry, *clever* would be an insult.

Henry said, "It seems I can do whatever I want and the authorities will never catch me. It's almost not fun anymore." He flexed his arms when he moved. It must've impressed someone at some time.

I laughed aloud. And it wasn't practiced. It was a sincere chuckle.

"And what's so amusing?"

I made sure to look Henry in the eye. "If I had a dollar for every half-assed crook who said something like that, I could retire."

"I can assure you, there is nothing half-assed about me."

"If you have to tell people, that means you probably are half-assed. It's sort of like when you have to tell people you're in charge. That means you're probably not." That little comment would get under his skin, too.

Henry was silent for a moment. Finally he said, "I've read about the great homicide detective. The newspapers say you never give up."

I didn't know where this conversation was leading, but it wasn't going anywhere good. I stole a quick look at the men on either side of me. They were both young and fit. They didn't look like computer programmers. One of the men had a blue teardrop tattoo near his right eye. The other was tall and sleek. His shirt almost looked like a uniform with his broad shoulders and narrow waist. He was ready for action right now. I also knew if I went for one, the other would be able to strike me from behind. I didn't think it was time to pull my pistol.

I looked up at Henry and said, "It's true I'm not known for giving up. But I'll make you a deal right now." I noticed how our voices echoed in the wide, open room.

"I'm intrigued. Please, go ahead."

"If you give me Natalie right now, I'll leave and you'll never hear from me again. I won't say a word to any law enforcement entity. All I want is to bring the girl back to her parents."

"And you leave Estonia?"

"Tonight. I already have a flight."

Henry chuckled and clapped his hands together. I was starting to wonder if this asswipe believed he was some sort of super villain from a James Bond movie.

Henry said, "Ah, the great savior. I'm afraid you're too late to save Natalie from a life of crime and return her to her loving parents."

My heart sank. Had this asshole killed her? I stood there in stunned silence. I considered pulling my pistol right then.

It would've been a pleasure to show this arrogant prick how smart he really was.

CHAPTER 69

I STILL HADN'T said another word, but the way I'd turned my body must've alerted Henry's hired thugs. Gunnar and the other two changed positions slightly and looked like they were ready to jump me.

The one with the teardrop tattoo worried me. At least in the US you had to earn that particular tattoo. And it wasn't from winning a softball tournament. He wouldn't hesitate to pull the trigger.

Then a thought flashed through my head. If I was going to die anyway, maybe I really should dispense a little *street justice*. I wasn't sure what my grandfather would say about something like that. And I knew it wasn't what Jesus would've done, but he was a pretty high standard to live up to.

I calculated the shot. There would be no time to aim carefully with the pistol. And it was a pistol I was unfamiliar with.

But I reckoned it could be done. I'd have to tune out all the others. That meant I'd be plugged a dozen times before I fired five shots.

The alternative was to do nothing and get plugged only once later, while kneeling. Either way, the outcome wasn't what I would have preferred. But by shooting Henry now, I might help another girl in the future.

I said a silent prayer. I said to Maeve: *Keep watching over the kids.*

Then a door on the catwalk, to the right of Henry, opened. A young woman walked out. She was in a simple dress with a heavy wool sweater. Her light-brown hair was now cut short. She wore stylish, wide-framed glasses.

It was a new look, but after a moment I recognized her: Natalie Lunden.

I turned my attention back to Henry and said, "What kind of asshole plays a game like that?"

He grinned.

Natalie spoke up. "I wasn't forced here. No one made me leave New York and come to Tallinn. I even paid for my own airline ticket. There's no reason for you to worry about me or cause problems here."

Her voice was steady and calm. She still sounded like a young person, but she didn't sound nervous or under duress.

I thought of the photo her father had on the wall of his office. She wore a little dress and was about five or six years old, smiling from ear to ear, holding the mayor's hand. What had happened?

I said, "Your dad and mom are worried sick about you." That had the effect I wanted. She looked stricken. Then I threw in, "Why haven't you called them?"

She took a moment, then her brown eyes settled on me. "I wouldn't bother my father about anything. He's too tied up trying to save the world and raise his new sons. But I don't want my mom to worry. I've thought about calling her, but I can't risk exposing our operation. We still have a lot of work to do. I'll figure a way to get a message to her tonight."

Damned if she didn't sound sincere. I was starting to think I'd wasted a trip. I hoped I hadn't wasted my life. I wasn't here to compel someone to return to the US. I was here to save a girl I thought had been forced into doing something she didn't want to do. I knew she was smart, but I'd still been worried about her.

When she put her arm around Henry's waist, then dropped her head to his shoulder, I understood the situation.

The door behind me opened and closed again. I turned and watched an odd pair of men strut toward the center of the room. One was tall with neat, blond hair. The other looked like a character actor in a cheap stoner movie. His stringy, dark hair spread out over his shoulders. The T-shirt from an AC/DC concert drooped over his belly like an awning.

Henry stepped up to the railing and leaned over it. He was clearly annoyed. He said, "Finally Ollie and Christoph have decided to grace us with their presence. And they never completed their assignment. I had to do it for them."

The slovenly man smiled and said, "Thanks, Henry. It's nice to get a little help once in a while."

I didn't try to hide my smile. I liked a radical, no matter who he worked for. Radicals tended to make life more interesting. It was the kind of comment I might have made. But I couldn't shake the feeling that I knew this guy. At least I knew I'd seen him.

I studied the two men. They looked so familiar. Then it hit me. They were the shooters from the coffeehouse, Brew, back in New York.

CHAPTER 70

I WASN'T IN New York, where someone might call in the cavalry, or at least the cops. I would've loved to see a SWAT team about now. I'd never again make fun of their fixation on tactics and training. In fact, if I got out of this, I had some apologies to make. Maybe to some cybercrime experts in the Intel Bureau as well.

I felt like I was doomed. Henry wouldn't have called in these two if he was going to let me walk away. These were the kind of men who killed you, then stuffed you in the trunk of a car. The irony of it was, now that I knew Natalie was safe, I would gladly walk away. That is, if I was given a choice.

The guy with the teardrop tattoo and the sleek thug were still on either side of me. I couldn't just break and run. They'd have no qualms about shooting me in the back.

Still, no one had searched me. That was going to be a hell of a surprise. I calculated the advantages of pulling the pistol now or waiting. The longer I waited, the better chance someone had of discovering the gun. It also gave them the opportunity to bind my hands and keep me from moving.

But if I waited, I could surprise whoever drove me in the car. It would probably be just the three of us. I liked those odds if I had the element of surprise.

I still had hope. That was the key to a happy life. Hope. Just like I *hoped* to see my children grow up. I still had *hope* that Brian would get out of prison. I *hoped* to marry Mary Catherine soon, and I *hoped* these assholes would be careless enough not to search me.

I looked up at Henry. "You don't have the guts to do your own dirty work?"

"I see you still haven't given up. Good for you. I don't know what kind of trap you're trying to walk me into, but I already told you I'm too smart for that. No matter what you think you've worked out. I'm a step ahead of you."

I could tell by the way he'd delivered the little speech that he believed it. Absolutely and completely. In his eyes, he was equivalent to Einstein. And that would be his weakness. Maybe not today, maybe not tomorrow, but eventually someone with that high of an opinion of himself always got knocked down.

The main problem, at least in my mind, was that if he was knocked down in the future it wasn't going to help me now.

The two men I'd seen in New York—Christoph and Ollie—stepped closer to me. They spoke English with an accent different from anyone else's in the room. It sounded German or Dutch. It wasn't anything I could use at the moment.

I said to the slovenly man in the AC/DC shirt, the one who looked like an Ollie, "I was in the coffeehouse in New York when you and your buddy opened fire."

He chuckled. "Wild show, eh? Good thing those don't happen every day, no?"

"I imagine in your line of work they happen more often than most people think."

It was his buddy, the tall guy—probably Christoph—who answered. "We're professionals. It depends on the circumstances and what our assignment is. If we don't want a public shoot-out, we don't have one. You were just in the wrong place at the wrong time. If it wasn't for Alice and Janos, there wouldn't have been any problems at all."

"Are those the other killers you gunned down?"

The neat, well-groomed Christoph smiled. "We're used for contracts on professionals."

The heavy, sloppy Ollie added, "And on cops." He had a breezy, endearing smile. It'd be hard not to like him in other circumstances.

Christoph said, "Aren't Americans used to public shootings?"

"Not by slipshod amateurs like you. It must've been embarrassing knowing you had to use that kind of firepower on two unsuspecting people. Now you had to get extra help just to deal with me. Don't you have any standards?"

I could tell I was getting to the neat killer. He had an image he was trying to maintain. Just like Henry. The fat one, Ollie, couldn't have cared less. He said something in Dutch and his buddy didn't say another word.

From the catwalk, Henry called out, "Enough. You can chat with him on the way. Just get him out of my sight. We have work to do. We need to go to the new office." He clapped his hands to get everyone moving quickly.

It was more information but nothing that could help me right now. I felt a little desperation creep into my mind. I might have to do something drastic soon.

Then the door behind me burst open, and I turned quickly. The door hung at an odd angle, swaying on broken hinges, as someone began to enter the room. I saw the gun first.

It was the FBI's finest: Bill Fiore.

CHAPTER 71

ALL EYES WERE on the FBI agent. Fiore looked focused as he stepped all the way into the room. He took a position near a concrete support column close to the door. He showed good tactical sense.

Everyone stood perfectly still. Including me. They just stared at the portly FBI agent with his Glock 9mm held out in front of him. Just as I was thinking, *Don't say something like "Freeze" or "You're all under arrest,"* Fiore opened his mouth.

He said, "Nobody move."

Great. That should scare them into submission. I stepped backward until I was close to him. The heavy support column was a few steps to our left. I checked it out because something told me we might need it.

Then the handsome Christoph, the one who'd started shooting in New York, pulled a pistol from behind his back.

At almost the same time the "janitor," Gunnar, did the same thing.

Out of instinct, I yelled, "Gun." It was the universal signal among police that there was real danger in real time.

Fiore fired three times quickly before we both jumped to our left, behind the column. Before I did, I saw Gunnar go down. His pistol clattered on the hard, tiled floor. Blood quickly leaked into the grout and spread all around him. There was nothing neat or clean about a bullet wound.

I had to ask Fiore, "How'd you find me?"

"You gave me the address, you moron. You said it was across from Toit's City."

The FBI agent was starting to impress me.

Now shots echoed as Henry's people fired on us. Fragments from the column burst into dust, clouding my vision. There was enough dust to make me cough. I still wasn't going to move from my position.

I crouched next to Fiore as he returned fire, and I drew my own pistol. I wanted a quick shot at Henry. It was the old theory that if you cut off the head of a snake, the rest of the snake is no threat.

When I popped out from behind the support post, no one was on the catwalk. Henry and Natalie had disappeared.

Fiore stopped firing for a moment. I ducked back behind the post. When he looked at me, he was astonished. "Where the hell did you get a gun?"

I shrugged and said, "Just picked it up."

I heard him mumble something foul about the NYPD. Then he started to shoot again.

I knocked down the guy with the teardrop tattoo. I hit him

in the leg and then the pelvis. He flopped down onto the floor, screaming in Estonian. He ignored his gun and desperately tried to stem the bleeding next to his groin. I knew he was out of the fight.

The sound of the gunfire boomed in the big room and shut down my hearing. We still had to deal with the main killers I had seen in action before. I didn't know where they had dropped back to. I couldn't get a bead on them.

Then I heard Fiore grunt. I leaned back and saw blood pouring from a bullet hole in his shoulder. It also seeped between his fingers where he was holding the side of his abdomen.

He started to pant. He was losing color.

All I said was "How bad?"

He turned and lifted his hand so I could see the wound. Even through his mangled shirt, I knew it was nothing to fool around with.

"I have an idea."

Fiore said, "Is it better than your idea to come here alone?"

"Only marginally."

"Better than nothing. Let's hear it."

"I'm gonna lay down some heavy fire. And you scoot out the door."

Fiore said, "I'm not going to leave you here."

"You're not going to do either of us a favor by bleeding out on the floor. Go get some help. And some immediate medical attention."

I could see him thinking about it.

Then I said forcefully, "You need attention right now. On the count of three, you get out that door. And don't forget to get me some help."

I counted quickly. "One, two, three." Then I slid to the right of the post and emptied my magazine. I spread the fire around, trying to keep anyone with a goddamn gun in the room from raising his head.

One bullet struck the metal handrail along the catwalk. It caused an impressive spark. The air was thick with dust and gunpowder. The slide on my pistol locked back. I was empty. I threw myself behind the support column.

Now I needed time.

CHAPTER 72

AS I CROUCHED behind the post, I said a quick prayer for the FBI man to make it. The ploy had worked. Bill Fiore had slipped out the door while everyone's heads were down. I couldn't buy him any more time with the gun. But I didn't need to surrender immediately, either.

Sweat stung my eyes. Suddenly I realized I was dehydrated. And exhausted. Gunfights can do that to you.

I called out, "Hang on, hang on. Can we talk about this?"

I was surprised to hear Henry's voice. He was apparently up in one of the offices around the catwalk. He shouted back, "Drop your gun and surrender. Then we can talk."

"How do I know you won't kill me?"

"Christoph and Ollie will *definitely* kill you if you don't. Now both of you drop your guns."

I smiled at the idea that they thought the wounded FBI

agent was still with me. I milked it for as much time as possible.

Finally I said, "I don't know what you mean by 'both of us.' I'm the only one here."

"Where's your partner?"

"I don't have a partner. That was just a guy who'd been bothering me before."

I heard the slovenly Ollie call out from the other side of the room, "He's telling the truth. He's the only one behind the post."

I slid my empty gun across the floor. Then I stepped out from behind the post with my hands up. Gunnar was, of course, still there on the floor. A giant puddle of blood had spread out around him. His eyes stared straight ahead. I guess he'd had more to worry about than closing his eyes when he bled out.

The other man I had shot in the leg was whimpering, still clutching his upper thigh. Real tears matched his tattooed teardrop. Strands of his dark hair hung across his face. His pants were soaked with blood, but he hadn't lost a bucketful like poor Gunnar.

The two killers from New York, the ones I now considered the professionals, rushed toward me with their guns up. Christoph showed some sense when he immediately put my hands behind my back and fastened them with something. It felt like rope, but then I realized it was a pair of disposable handcuffs. I'd seen them at police trade shows. They looked like shoelaces with a sturdy plastic bracket that locked the two thin cords in place. I tugged on my arm and was impressed at how well they worked.

Ollie searched me carefully and kept my wallet, leaving behind the few euro coins I had in my trousers pocket.

"I got twenty-eight euros in there."

He smiled. "If you need them, I'll give them back to you."

"What if you're not around?"

Ollie chuckled. "Trust me, I'll be close by until you really won't need cash anymore."

That was a little disconcerting.

Now my main hope was that Fiore could get help here immediately.

Henry came down the stairs from the catwalk with Natalie right behind him. He walked quickly across the floor, shouting for men to starting sterilizing the place. He paused briefly to look down at the injured man with the teardrop tattoo. Then he spoke in Estonian to the remaining shooter, the other man who had crept up next to me when I first stepped into the room.

The man shrugged, then shot his injured comrade in the face. Aside from a surprised gurgle just before the shot, there wasn't time for the injured man to react. Now he lay flat on the floor, blood leaking from the hole between his eyes. The blue teardrop was still visible.

Henry casually looked my way and said, "No witnesses, no links to me. You see? I really am smarter than any cop."

Christoph and Ollie pushed me forward as we all rushed out of the building. They shoved me into the back of a surprisingly clean Volkswagen Passat. It had a remnant odor of pot but was otherwise immaculate.

Ollie turned around in the passenger seat and pointed a Smith & Wesson revolver at me. "Lie down on the floor and don't sit up again. If you do, I'll have to shoot you."

"If I don't, does that mean you'll just shoot me later?"

"Is that something you want to test right now?"

He was eloquent in his own way.

CHAPTER 73

THE RIDE IN the back of the Dutch killers' Volkswagen had been short, probably less than ten minutes. I'd had a hard time calculating the speed with my face on the floor of the car. I believed Ollie when he said he'd shoot me. After years as a cop, you get a good sense for someone who's full of shit. Ollie was not, even if his looks said otherwise. Stuck on the floor, with an utter lack of knowledge of Tallinn, Estonia, I was up shit creek. I had no idea where I was or why they had taken me instead of killing me on the spot. Perhaps I'd been spared just because Natalie would've been a witness to Henry ordering it. I might never know.

I had gotten a quick glimpse of the street and the fairly nice stand-alone office building I was rushed into after they stopped the car and hauled me out. Then they'd shoved me down a flight of stairs to some kind of basement with an empty loading dock area at the back. The building had to be perched on a hill, then, the dock at the far end lower than the main entrance. I'd been lucky to stay upright on the hard, concrete steps with steel strips embedded along the edges. At the bottom of the stairs, they'd crammed me into a small room with stained cinder-block walls sweating tiny beads of water. It wasn't that humid, but basements did weird things all over the world. Dead bug carcasses littered the bare concrete floor with a drain in the center of the room.

It was dark and smelled of urine. Not the image I had of a cybercriminal's hideout at all. Not even a decent super-villain lair. This sucked.

I had tried to pick up some intel on the ride over, but the men had spoken to each other only in Dutch. I worried about Bill Fiore and his wounds. I hoped he was getting treatment right now. That would mean he'd also alerted the local police to my kidnapping. I wasn't a hopeless case yet.

Now I found myself in a room where the only light was a line along the bottom of the door, from a bulb at the base of the stairs next to it. I sat on a hard, wooden chair, like I was waiting to see the principal at a Catholic school. My hands were still secured by the cord handcuffs. And just like in a holding cell of a police station, there was a bolt in the wall with a ring on the end big enough to tie a rope through. That rope was attached to my handcuffs and kept me in place. I wasn't impressed with Estonia's restraint technology. I felt like I was in the Alabama of the Baltics. But I was secure. I had already tried to break free and only had sore wrists to show for it. Maybe I should watch my New Yorker's natural tendency to make fun of Alabama.

Several times I heard people on the stairs who then walked past my room and toward the loading dock. After about thirty minutes, someone came down the stairs and stopped, then turned toward my room. Finally I was going to have some human contact.

Whoever it was, they hesitated outside the door. After another minute, a head popped into my room, allowing in some dim light. It was Natalie Lunden.

She didn't say anything. I think she was shocked by the sight of an American police officer held prisoner in her boyfriend's office building.

I managed to say, "Where are we?"

She didn't answer. Natalie stepped into the small room and kicked away dead bugs near her feet.

"Are they going to torture me?"

She shook her head and said, "Henry doesn't do that kind of thing."

"Tell that to the guy Henry had shot in the head."

I could tell by the look on Natalie's face she had already been thinking about that. She looked like she might be ill. That's just what this little shithole of a room needed: vomit.

Natalie said, "Henry acted rashly. He wasn't thinking. He's been under a lot of stress." Everyone wanted to make excuses for criminals. Sometimes they were just assholes to the core.

"You're kidding yourself. You're not some wide-eyed country girl, for Chrissakes. You went to MIT. Can't you see Henry is bad news?"

Natalie thought about it for a moment, then said, "I know what you think. But I'm here by choice. I wasn't lying when I told you I bought my own ticket. It wasn't my mom's choice or my dad's. I did it."

"But why? For that little twerp with a Napoleon complex?

How many steroids does he take to look like that? He looks like Arnold Schwarzenegger and Tom Cruise had a baby."

Her pretty face flushed. She swallowed and said, "He loves me. And I love him."

Then I understood. The one thing in the world that can screw up a good education, derail career plans, and generally mess with your head: love.

CHAPTER 74

OLLIE AND CHRISTOPH sat in an office on the ground floor of the new building. There were six offices on this floor and ten on the floor above them. Plus there was a loading dock and four storage rooms in the basement. It was dreary— that was the word Christoph thought of. No style or splash.

Henry was expanding. And getting crazier.

Ollie said, "I can't believe Henry had Joseph shot. I think he was just trying to impress the American cop."

Christoph said, "No doubt Henry can show off, but in his defense, gunshot wounds are hard to explain at hospitals." He had his doubts about their employer, but he didn't want to fuel Ollie's growing dissatisfaction.

"But it's like he thinks he's some kind of god, ordering death sentences."

Christoph nodded. "He pays well and is making money. Don't

worry about it. He said we could have this office space for our-selves." Christoph liked the idea of them having their own office. Henry had designated this room just for them. At the moment, there was only a table and two folding chairs in it, but they had already ordered two desks and a bookshelf.

Ollie had a different take on it. He said, "Why on earth would we want an office? It's just another way for Henry to keep track of us. Next thing you know, he'll tell us to work regular hours. Do you want to get high at night and wake up at seven thirty the next morning for the rest of your life?" Ollie shuddered.

The way Ollie put it, Christoph wasn't nearly as excited. He did like the easy hours they could generally set on their own. He was too lazy to go to school—that's why he had to make the most of his youth and lack of conscience. He didn't think he could be doing this kind of work into his forties.

Christoph said, "Doesn't it make you feel more professional?" But looking at his partner, and his nasty black AC/DC T-shirt and long, greasy hair, he realized Ollie didn't care anything about feeling professional.

Ollie said, "There's only one thing that makes me feel profes-sional: getting paid. If we didn't get paid for killing people, we'd just be psychopaths. I don't care about offices or if the boss likes us. I just want to get paid for our work."

Christoph had told Ollie his plan to save enough money to buy an apartment for himself in Amsterdam and set up his mom in a nice house. He had about €130,000 saved. He needed more. A lot more. The idea of sharing a house with his mom was unattractive. Unless he talked her into still doing his laundry.

Christoph said, "I don't want to have to find new work. Henry keeps us busy. I need the steady income."

Ollie said, "Henry keeps us busy for now. The way he's been acting, who knows how long this job will last. We need to get rid of this cop and start looking for a backup job." He paused, thinking. "For the record, I don't think it's cool to kill an American cop. It could stir up all kinds of shit. I prefer it when we have to kill other criminals. No one cares much about that. We just need to be careful with this cop."

Christoph said, "How do you want to do Bennett?"

Ollie pulled out of his pocket a Dutch two-euro coin with an engraving of Queen Beatrix on it. "I'll flip this coin. Heads you get to kill Bennett, tails I do."

Christoph nodded.

Ollie caught the coin in midair, then opened his hand. It showed the head of Queen Beatrix.

Ollie looked at him and said, "Gun or knife?"

Christoph shrugged. "If we're going to take him out near the port to kill him, I'll try my hand with a knife. I've shot plenty of people. I've only stabbed one."

Ollie stared in disbelief, then said, "Who'd you stab?"

"Just someone a long time ago, when I was a teenager."

"Really? I've never heard this story. I told you about shooting someone when I was seventeen over money, but now you're all secrets and lies. You think you're a spy or something?"

Christoph thought about it. Ollie already knew everything about him. He had seen some terrible things. There was nothing Christoph could tell him that would get him in more trouble if Ollie ever went to the police.

Christoph hesitated, then said, "I stabbed my cousin. We were fourteen. She's still listed as a runaway."

Christoph saw what he thought was a look of admiration on

Ollie's face. It was the first time he'd ever told anyone about his cousin Elizabeth. His first-ever murder victim. She had called him a pervert when he tried to sneak a peek down her shirt. When she threatened to tell Christoph's mother, he panicked. He didn't know what else to do and stuck his new folding knife right into her throat.

He even tried to help her afterward, but the blood just kept coming and coming. A few minutes later, she looked like she'd been left outside all winter. There was no color at all in her face. Her brown eyes just stared up at the sky.

They were in a field about a mile from his parents' house. It didn't take anything at all to weight her down with the rim of a tire and drop her into the pond on the edge of the field.

Aside from his aunt crying about her every once in a while, he'd never heard another word about it.

He figured he'd do the same thing to this New York cop.

CHAPTER 75

NOW I HAD Natalie's complete attention. She realized Henry loved the thrill of cracking security systems as much as making money. He'd never love anyone as much as he loved himself. She'd worked her way through an array of emotions, and I knew she was starting to assess how she fit into Henry's plans. Smart people usually catch on when you point out something that's not right. It just takes them a while to see what they don't want to.

I said, "Henry is a batshit-crazy criminal. That's all."

Natalie said, "No, you're wrong. Sure, Henry crosses some lines to make some money from corporations. He supports a lot of people. But he's not a killer. I mean, he doesn't just kill for no reason."

"What's the reason that justifies murder?"

She stared at me without saying a word. I saw my own children in her face. I knew people made mistakes. This girl wasn't a killer. She probably hadn't done ten things wrong in her whole life before she met this asshole, Henry. She might say she wanted to be here, but I didn't think it was true.

I decided to lay it on heavy. I said, "You really think that's the first person Henry's had killed? I've seen his handiwork in New York. I personally witnessed the two Dutch guys shoot up a coffeehouse. They even hit a witness I was talking to. A witness who knows you."

Now Natalie looked like a little girl. Her mouth was open slightly, and she was just staring at me. Then with a childlike voice she said, "Who were you talking to?"

"Jennifer Chang."

She sucked in some breath and steadied herself. "Jen? Really? Is she still alive?"

"Even with a bullet in her back, she pulled through. She's going to be in the hospital for a good long while. Plus, there were other fatalities at the coffeehouse. And then another witness named Tom Payne. They strangled him and left him in a parking lot near Penn Station."

Her eyes moved off into space. "Tommy? Dead?" She tried to reconcile what had happened. Finally she was grasping at straws. Natalie said, "Henry didn't do any of that. He hasn't been to New York in over a year."

"Henry *ordered* it all done. You can't be this blind. Will you think the same thing after they murder me? See if you can live with that, knowing ahead of time what he intends to do."

She stared straight ahead. Torn between ignoring what I was saying and recognizing the truth. She looked like the college student I had thought I would rescue: impossibly young and scared.

I was getting to her. The indecision was etched on her face. There was a certain panic starting to run through her as she connected the dots and realized I wasn't lying. But I didn't know the extent to which Henry would go. If he was as crazy as everyone claimed, he might change the focus of his criminal organization and go even bigger. He could shut down power grids and really put a lot of people's lives at risk.

I looked at Natalie and said, "Anything happens from here on out, you're complicit. I'm not saying you'll be arrested for it, but you're a decent girl, raised by decent parents. You know what's right and wrong."

"I don't know how decent they are. My mom is busy with her new boyfriend and my dad has an entire family. No one misses me. No one needs me. Except Henry. He told me I'm one of the only things that keeps him going."

"Your parents cared enough to spin up the NYPD to look for you. And now it looks like they cared enough that I'm going to be murdered because of it."

"Don't say that."

"The truth is hard to face. That's why people turn to alcohol and drugs and make all kinds of crazy choices. But it's never too late to face it. It's never too late to correct mistakes. Believe me, I know that better than anyone." Brian flashed in my brain. Suddenly I had an incredible urge to speak to my kids.

I heard someone on the stairs. It didn't sound like the

rushing footsteps of police rescuing me. It was a measured, casual pace.

A shadow fell across the light from the stairs. Then a form filled most of the doorway.

It was the tall Dutch killer, Christoph.

CHAPTER 76

BEFORE THE DUTCHMAN could say anything, I heard another set of footsteps on the stairs. Henry appeared just behind Christoph, stopping on the final step of the staircase, right next to the open door. He had changed clothes. He wore a dark sport coat, like he was going to a party. He stood on the stair above Christoph to make himself look taller. I noticed men who did that kind of shit at the PD all the time.

Henry said, "I hope you have a pleasant trip home, Mr. Bennett. Now that you see Natalie is safe and here of her own free will, maybe her parents will leave us alone. I'm sorry you have to be treated this way. Perhaps if you behave better at other people's businesses you will be treated better in the future."

I gave him the best smile I could. I also sat up straight. At least as straight as I could with my hands tied to the eyebolt in the wall. Then I said, "Who are you trying to fool? The only trip I'm going on is a short one. And I'm certain I won't like the destination."

It would've been easier to play along with him, and his killers might be less vigilant if I kept my mouth shut. But I needed Natalie to see who this guy really was.

Henry gave a nervous glance toward Natalie. "I'm sorry I can't feed into your conspiracies. Christoph and Ollie will drive you to the airport shortly."

Natalie looked like she was buying it. She said to me, "See, Mr. Bennett? You have nothing to worry about." A smile ran across her pretty face. "Have a good flight and tell my dad to leave me alone." She excused herself and darted past Henry and up the stairs. She'd taxed her view of reality enough for one day.

Henry said, "Excuse me, Detective. We've got to get things set up to get back to work quickly. You know how the corporate life can be. Always something. Am I right?"

"I wouldn't know. I've always been in public service. We're busy in different ways."

"Like looking for young women sick of their parents, instead of solving murders."

The way Henry had said it, I understood why Natalie believed in him. He seemed reasonable and rational. Then again, every good criminal did. No one who was arrested was ever guilty. I said, "You really think I buy into that bullshit?" Now it was just Henry, me, and a known killer. "Let's be honest. You're going to kill me, right?"

Henry chuckled as he brushed unseen dirt off his sport coat. Just a way to move and show off his arms. He didn't look like a computer genius in this setting. He could've been any psycho I'd met over my career.

He said, "I don't kill people." He started back up the stairs, out of sight. Then he called down, "I order other people to kill. Good luck, Detective Bennett."

Now it was just me and the Dutchman, Christoph. He looked more imposing up close. Thick arms and no hesitation in his movements. He knew exactly what he was going to do.

He pulled a steel, four-inch, fixed-blade knife from a sheath secured at his waistline. He held it up high, so I could see it and his face at the same time. These younger guys, raised on action movies, loved doing that kind of stuff. Like there was a camera watching their every move.

That didn't mean I wasn't unnerved by the knife. That's the main function of a knife in a criminal's hands. Stabbing is a last resort. Besides, it was a combat knife. A Gerber. It wouldn't snap or break when it hit a bone. I shivered at the thought.

Every step he took toward me made my stomach tighten. There were few things as frightening as an edged weapon. Every cop remembers the training video they saw in the academy about defending against edged weapons. The testimonials of cops who'd survived stabbings were horrifying.

Now I realized why the force toughens us up about potential knife attacks. They just want to keep us from panicking at the sight of a blade intended for stabbing. I wasn't sure how well the training was working right about now.

Christoph stopped directly in front of me with the handle of the knife in his right hand. He didn't move or say anything.

I stared up at him. I had my feet ready in case I needed a desperate defense.

Christoph said, "Well?"

"Well what?"

Christoph's accent was more pronounced as he said, "Turn round so I can cut you loose from the metal ring."

Oh. I had misread that. I let out the breath I was holding. I turned on my seat and felt him work on one of the ropes behind me. In a moment, I was free of the bolt on the wall. My hands were still cuffed behind me. And I was down a few ounces of sweat.

I said, "Can you do me a favor, pal?"

"Perhaps."

"I'm a little older than you. My shoulders are really bothering me with my hands cuffed behind my back. Can you cuff me in the front?" It was a request I had heard from virtually every person I'd ever arrested. And I always told them, for safety reasons and because I had to follow policy, they would stay cuffed behind their backs.

Christoph didn't have the same policies. All he said was "These little cord handcuffs cost three euros each."

"I've got maybe ten euros in my pocket. I'll give it to you."

"That's okay. We're going to keep anything in your wallet or pockets anyway." He paused for a moment, then added with a smile, "It doesn't bother me too much that your shoulders hurt."

A Bronx beat cop couldn't have said it better.

CHAPTER 77

THIS WAS IT. The Dutch killer, Christoph, had me secured. I could barely move my arms, and his little cord handcuffs were strong. He kept a hand on my right arm and stood behind me where I couldn't get a decent kick at him. We walked out of the room and turned down the hallway aiming for the loading dock at the back of the building, where his partner, Ollie, could presumably shove me back into their car and drive me to God knows where. I needed some kind of plan. Like right now.

My best chance would be to face only one of the killers at a time. I'd been watching them both carefully. The other guy, Ollie, looked like a slob. No one gave him credit. But I could see he was the brains of the operation. Really smart people try not to let others realize just how smart they are. His partner, Christoph, didn't notice that Ollie *allowed* him to make decisions while guiding him to it.

There was something unsettling about Ollie. It was probably his appearance and the fact that he did everything to hide who he really was. This was the guy I wanted to escape from.

Christoph might give me that opening. The way he held my arm and stood just behind me and to the side was textbook NYPD. I knew veteran cops who didn't transport prisoners as safely. I wondered if he'd learned it from being walked by the police himself.

I tried chatting with him, to maybe distract him. I said, "Is this something you really want to do? Think about it. You want this on your conscience?"

He slowed his walk and looked at me. "Those are separate questions. No, I don't *want* to do this. But I *need* to be paid. As far as my conscience goes, this is business. It has nothing to do with my conscience."

Great. I couldn't tell if he was a psycho who lived in a little fantasy world or an actual professional hit man. Hit men for the mob in New York mostly lived seemingly normal lives, with wives and kids. That wasn't this guy.

I said, "Keep telling yourself it's just business. Maybe it'll keep you from going crazy as you get older. I've seen a lot of killers in my career. Most of them don't live particularly long. And the ones who do don't have much left between their ears."

"Good to know. Thank you for your advice. Now I would ask you to stay quiet. It will go easier on all of us if you do that."

"Not to contradict you, but I have a feeling it's going to go the same way for me no matter what I say or do."

Christoph just shrugged his broad shoulders. He didn't seem concerned about my feelings. I find that common among killers.

Nothing I said could distract him enough to give me a reasonable chance to escape.

As we approached an archway at the end of the hall that led into the loading dock area, he stepped in front of me to lead me through. On the other side of the archway, a fast blur of movement caught my eye. It took me a second to register the movement and the loud *thwack* sound that accompanied it.

Natalie Lunden had hit Christoph square in the face with a two-by-four. The pine board broke in half.

Christoph staggered, but he remained upright as he slowly glared at Natalie and said, "Not funny."

I could see Natalie was scared as she looked up into the killer's eyes. She managed to say, "Henry won't let you hurt me."

"Only if I ask him first." He seized her wrists and started pulling them up like he intended to rip her arms from her body.

CHAPTER 78

I FELT HELPLESS with my hands tied behind my back. I also couldn't believe the tall Dutchman was still on his feet. He'd taken a hell of a blow.

Christoph held Natalie's wrists like she was an insect and he was about to dismember her. She knew she'd made a mistake. She started to whimper. Her glasses slipped off, and one of the lenses popped out with a clatter as they hit the concrete floor.

I had to do something. I couldn't just watch Natalie be murdered.

Christoph was focused. On her. This might be the best chance I got. I wasted no time as I stepped a little to my left and used my right leg to kick the big man in his thigh. I was aiming for the common peroneal nerve. It's tricky to target. But if you connect just right, it can crumple your opponent.

The nice thing about the nerve that runs from the hip past

the knee along the back of the leg is that if you miss, the kick still hurts. And I had missed. I didn't know by how much, but it hadn't been a direct hit on the common peroneal. Instead, my heel had ground into his muscles and compressed the nerves against his femur, which had a similar effect.

Instead of crumpling him, I managed to send him reeling. He lost his balance and dropped Natalie, reaching for his injured leg as he let out a yowl like an injured cat.

That's when I threw my whole body into him. He was already off balance, so even with my hands fastened behind my back, I was able to lower my shoulder and really plow into him like he was a tackling dummy. I assumed he didn't have the benefit of regularly watching the NFL.

Christoph slammed against the edge of the archway. His face made a sickening sound as it hit the rough concrete. When he staggered back and I could see his face, I realized it had been a good blow. Blood poured out of his nose like some kind of emergency ballast release.

Then his knees gave out and he sat down hard, then rolled onto his side. He was done. At least for now. Blood still poured out of his ruined nose.

Natalie stood staring at me, stunned.

I said, "Natalie. Listen to me. He has a knife in the waistline of his trousers. See it?"

He wasn't dead. I could feel him breathing. We had maybe a minute at most.

When she didn't move or acknowledge me, I shouted, "Natalie, snap out of it." Then my message sank in. She inched closer to Christoph's inert form, paused, then quickly crouched and with both hands jerked the knife clumsily out of its belt-line sheath.

After she backed away from him again, she let out a deep, uneven breath.

I turned around and pulled my arms as far apart as I could so the cord would be taut for her. I felt her sawing on it, and my arms burst free in no time. I wiggled my stiff fingers, trying to get blood back into my hands.

I spun and checked Christoph. He was starting to move. I patted him down roughly. His pistol wasn't on him. Damn.

I turned and gently took the Gerber from Natalie's trembling hands. Not my weapon of choice. I tossed it to the floor before I was tempted to take it with us. Then I said to Natalie, "Where's his partner?"

"He went to get their car. He's probably already outside this door, waiting." She tilted her head toward the loading dock's roll-up door. She had regained some of her composure.

I said, "Now you *have* to come with me."

She nodded. "I know. Once I realized they really were going to kill you, I couldn't just sit back."

"Me and my whole family are glad you came to your senses. Now we gotta get out of here."

"But where? Henry knows people all over the city. And I'm not sure if he owns any police. I don't know who we can trust."

I said, "I do."

CHAPTER 79

CHRISTOPH PANICKED FOR a moment when he snapped out of the pain-induced blackout. His eyes wouldn't focus. He wasn't even certain where he was or what had happened. Then it came back to him in a rush. He didn't think he'd been unconscious for long, but it was still going to take some time to get going. Then the lightbulb in the middle of the ceiling above the loading dock came into focus.

He blinked a couple of times as he lay on his back, assessing his injuries. His head throbbed like the bass from "Smoke on the Water." Then he moved his leg and it hurt so badly he forgot about his head.

He rose onto his hands and knees, and thought he might be sick. The splash of blood on the floor made him lift his fingers to his face. Blood was still trickling out of his nose. His beautiful, straight nose. Which was now broken. Badly. It was so flat, it felt like he just had two holes in the middle of his face.

He was startled when a new sound ripped through his brain. He was worried he might be having a seizure. Then he realized it was Ollie knocking on the steel loading dock door.

Slowly, he managed to make it to his feet. He felt his face again and thought, *That son of a bitch really clobbered me.* And Natalie had been part of it. The pounding resumed in his head.

Christoph stumbled over to the wall where the control for the door was at chest level. He had to lean against the wall and focus just to hit the right button. Then he heard the slow pulse of the motor pulling up the door. The rattle of the steel felt like someone running their fingernails over a chalkboard.

As the door rose at its glacial pace, Christoph tried to wipe the blood from his face. Now he noticed his eye was tender. His nose, his eye, his leg. That cop was going to suffer. So was Natalie. He needed his knife. He spotted it on the floor.

The door was finally up and the gray Volkswagen Passat sat puttering beside the loading bay.

Ollie shook his head and said, "What happened to you, brother?" He tried to hide his shock at the sight of his partner.

"It was a combination of Natalie and that cop. She ambushed me and he caught me while I was distracted." Christoph limped over to the knife and scooped it up with no small amount of dizziness.

Ollie thought for a moment, then said, "If you want to do something to Natalie, it's probably best we leave without talking to Henry. He still pays the bills."

Christoph clutched the handle of the Gerber tightly. "I'm going to use my knife on both of them. Slowly."

"Another reason we should wait to talk to Henry. I say we jump in the car and start looking for them. We'll call Henry and tell him to do some of his computer magic and see if he can find anything. But we don't call him until we're already out of here. Just in case he has one of his fits and tells one of the locals to shoot us."

Ollie ran up the short flight of steps next to the loading dock and found a rag on a workbench inside, then used it to clean up Christoph. He wiped his partner's face like a mother cleaning up a three-year-old. Blood sloughed off the rag onto the floor.

Ollie said, "Hopefully people will think the blood on your shirt is a design."

Christoph shoved his knife into its sheath. He was in no mood to listen to his partner. He wanted blood for blood.

They had a brief discussion about who was going to drive. Christoph wasn't interested in debate. Finally he said, "I'm driving," and pushed past Ollie.

The two Dutchmen got into the car and scanned the sidewalks for Bennett and the girl as they drove. It was early evening and there weren't that many people on the street.

Eventually Ollie pulled out his phone and dialed Henry. He put the phone on speaker, in case Christoph wanted to add anything.

Henry answered the phone with an impatient "What now?"

Ollie started with the touchy subject first. "Your girlfriend attacked Christoph and helped Bennett escape."

After a long silence, Henry said, "Is Natalie still here, or are they both missing?"

"They both fled."

"Are you certain Natalie helped him?"

"Absolutely. She hit Christoph with a board and shattered his nose."

"Her phone is still here. Too bad. That would've made finding her much easier."

Ollie said, "Sorry, Henry."

"I'm really disappointed in you two."

Ollie said, "So are our families."

"Always with the smart answer."

Ollie let the silence hang there for a moment, then said, "We'll keep searching and let you know if we find them."

"Let me see what I can do on this end. I'll call out some more help since you two morons can't seem to handle anything yourselves. If I hear anything, I'll send you to their location."

Ollie cut off the call. "He sounds pissed."

Christoph said, "He always sounds pissed. That's how crazy people sound."

"Exactly why I'm not sure we should even waste time looking for Bennett and Natalie."

"What? Have you lost your mind as well? Look what they did to me."

Ollie thought for a moment. "This is still business. We need profit, not problems."

"Then I'll finish this alone."

"Wait—"

"No, I'm serious. This *has to* get done."

Ollie said, "All right, we'll finish this, but then we walk away from Henry. This is getting to be a pain. I don't care how well he pays. You get your revenge, we collect our pay and head straight back to Amsterdam."

Christoph smiled. That's all he wanted. A chance for some revenge.

CHAPTER 80

WITHOUT A SOUL noticing, Natalie and I had slipped back upstairs in the building to what seemed like an empty ground floor and out the front entrance. Then we ran, trying to stay off the main roads. Neither of us was hurt. Natalie squinted at the street signs, and I remembered that Christoph had knocked her glasses off.

"You can still find your way around town, right?" It went without saying that I was a tourist. Most of my travels around this town had been out to St. Laszlo's with Fiore driving and on the floor in the back of Christoph and Ollie's car where I couldn't see anything.

As we trotted down an alley, I said, "Do you have any money? Anything we can use to get a ride?"

"I have a few euros, that's it."

"I don't know if that's going to help us much." I found the euro coins in my pocket that I'd told Christoph about, which I doubted amounted to enough for a cab.

When Natalie stood on a street corner, looking for an approaching bus, I snapped at her. "Keep off the street. They'll be looking for us."

Natalie turned and frowned at me. "Sorry, I've never been on the run before. How about cutting me a little slack?" After a few moments, she said, "Where are we running to, anyway?"

"Do you know St. Laszlo's Church?"

"Yeah, but it's on the other side of the city. The Alexander Nevsky Cathedral is nicer and a lot closer."

"I'm not going there for mass. I know someone at St. Laszlo's who can help us."

Natalie led me through an alley and then over a few blocks, where we caught a bus. We transferred after a few minutes. The second bus seemed to stop every two blocks.

Natalie said, "I could walk faster than this."

"Go ahead. I'll meet you at St. Laszlo's." I was done with whining. As long as we were moving and on the bus, we were relatively safe. I would gladly ride it all night long.

About forty minutes later, I recognized the neighborhood and soon saw the lighted cupolas of the Orthodox church. I hoped we weren't too late to catch Father Marty at the office.

When I raced into the building, Natalie followed me through the door. Almost immediately, we ran into Father Marty.

He smiled and clapped his hands. "You found her. Good for you." He looked at Natalie and said, "I prayed for you, my dear."

She mumbled her thanks, and I gave him a quick rundown of what had happened. I left out some of the bloodier details, but he now knew the facts. I ended by asking if he had heard about the shoot-out near Tartu Maantee.

Father Marty said, "No, I haven't heard anything about a shoot-out in Tallinn."

"The FBI agent who was chasing me was injured trying to save us."

"Oh, dear. And you don't know how Mr. Fiore is doing?"

"No, Father, I don't. As soon as I make sure Natalie's safe, I want to check on him. He saved my"—I paused for a moment, then came up with—"life."

"Mr. Fiore was quite angry at me after I helped you escape. I told him I followed my heart."

"And what'd he say to that?"

"He had another suggestion on showing my love for myself." The priest smiled.

I hid my own smile as I imagined the exchange. I said, "I'm sorry, Father."

"No. One needs a diverse experience. It's sometimes nice to hear new phrases. And in his defense, he did appear to be a dedicated law enforcement officer."

"He absolutely is. And I hope he's safe."

Father Marty said, "I can have a car here in an hour. A man I know can drive you down to Riga, in Latvia. I think that's the safest course of action. It will be easy to arrange a flight back to the US from Riga."

Natalie said, "Can I send a quick email to my mom? I left my phone back at Henry's building."

"Of course, my dear. Use my office. There are some drinks in the little refrigerator if you need them."

I plopped down in an overstuffed chair. Suddenly the events of the last few hours hit me in a wave. I dozed off before I even realized how comfortable I was.

CHAPTER 81

CHRISTOPH WAS BEHIND the wheel of the Volks-wagen Passat. He hated this car. It didn't fit his image. Ollie had tried his best to talk his partner out of driving. With blood still leaking out of Christoph's nose and his face turning a dark purple, Ollie had thought it would be best if he drove. The debate had lasted almost a minute, until Ollie had relented.

Now, as Christoph's vision blurred, he wasn't about to say anything to his partner. He blinked harder to get a better view of the streets of Tallinn. A woman, walking hand in hand with a little girl on the edge of the street, had to spring out of the way as Christoph swerved. Ollie turned quickly to see the woman on the curb, holding the girl and cursing them.

Christoph thought the vision issues might have more to do with his feelings than a physical injury. He was furious. And his fury was focused on two people. All he could think about was sticking his knife into Bennett's throat. He imagined the blade when it first broke skin and he smiled. He wanted to do it just like he had done it to his cousin all those years ago. He never would admit to anyone how satisfying it had been. She had been laughing and threatening to expose him, and he had put an end to it with a simple, single thrust of his pocketknife.

He pictured Bennett in the same situation, grasping his neck as blood pumped out of severed arteries and veins. This time Christoph wouldn't panic. Instead, he'd enjoy it.

Natalie was another story. He was thinking he wanted to watch her die slowly. Maybe by strangling her. He could picture that pretty face staring up at him as he choked the last breath out of her. Her brains wouldn't count for shit when that happened. Natalie had brought this on herself. To Christoph, she was just another of Henry's many girlfriends. Until she'd hit him in the face. Now she was a target. Henry hadn't given him explicit permission to kill Natalie. But as far as Christoph was concerned, it was implied.

Henry was hard to figure. He never confided in anyone. But there was no doubt he was a business genius. The operation ran flawlessly, and they raked in a lot of cash. To Henry's credit, he generally wasn't shy about spreading the money around.

On the downside, he could lose his temper and order one of his hired thugs to kill anyone at any time. The perfect example was Janos and Alice in New York. They had apparently questioned his authority. Now everyone knew he was the king. Even if the king was a little crazy.

Christoph had known Henry since the beginning. The computer geek never would admit it, but he had changed. Some people speculated it happened when he got into weight lifting and using steroids. But Christoph had seen his dark, murderous side even before that.

The first killing Henry had ordered them to commit was a programmer who'd stolen some of Henry's ideas and applied them to businesses in his native Canada. They had flown first class to Toronto, rented a car, and driven for what seemed like days, just to shoot the young man in the head at his parents' house.

Now it was absolutely personal for Christoph. He didn't care if Henry even paid them for these killings. They were going to happen.

Ollie said, "What happens once we catch them?"

Christoph tried not to show his anger in his voice. "We've already spent too much time and blood on this. Once we find the cop and the girl, I know exactly what I want to do. We take them to our favorite dumping ground in Kopli Liinid. With all the new construction there, no one will notice a couple of bodies stuck in the foundation of one of the new houses."

Ollie was quiet. Finally he said, "Maybe we let this one go. We can find other jobs."

Christoph flared. "No way. Not these two."

"Perhaps we should talk to Henry first."

"He's busy. He's got other problems."

Ollie said, "I'm worried about the fat guy who escaped. He has details about us."

"You worry about things too far ahead of time. We need to live for today. And today we're going to kill Bennett and Natalie."

"That's the kind of shit Janos used to say. Look where it got him and Alice. I like looking into the future. I enjoy life too much to waste it. The fat guy could give the police everything. Maybe we'd be better off to end this and head back to Amsterdam right now."

Before Christoph could rebut his partner's logic, Ollie's phone rang. It was Henry. Ollie put it on speaker.

Henry's agitated voice was scratchy on the tiny phone speaker. He said, "Looks like Natalie accessed her email on a Wi-Fi network."

Ollie asked, "Do you know where the network is physically located?"

"St. Laszlo's Church."

Christoph said, "Damn. We followed him there yesterday. He must be friends with the priest. We'll call you when we're done." He ended the phone call before Henry could say anything else, just in case their fearless leader had second thoughts about his girlfriend.

CHAPTER 82

I CAME AWAKE suddenly when a hand gently shook me. Father Marty and Natalie were standing over me, smiling. The giant chair still felt like a wide, soft pillow, and the remnants of a dream stuck in my head. I was marrying Mary Catherine. My grandfather was officiating, and Brian was with us. Pretty nice dream, but now it was back to a rougher reality.

Father Marty said, "It's impressive you can fall asleep so quickly."

"How long was I out?"

"About an hour. Your car is out front. Natalie told her mother she's safe, and my colleagues in Latvia are expecting you."

I said, "Thanks. Sorry we're tying up one of your people."

Father Marty waved me off. "Latki was driving to Riga anyway. He's our IT manager for the entire region." The Orthodox priest smiled. "It's an old church with new ways. We find that social media keeps us up-to-date on what people are worried about."

A red Volkswagen sedan sat in front of the church. The young man standing next to it smiled and introduced himself. He was tall and a little awkward, with thick glasses and shaggy hair. He couldn't look Natalie in the eye. He looked like an IT character in a TV show, only a lot taller.

A box of files sat on the front passenger seat. Natalie and I slid into the comfortable back seat.

We made our good-byes, and our driver waved to Father Marty. He looked over his shoulder and said in accented English, "Make sure of seat belts. We are going on some bigger roads. If police check, the fine is unbelievable."

Natalie said, "You make this drive often?"

He hesitated. It looked like he was screwing up his courage. It must've worked, as he turned and looked directly at Natalie. "Once every two weeks. How do you say in English? Semi-weekly?"

I had to think about that one for a moment. I was pretty sure he was looking for *biweekly*.

I wanted to get moving. I needed to know Natalie was safe and then I needed to check on Bill Fiore. The longer we waited, the more anxious I felt.

As I sat there, thinking about it for a moment, I saw a flash in the corner of my eye. Another car was barreling directly toward us. It had hopped a curb and was cutting across the stretch of park across the street from the church like a missile.

The crash was tremendous. It was as if sound faded away, then my whole world spun in every crazy direction. Our car flew across the sidewalk, spinning 180 degrees before plowing into the bushes in front of the church. The driver's soda, which I learned that moment was called Lumivalgeke, floated into the air and seemed to freeze in space as gravity worked its magic on everything else.

It felt as if the laws of time had been suspended. Everything happened in slow motion. Until it didn't.

The engine creaked and shifted under the crumpled hood as the car came to a stop. The windshield crackled, then tumbled into the car, a spider-webbed mass of glass.

Our driver was moving. Slowly. He called out, "Are you injured?"

I was relieved. If he was asking, it meant he wasn't too badly hurt.

I turned to Natalie. She wasn't moving and her eyes were shut. I thought the worst. I gently touched her arm. When her eyes popped open, I almost fainted with relief.

I leaned in close and spoke clearly. "Are you okay?"

She just sat there for a moment. Then she turned her head to face me. Her voice was weak. "I'm okay, I think."

Then I looked past Natalie out the window. I could see that Father Marty had leapt out of the way.

The other car was also a Volkswagen. A slightly smaller one. The front end was smashed. The car would never run again. It rested partially on the street and partially on the sidewalk.

Then I saw the other driver. The Dutch killer Christoph glared out of the driver's side window directly at me. This collision was no accident. And it left no doubt what Henry wanted done with me and Natalie.

I tried my door. Jammed shut. I fumbled with my seat belt, finally managing to open the buckle. I hit the door with my shoulder. Still nothing.

No one emerged from the other car, either.

CHAPTER 83

I'D BEEN IN car accidents before. Shock was one of my immediate concerns. Shock did crazy things to people. They couldn't think clearly, and their perception was faulty. That was the last thing I needed right now.

I had to do something. My door was jammed, but if we waited much longer, that would be the least of our problems. The interior of our car started to fill with a foul smell. I'm not a mechanic, but it had to mean that the engine was leaking oil or some other kind of fluid. Either way, I knew we couldn't stay in the car.

Latki moaned, then coughed, but kept moving. He pulled the handle on his door and almost fell out into the bushes. One of the hinges on his door snapped and the door fell onto the torn-up grass almost on top of him.

I reached across and unhooked Natalie's seat belt. She opened her door easily, got out, then turned and reached back to make sure I got out of the car as well. She may have been scared, but she wasn't clueless. I appreciated that.

I stepped out on shaky legs. Natalie grabbed me under the arm and helped me stand. I turned to her and said, "Go with Father Marty, right now."

It was as if saying his name made him appear. He kneeled down and quickly checked Latki, who waved him off.

Father Marty said, "You *both* need to run. I'll see if I can delay those men." From what I'd told him earlier, he'd figured out who was in the other car.

I said, "We'll run, but you can't confront these men. They're not like us. They won't listen to reason. They don't care about your standing in the church or if this is holy ground. You and Latki need to get out of here, too."

Father Marty nodded, then shoved me toward the church to get me moving. My ankle and knee felt like someone had hit them with a hammer. But I followed Natalie as she urged me along, just as Father Marty and Latki trotted roughly off in the opposite direction, away from the church and hopefully to safety.

Each step was agony. I knew I wasn't in shock because I rationally considered what a torn meniscus or damaged ankle might mean in the long run. I didn't want Chrissy pushing me in a wheelchair before she graduated from Harvard.

Then I had an idea and was able to pick up the pace a little bit. I didn't have a gun and I didn't have backup, so I had to use our only advantage. I'd been here before and knew the terrain. These two Dutchmen had gotten in a surprise blow, but I knew not to underestimate them.

With my new burst of energy, Natalie was having a hard time keeping up with me now as we raced through the church and past the altar. I had a little difficulty remembering the exact path to the hidden corridor Father Marty had shown me earlier that day, but after some turns and a couple of fruitless shoves against the wall, I found the right panel. I shoved it hard, and the entryway to the hidden corridor opened. When Natalie hesitated, I pulled her into the tight passage. There was no time to be subtle.

We hustled down the narrow hallway, as dark as it had been the last time I'd traversed it. My knee started to scream at me again. I had a hop-limp in my run now, but it wasn't much farther. I could hear Natalie taking deep breaths. The stress and accident had taken a lot out of both of us. I hoped it was having the same effect on the men chasing us.

Natalie said, "I hate enclosed spaces. I'm having a hard time catching my breath."

"You and me both. But we can't stop now."

We finally came to the long sequence of steps that I knew would lead us to the bottom of the hill. The stairway was even darker here and Natalie hesitated.

I didn't have time to argue as I gently pulled her along. I held her hand the entire descent. Finally we were at the base of the stairs.

I burst through the last door into the darkness of the Estonian night.

Standing by the open door, I froze when I heard something.

The Dutch killers were in the corridor and still chasing us.

CHAPTER 84

CHRISTOPH SPRAWLED IN the smashed Volkswagen for a few more moments. All he heard were the sounds of metal creaking and something sizzling on the hot engine block. He could feel his toes and his fingers and move his head. He called it a win. When he'd driven along the street leading to the church and seen Bennett and Natalie getting into the car by the curb, something inside him had snapped.

He'd wanted—no, *needed*—to see them dead. He'd never experienced this feeling. Not naked, premeditated murderous urges.

He and Ollie were slow to move. He saw Natalie and Bennett struggle out of the other car. He tried his door, but it was jammed shut. There was nothing he could do. Christoph screamed in frustration and slammed his shoulder against the door. Finally it started to give.

Ollie stirred next to him. Then he seemed to snap into alertness. His first words were "Are you insane? You could've killed us."

Christoph's eyes were fixed on Bennett. "Get moving. They'll escape if we don't get to them now."

As soon as Christoph stepped out onto the sidewalk, his legs gave way for a moment. He had to steady himself on the car.

On the other side of the vehicle, Ollie managed to stand up, and he took a moment to check himself. He said, "My ribs are cracked. It hurts like a son of a bitch. Satisfied?"

Christoph had almost tuned him out completely. He marched toward the priest, now trying to move quickly away from the church with a young man.

Ollie caught up to Christoph and put a hand on his shoulder. He had to wheeze for a moment because he was having difficulty breathing. "I'm not about to threaten a priest," he said. "We know they're in the church. We'll figure out where they went." With some effort, Ollie managed to turn him toward the front door of the church.

Inside, without any pews to look under, they were quickly able to tell that no one was inside the nave.

Ollie, walking along slowly because of his injuries, said, "Back here and toward the offices."

Christoph followed his partner down a long hallway. Ollie mumbled, "This place is built on a hill. I'll bet there's a way to get downstairs and out the back."

Christoph grumbled and pulled out his knife. He didn't want to be surprised by this cop again.

CHAPTER 85

THERE WAS ALMOST no light at the bottom of the hill behind the church. I was startled when I looked straight up and saw the night filled with stars. It wasn't easy to see any constellations in New York. On the other hand, I would know where to get help in New York. Help I could trust.

We were outside but not safe. When we reached a narrow road, we broke into a jog. I kept looking over my shoulder at the church sitting up on the hill. I didn't know what to expect: someone shooting at us from the top or someone chasing us along the road.

We had to walk back up two flights of concrete stairs built into the hillside to get to the main streets of the surrounding neighborhood. This was our best chance to disappear.

Natalie said, "I recognize the area. We're in Sikupilli."

"Is that good or bad?"

"I just know where we are. There's a lake and a park just over there. There should be some thick bushes. Somewhere we can hide."

I liked the way she was thinking.

At the top of the stairs, I didn't see a park. I didn't see much of anything except a few houses. There was almost no traffic at this time of night.

I hurried Natalie along, desperately looking for the park or anyplace else we could hide. I was ready to hunker down for the night and see if we couldn't find some help in the light of day.

Then Natalie pointed. "Over there. Pae Park. And look, Pae Järv." She was excited now.

I said, "What does *järv* mean?"

"It means *lake*. There's a big lake in the park. See that bridge? If we cross it, there should be plenty of places to hide."

I studied the bridge for a moment. It was about twenty-five feet off the water and built for pedestrian traffic.

We'd come this far. It was as good a plan as any.

It took longer than I'd thought to reach the bridge. Natalie didn't look tired, but she was scared. I was, too.

We rested for a moment, looking across the bridge. Was there another way out of the park or across the lake? I didn't want to get stranded with our only way out blocked by a killer.

Then I heard a gunshot, and a bullet pinged off the rail of the bridge. A second later, I heard the report from the pistol. This time I didn't need to prod Natalie to move. She sprinted across the bridge with me following her. Another shot rang out behind us.

About halfway across the bridge, near a red support beam, we paused. I'll admit I needed to catch my breath. But I also wanted to see if both of the killers were chasing us. We might have a chance to overpower one of them.

I looked back down the length of the bridge, and standing a few feet in was the Dutchman I had escaped from. Christoph. Even in the faint light from the neighboring streets, I could see him clearly enough. He stood there like some kind of specter with a pistol in his right hand, dangling by his side, and what I thought might be that Gerber knife in his left. He no longer looked like an underwear model, all neat and groomed. Now he looked like a crazy person. His shirt was covered in dried blood, hair whipped out in every direction, and I thought I could see bruises covering his face. He just stood there, staring at us. If he was trying to look creepy, it worked.

In an attempt to stall, I yelled to him, "Impressive. You found us."

The tall Dutchman called out, "A child could see where the church's basement should be. Many old buildings here in Tallinn have elaborate back exits."

"If I surrender, will you let the girl go free?" I didn't like the smile that crept over the tall Dutchman's face.

He raised his right arm and aimed the pistol. There was nowhere to hide on the bridge. If we started running, he'd have a clear shot at our backs.

I looked over the railing into the water. This part of the lake was more of a canal with a slight current. It was a longer drop than I'd prefer. But I would've preferred no one was shooting at us.

A bullet struck the giant support beam a few feet from us. I felt the shot through the handrail. I heard Natalie gasp.

I turned her to face me and said, "Can you swim?"

"What?"

I raised my voice like it was going to help. "Can you swim?"

"Yes. I mean—"

I didn't have time to hear any explanations. I took Natalie by the arms and said quickly, "Don't look back this way, no matter what happens."

Then I threw her off the side of the bridge.

CHAPTER 86

ON THE BRIDGE, I had my doubts. If we got out of this, I knew I'd have a lot of explaining to do to Natalie. I hadn't had time to go into the fact that I was afraid we were too isolated for anyone to hear the shots. Christoph had lost all reason and was just intent on killing us. And I hadn't had any other choice but to throw her into the lake.

I looked over the side of the bridge and felt a little twinge of vertigo. But I had to focus. I had to think. That might be the only advantage I had over Christoph. His brains had to be scrambled.

The problem was that the only thing I could think about was my family. Maybe it was because I was reconciling the fact that I was about to be confronted by an angry man with both a gun and a knife. And I was absolutely defenseless. That gave me an instant flash of all of my children's faces. I could see Mary Catherine. Maeve. And even my crusty old grandfather.

I shook my head to clear my thoughts. I needed to buy time for Natalie to get away. I heard her shout something from the water, but I didn't look over the railing again. Now I was focused solely on Christoph. And he appeared to be concentrating completely on me.

Not only did I want to stall, I also needed to get nearer to Christoph. My only chance was to engage him up close. Preferably after he ran out of bullets and somehow lost the knife. Sometimes you don't get to choose the exact time and place of a fight.

I held up my hands and started to walk toward him very slowly. I called out, "Okay, I'll come with you."

I kept walking, desperately praying that Christoph wouldn't just raise his right arm and shoot me.

As I got closer, I could tell he was confused.

Natalie screamed something from the water.

Christoph casually looked over the railing, raised the pistol, and fired three times into the dark water.

There was no way he could clearly see where she was. But I was scared by the fact that she'd stopped screaming.

I picked up my pace with my arms still in the air. The thought of that girl being shot by this jerk infuriated me. I'd like to say that I had been counting his shots. The best I could think was he had fired six times. But I couldn't be sure exactly how many rounds his pistol held. If it was a single-stack 9mm he'd be down to at best two shots now, at worst five.

When I was within twenty steps of Christoph, I made up my mind. This was going to be a fight. I didn't care if I ended up with five bullets in me. I was going to stop this asshole.

Ollie shouted from a field near the approach to the bridge.

Christoph answered him in Dutch. I didn't follow it exactly. Then I saw Ollie sprint toward the banks of the lake. Christoph had told him to get Natalie.

Ollie's gait was off. It almost looked like he was skipping the way he moved, favoring his left side. He'd been injured somehow. Probably the car crash. That was information I might be able to use later.

I continued to march slowly toward Christoph. I wanted his attention on me and not Natalie. I came to a stop with my hands still raised.

We were only five feet apart.

CHAPTER 87

CHRISTOPH WAS STILL trying to understand the anger he was feeling. He didn't just want these two dead. He wanted to do it himself, up close. Everything was boiling over now. And instead of fighting it, Christoph embraced it. Maybe this was what he should have been doing all along, going wild instead of trying to suppress his instincts.

His thoughts of rage beat through his brain like a drum. If Henry complained about anything they did tonight, he might have to go, too. Henry wasn't so dangerous on his own. He had to *hire* muscle. Christoph and Ollie *were* muscle. Without them, he was defenseless. Sure, Henry was trending toward being a psycho. He liked to think of himself as a crime lord. Some kind of drug kingpin. But the fault in his reasoning had to do with surrounding himself with nerds. A true kingpin has to be tough on his own. You never know when someone will try to rise up through the ranks and snatch the throne.

In Henry's case, there was no one to threaten his power. The computer people he hired wanted nothing to do with violence. Most of them wanted very little to do with other people. That gave Henry a false sense of superiority and security.

But Henry could wait until later. Now Christoph had to deal with Natalie and this infuriating cop. Bennett had tossed the girl from the bridge into the lake. Christoph admired that kind of thinking. Doing the unexpected. Taking risks. That's what Christoph and Ollie needed to do more.

He'd sent Ollie down to the bank to grab the girl. That meant he could keep his attention trained on Bennett.

Bennett had his hands raised and was walking toward him slowly. Christoph didn't trust him. But this was falling in line with his own plan. He wanted to see the cop up close. Preferably, he'd use his knife. Instead of one jab to the throat, he'd take a few practice slashes, then take an ear or cut off his nose. Maybe make it last a little while. Then move on to cutting off something more delicate.

He knew Ollie would argue against that. He just wanted to take both of them to the area in Kopli Liinid with all the new houses. A lot of concrete was poured every day; there was always someplace convenient to leave a body or evidence they never wanted found. Having two people walk to the site would be much easier than carrying their bodies, and it would leave less blood everywhere they went. Christoph hated cleaning blood out of the car. And he'd done it more than most people.

All that ran through his brain as Bennett kept walking toward him slowly, his hands clearly empty and up over his head.

He didn't blame the cop for surrendering. The guy had been through a lot. Maybe he'd realized there was nowhere else to run. At least not in Estonia.

Christoph was about to warn him to freeze in place when the cop came to a stop on his own.

Now they were only about a meter and a half apart.

CHAPTER 88

AS WE FACED each other on the bridge, Christoph stared me down, then gave me a little grin. I'd seen it before. He was showing me he was in charge. He had won. I have no idea why these idiots think something is over before it's even started.

I glanced over the side of the bridge into the lake. I heard or thought I could still hear Natalie, but I really couldn't see anything in the darkness of the lake. I tried to gauge where the slovenly hit man, Ollie, was on the bank, but I had to deal with a younger, fit, armed killer right in front of me.

The first thing out of Christoph's mouth surprised me.

He said, "Why did you throw the girl off the bridge?"

"She's so light I thought she could fly." Right now I was willing to say anything to buy a few more seconds for Natalie to escape. The problem was I had no idea where she or the other killer were. It had been quiet for too long.

I needed to do something. Fast. I also wanted to make Christoph scream. I was hoping that might bring his partner away from the lake and back to the bridge. It was a lot of speculation on my part.

I kept watching the Dutchman. He seemed pretty confident. Natalie's blow across his face and my full-body block hadn't seemed to slow him down too much. Sure, his nose still leaked a little blood. It was clearly broken and almost flat against his face, but that wasn't affecting his reflexes. At least not that I could see.

Then I realized he was waiting just like me. He was waiting to hear Ollie call up and say he had caught the girl. That wasn't going to fly with me. I'd taken all the abuse I wanted to take.

Christoph finally turned his head and looked toward the bank, hoping to see his partner. His gun was still in front of him, pointed right at my stomach, and the knife was gripped at the ready by his hip. It wasn't a long look, but it was enough.

I made my move.

The situation was almost identical to what they put us in during training with the NYPD. It's tough: a gun is extended toward you, the shooter's reaction is slower than the captive's action, and you have no other choice. Though there was the added complication of that knife.

My hands and feet moved at almost the same time. My hands came down, one arm swinging to knock the knife out of his left hand almost too easily, just as I stepped forward and closed the distance. My other arm swung toward Christoph's gun hand a fraction of a second later.

Then the gun went off.

CHAPTER 89

I HEARD THE roar of the gun as soon as my body had cleared the path of Christoph's pistol. It echoed along the dark banks of the lake. The heat from the blast penetrated my shirt. That's how close it was. The smell of gunpowder crowded my nose. The bullet missed me on its way to God knew where.

As soon as he fired, the slide from the pistol automatically rocked back from the gases in the cartridge. It sliced the top of my left hand, which was holding Christoph's wrist. That kept the slide from slamming forward again.

While the gun was useless, I used my right hand, which was closer to the pistol, to reach down and press the magazine release. I didn't know the make of the pistol, but there are two main methods for dropping a pistol magazine. Thank God the button for the magazine was near the trigger. The other way would be on the butt of the pistol itself.

My index finger found the button and I heard the satisfying *click* followed by the *thunk* of the magazine bouncing off the bridge and dropping into the water below.

The fight was a little more even now.

I liked the way the Dutchman just gawked for a moment when I popped out the gun's magazine. I guess no one had ever fought back against him. Or, like most people, he had seen just a tad too much TV. That wasn't a move people saw very often. Honestly, I'd never done it before. But I wasn't about to fight fairly.

Christoph stepped back and stared at his useless gun. I took the opportunity to throw a knee into his thigh. As he grunted and took another step back, I got a chance to throw a big punch at his face.

He surprised me by blocking it with his left arm. There was fight left in him. And he was still pretty fast.

But I was able to also grab his right wrist and rip the pistol from his hand. The force drove us apart. When I turned, Christoph was standing with both hands balled into fists.

He smirked. "The gun's empty. What good is it going to do you now?"

It was a good question. I decided to demonstrate rather than explain. I flipped the pistol so I was holding it by the barrel, then swung it like a bludgeon. I kept swinging the pistol in wide arcs. Most of the blows bounced off his forearms, but I could feel the butt of the pistol dig into skin and bones. He yelped as each blow landed.

Then I threw a new wrinkle into the pattern. I kicked out with my left leg. I didn't expect it to do much. Just catch his attention. Which it did. As soon as he shifted and looked down at my leg, I swung hard with my right arm, the pistol still in my hand, like the head of a hammer. I caught him hard, across the chin. His head snapped back and blood sprayed out from his split lips.

I stepped back to give him room to fall. Instead, the tall Dutchman stood on wobbly legs. It was like a point of pride for him to remain upright. He was gasping for breath, and every time he breathed out, blood spewed from his mouth.

When he didn't drop to the ground immediately, I recognized I didn't have time to wait for his show. The fight had pushed him back almost to the end of the bridge, only four feet away. I quickly glanced over the side and saw that the muddy shore was underneath us.

I couldn't see or hear Natalie or the other killer. I couldn't wait any longer. I tossed the pistol far into the lake. Then I grabbed Christoph in a bear hug. I lifted the tall Dutchman off his feet and tossed him over the side of the bridge. It was a lot harder than when I threw Natalie over.

I knew he'd miss the water. That was the point.

CHAPTER 90

I RACED OFF the bridge and scrambled down to the banks of Pae Lake. Christoph had landed almost exactly like I needed him to. He was stuck in the mud up to his shoulders. His left arm was pinned under him in the dark muck that surrounded the lake. Just his head and right arm had escaped the gooey prison. He looked like an alien from a cheap science-fiction movie.

But he was conscious and appeared to be unharmed. He looked at me and screamed, "Get me out of here," the disembodied head turning frantically to see how close the water was.

I wondered if there were tides in the lake. That would be terrifying in Christoph's position.

"You're going to pay for this," yelled the Dutchman.

"Defiant to the end. Good for you."

"I'm going to kill you."

There was an edge of panic in his voice. I wondered if he had a phobia. Although, to be fair, I'd be a little freaked-out stuck in the mud like that.

As long as he wasn't sinking past his nose, I shifted my attention to the lake itself. I started running from the bridge and the half buried killer to search for Natalie. But I hadn't forgotten about the other killer, Ollie.

I sprinted as fast as I could away from the bridge. The bank proved to be slick and littered with boulders and drainpipes. This was not the place to run with no light at all shining on the ground.

I skidded to a stop fifty yards away from the bridge. I thought I'd heard something. I balled my hands into fists in case I stumbled into Ollie.

Then I heard it again. A faint cry and water splashing. I screamed, "Natalie."

I heard a response, I thought. And I just caught a glimpse of the water moving, twenty yards offshore just ahead of me.

I couldn't wait to ensure the other killer wasn't nearby. Natalie was in trouble. I dove in, shocked by how cold the water was. I knew that whatever I did, it had to be fast. If I'd known beforehand how cold the water was, I probably wouldn't have thrown Natalie into it. But at the time, I hadn't had a choice.

I had a hard time distinguishing the splashing sounds I was making in the water from the sounds I heard. There was very little light on the lake and I couldn't see anything past a few feet.

I knew I sounded panicked when I yelled, "Natalie, Natalie," on an almost unending loop.

Then I saw something just break the surface of the water a few feet in front of me. I kicked hard in the water and closed the distance in a couple of seconds. There was nothing there.

I frantically moved my hands under the water and felt something brush my leg. I ducked underwater and followed its path. My hand closed around something. It was a wrist. Oh, my God, it was Natalie.

I pulled with all my might, kicking my legs to counterbalance the force of pulling Natalie up. It felt like it took forever. It could've been wet cement I was pulling her through. Progress was so slow it hurt me physically.

Finally I had her head above water. I waited for that first big gasp to suck in air. It didn't come. Her face was ice-cold and her eyes were closed. I had to get her to shore to give her CPR. It was her only chance.

I swam hard with Natalie hooked under one arm. I hadn't done a water rescue since I was a patrolman and dove in for a kid who had fallen into the East River. When I brought him back to the seawall, there were a dozen people who helped us out of the water. That wasn't going to happen tonight.

CHAPTER 91

WE THRASHED IN the water as Natalie drifted in and out of consciousness. She'd wake up and panic, elbowing me and kicking wildly. Then she'd pass out and be deadweight. It was exhausting. Murky water splashed into my mouth, and I kept swallowing it.

My legs and lungs started to burn as I swam. It took me a minute to realize that in the darkness, I hadn't gone in the right direction. I had been swimming parallel to the shore. Wasting precious energy wasn't something I could afford to do right now.

Finally I got my bearings. A tiny red light flashed in the distance and gave me a focal point. I kept heading toward the tiny light until my feet brushed the sandy bottom of the lake. I lifted Natalie out of the water as I trudged toward shore.

It took longer than I had expected, but I pulled Natalie onto the shore and wasted no more time. I stripped off the wool sweater that had weighed her down. I fell right into the training I'd received over and over again from the NYPD. I shook her to make sure she wasn't responding. I checked her pulse, then cleared her mouth with my finger. There was nothing in her mouth, and she gave no reaction.

Water rescues are no fun and dangerous. But CPR in a situation like this was positively terrifying. I pinched her nose with two fingers. Since she was ice-cold, I wondered if some of her problems were related to hypothermia.

I sealed my lips over hers and started my first rescue breath. It was longer and deeper than I intended.

As I raised my head slightly to take in more air, I felt Natalie move. At least I think I did.

Just as I was about to give another serious rescue breath, she coughed. Gurgled is more accurate. I'd seen it a dozen times. I knew just what to do: jump out of the way.

She sat up quickly and turned to one side. Water cascaded out of her mouth as she coughed and vomited. She cleared her throat several times and coughed up more water. It felt like she'd been in the lake for hours, but maybe it'd been only minutes.

As long as she was coughing, she was breathing. That was a win. I sat by her and put my hand on her shoulder.

After almost a full minute, she turned and looked at me. Then she threw her arms around my neck and gave me a hug.

When I wrapped my arms around her and patted her back, she started to sob. At first, I thought it was a reaction to the drowning. Then she said, "How'd I end up here? With men trying to kill me. Almost getting you killed." She just started crying again.

I got it. I really did. I had experienced this with my own daughters. Maybe not in so dramatic a fashion, but I understood the release.

Then I remembered there was another killer out there. I let go of Natalie and stood up to scan the area. I could see the approach to the park because of the lights out on the street nearby. Just the lake and its banks were completely dark.

Then I saw him. He was standing on a hill not far from the street. Ollie looked a little like the Creature from the Black Lagoon, the way he moved. He had apparently jumped into the lake at some point. His wet shirt, plastered to his wide chest, showed that he wasn't just a big lump of fat.

He turned and faced me. It was pretty far for a pistol shot. I didn't know what I was going to do if he started shambling back toward us with that stiff-legged gait both the wet pants and the earlier car crash had given him.

But he stayed right where he was. Then he did something that surprised me. Ollie gave me a casual salute.

He called down to me in English, "You're both too much trouble. As a professional, I have to know when to cut my losses. Good luck." He turned quickly and disappeared across the street.

Then I heard faint sirens. That's what had scared him off.

I helped Natalie over to where Christoph was stuck in the mud.

He screamed, "Dig me out of this. You're just trying to torture me. Get me out right now."

I figured it was a job for a local fire-rescue team.

Natalie and Christoph both looked like they'd just survived the worst day of their lives.

I hoped this really was the worst day Natalie ever had. I knew Christoph was going to have many that would be worse.

CHAPTER 92

NATALIE AND I were checked for injuries at East Tallinn Central Hospital. There weren't a ton of hospitals in Estonia's capital, at least not by New York standards, and I was glad to find it was the same hospital where Bill Fiore was recovering from his gunshot wounds.

I was anxious to see the crusty FBI man, but first I needed to make sure Natalie was okay. I sat on a hard, plastic chair in the hallway outside an examination room.

It was midmorning, I'd been up more than twenty-four hours, and the bright lights of the hospital were brutal on my tired eyes. No one seemed to notice me. I wore surgical scrubs someone had given me and a pair of tennis shoes that were a size too tight. But I wasn't going to complain. I was alive. Natalie was alive. And we were both safe. All that was left now was the plane ride home.

Somehow I'd resisted calling Mary Catherine once we were safe. It would've been the middle of the night in New York. She would be just as happy to hear about my success and return after a full night's sleep.

I found the FBI agent's room on the fifth floor. None of the nurses gave me a second look. I guess it was the surgical scrubs that confused them. Or maybe they just didn't care as much in Estonia if you had extra visitors.

There was an Estonian police officer sitting on a stool outside Fiore's room. Luckily, he had met me earlier when I shared everything I knew with him and another police officer. He motioned me into the room without any fanfare. I nodded to him.

The police were clearly concerned about the security measures. Maybe Henry hadn't been pulling my chain when he told me what a badass he was. He hadn't yet been picked up, but I'd given the Estonian police and anyone else who would listen all I had on the cybercriminal.

The cops had been impressed by the way I'd managed to stick the Dutch killer, Christoph, in the mud. Apparently there were John Doe warrants for him in the Netherlands, Belgium, and Latvia. New York would throw some more warrants in for him and his former partner, Ollie.

It could've been a hospital room anywhere in the States. White, clinical, dull, with a TV anchored to the wall. The only thing that surprised me in the room was Father Marty Zlatic sitting on the far side of the bed, chatting with a silent Bill Fiore. The FBI man was sitting up, with the bed elevated. He had tubes in his nose and two IVs in his right arm, with one of them bandaged into his hand.

Fiore turned his head as I walked in. Father Marty let a huge smile spread across his face as he stood up to greet me. He came around the bed and embraced me. "I felt Agent Fiore deserved some extra attention from me. Especially after you told me how he saved your life. God surely guided him into our lives."

"It all worked out for the best, Father."

"You had us so worried last night."

"Sorry to cause you all this trouble, Father."

The priest laughed. "Trouble? This is the most interesting week I've had in years. I wouldn't trade this experience for anything. Especially since you rescued the girl. I've been filling in Agent Fiore on everything. He is most impressed."

I couldn't help but smile when I looked toward the FBI agent. No employee of the Federal Bureau of Investigation was ever going to admit he was impressed by the NYPD. Especially in another country.

Fiore motioned me over to his bed with a movement of his left hand. I came closer, but he couldn't speak clearly. He was weak and had too many tubes. He motioned me closer.

I lowered my ear toward his mouth in case he wanted to speak. I knew it would be hard for him to admit I had done the right thing saving Natalie. I didn't intend to rub it in his face. Much.

As I leaned over, he tried to form a word. At first, it was just air brushing over his vocal cords without much response. Finally, after great effort, he managed to make his word clear.

I steadied myself on the bed, my head just above his mouth. Then he said, "Asshole."

I started to guffaw. It was hard not to. A man who had risked his life, been shot twice, barely out of the operating room, and he still managed to summon enough strength to call me a name. I loved it. It completely restored my faith in the FBI.

I wouldn't repeat to Father Marty what he'd said, even after the priest asked.

I looked down, and Fiore managed a smile under the tubes. I said, "I agree with you. If someone had come into my jurisdiction and ignored every reasonable warning I gave them, I would have choice words as well." I patted the FBI man on his unbandaged shoulder. "Let me say it clearly in front of a witness. You saved my ass." I quickly looked up at the priest, ready to change *ass* to *life*. Father Marty motioned to me to continue.

"I'm going to tell you something I've never told an FBI agent." I liked the look of anticipation Fiore managed even under these difficult circumstances. I sucked in a breath of air and said, "You are one hell of a cop."

I meant it.

CHAPTER 93

I'D NEVER FELT so safe preparing to board a flight in my life. Natalie and I were in a lounge at Lennart Meri Airport with several Estonian police officers and Bill Fiore's FBI partner, Matt Miller. The Estonian police were growing more concerned about how Henry's operation had flown under their radar for so long.

The cops could've been from any country. Command staff in suits, detectives in cheap jackets, and a few patrol officers, years younger than the others. Lots of bald spots and graying hair, a phenomenon that happens to all police officers, regardless of nationality—stress takes years off our lives. One of the less-talked-about aspects of police work, and one of the contributing factors to an early death after retirement.

I knew how uncovering an operation like Henry's would lead to speculation about corruption, and that sometimes affects an investigation, because no one is sure who to trust.

Besides all the damage to the concrete columns, they'd found only a couple of casings and some blood in the warehouse room where the big shoot-out took place. I wasn't much help finding the second office. Natalie was able to point them to where it was located, but Henry and his crew had cleaned the place out by the time the cops showed up.

As I sat in a comfortable cushioned chair, I muttered, "This is a lot of protection."

Matt Miller, who sat next to me, said, "There's no way the Estonians want to explain how a cybercriminal like Henry whacked you at the airport. They're going to cover you like Secret Service agents around the president."

I smiled and checked my watch. It was seven o'clock in the morning in New York, and I made the call I'd been avoiding. Telling your fiancée that you were almost killed is never fun. I figured I would gloss over a lot of the trip.

As soon as I heard Mary Catherine's voice, any concerns I had vanished. All I wanted to do was get home. She had a million questions.

She quickly spit out, "Are you okay? How can I help? What's Estonia like?"

"I'm fine. Don't need anything. Estonia is nice."

Before I could ask about the kids, she said, "Did you find the mayor's daughter?"

"Yes. She's coming home with me."

Mary Catherine let out a squeal. "When will you be home?"

"This evening." I gave her the flight information.

"Did you have any trouble? Was the mayor's daughter really in danger?"

I thought about saying we had a bad connection. Instead, I

deferred answers until I got back. I spent about a minute talking with each kid. Everyone said they were looking forward to me coming home. So was I.

At the first boarding call for the flight, Agent Miller gave me a quick rundown of what he knew. He said, "I was waiting to catch you up in case I heard something new. The Estonian authorities are chasing down a ton of leads."

"They seem like they're squared away."

"The local cops are very impressed by you. They're saying the guy you caught, the Dutchman, is a really big deal. He's not talking except to say how much he hates you. Kind of the same thing Bill Fiore was saying for a while."

We both had to laugh at that.

I said, "What about Christoph's partner, Ollie, the sloppy guy I told you all about?"

"He's in the wind. We've got no idea who he is or where he went. Based on some of the details about Christoph, we're in touch with the Amsterdam police. They might have something on him."

The flight itself was uneventful. I noticed that Natalie, wedged into the seat next to me, didn't want to venture too far on any topic. After everything she'd gone through, I could understand her feelings.

She asked me why I really had started looking for her. My natural inclination is to always tell the truth, but this was a family issue, and I wasn't sure what was best for that family. Finally I explained, "I had a few problems on the job. I was in a shooting. Your dad thought it was best if I stayed off the streets of New York for a little while. He was worried about you, so I started looking. Not much more to tell."

"What about your shooting? Is it resolved?"

"I don't know about officially, but there was plenty of video. I've been told I'm going to be cleared officially."

She asked for the details.

I said, "I was up in the Bronx working at the site of the homicide of a nurse and her young daughter. It was horrific. I stepped outside to grab a Gatorade and two men confronted me with a gun. I shot one. The other, a guy called Tight, ran away. After looking at it more, we now think he might have been involved in the homicide of the nurse and her daughter."

"That sounds traumatic all around. That would keep me up at night the rest of my life."

"The thing that bothers me most is that Tight is still running free. I'd do anything to lay my hands on that guy."

Natalie said, "It's sad to say, but I don't know much about police work other than what I've seen on *Law and Order*. After watching you firsthand, I can tell you I could never be a cop."

I laughed and said, "That is the exact opposite of what most people think. The public believes they understand what a cop goes through, and everyone seems to have advice on how to do police work. I appreciate you admitting a blind spot."

"Trust me, it's not a blind spot anymore. I'll never forget what you did for me." She placed her hand on top of mine. It was one of the most sincere thank-yous I had ever heard.

CHAPTER 94

I WATCHED THE Manhattan skyline as the Lufthansa 747 landed at JFK. It was always good to get home.

Twenty minutes later, Natalie and I hurried down the Jetway to the main terminal. I'm sure she never would've admitted it, but I could tell the young computer genius was excited about seeing her parents. I was just as excited to see my family.

I noticed a group of official-looking people not far from the gate. They had a uniformed NYPD officer with them, probably to help them slip through security. Before we had even cleared the gate, an attractive woman in a smart pantsuit rushed forward and embraced Natalie.

I hesitated, not wanting to intrude on the touching reunion. Natalie and her mother started to cry. As I continued to walk, Natalie reached out and grabbed me by the arm.

She broke her embrace with her mother and said, "This is the man who saved me. You have no idea what he risked looking for me in Estonia. We have to tell Dad about it right away."

The look on her mother's face told me everything I needed to know about the mayor at that moment. She turned to her daughter and said in a soft voice, "It'll have to wait. Your dad had an event he couldn't miss. He also didn't want to turn this into a media circus. We're all going to meet for dinner."

Now *I* felt like giving Natalie a hug. She looked more like a lost little girl at that moment than at any time during this investigation. Even after all of her talk about not caring what her father thought, she was devastated he hadn't come to the airport to welcome her home.

She looked at her mother and said, "Dad didn't want a media circus because he doesn't want anyone to know about the mayor's wild daughter." She started to cry but buried her face in her mother's shoulder.

Her mother looked at me as she patted her daughter's head. She said quietly, "I don't know how we can ever thank you."

Before I could even acknowledge her words, I heard a shriek and had just enough time to look up and prepare for Chrissy coming at me like a guided missile. As I suspected, she was followed in short order by Shawna, Trent, and Fiona. I was lucky to stay on my feet.

Before I could give these four the hugs they deserved, Mary Catherine appeared out of the crowd. She started to cry as she kissed me on the lips and wrapped her arms around my neck.

I was enveloped by a giant hug from all of them. Shawna started to cry. That was unusual.

I picked her up, which was not as easy as I remembered. I

brushed a tear off her beautiful face. "What's wrong, sweetheart? It's okay. I'm home now."

She sniffled. "I'm sorry, Dad. I had dreams, bad dreams, about what you were doing in Estonia. I'm just so glad to see you." She hugged me around the neck and kissed me on the cheek.

I had to wipe a tear away from my cheek after such a touching admission. All I wanted now was to get home.

Thankfully the NYPD told me I could hold off on a debriefing until I got back in the office. They knew the story. The FBI would've already produced a detailed report. No doubt the mayor had told everyone not to bother me too much. I could live with that.

I spent the ride from the airport to our apartment catching up on all the kids' adventures and achievements while I was gone.

Bridget had started an arts and crafts club at Holy Name. She was very excited that she already had four members besides herself. Five if you counted her twin, Fiona.

Jane had absolutely killed an AP world history exam. There had even been an announcement at the school about how well she'd done.

Juliana had won a lead role in the latest school play. It was a retro musical based on the works of Neil Diamond. They were still working out the copyright issues and realized they might have to change the names of some of the songs. I couldn't imagine what "Sweet Karen" or "I Am, I Declared" might sound like.

Once we were home, I couldn't believe how relieved I was to embrace my grandfather. He, of course, had talked to Father Marty Zlatic and knew the whole story. He looked me right in the eye and said, "I know I don't say it often, but you make me very proud every day."

"Often? You've *never* told me that."

"In words."

"In any form of communication, verbal or nonverbal, written or in any other form. How's that for being specific?"

"It just makes me more proud."

Damn, I do love that old man.

CHAPTER 95

LATER IN THE evening, after I tried to spend a little time with each of the kids, we waited for a special phone call from Brian. Everyone circled around the phone and it rang right on time.

Trent snatched it off the cradle and immediately said, "Hey, Brian." Then he put it on speaker and placed the receiver back in the cradle. It was just his little way of trying to get some personal contact with his brother. I got it.

Brian was upbeat and filled us in on passing more of his certifications to be an air-conditioning repair mechanic. He also had started his first college courses. He said, "In case I want to earn my degree, I thought it was a good idea to get the basics out of the way now. I'm taking English and US history."

Chrissy said, "I'm great at history. I can help you with anything you don't understand."

I liked how everyone in the room over the age of fourteen effectively concealed a smile at the little girl's offer of help.

Brian asked me about the trip to Estonia, but I didn't go into any detail. I was often vague about work around my family. Some people said it wasn't right to keep them sealed off from my professional life, but it was a choice I made to save them the details that no one else had to hear.

We ended the call like we always did, with tears and good-byes. But I felt pretty good about the progress Brian had made. Like I had told Natalie in Estonia, people make mistakes. Brian had made his and was doing his best to overcome them. I was proud of him, and I told him that. Frequently. Sometimes in front of my grandfather, just to make a point.

After the call, I sat down next to Eddie at the computer. He was working on some sort of programming problem they'd given him in the special class at Columbia he and Trent were enrolled in.

He turned to me and said, "I have to say, Dad, that I've been looking at a number of the hacker forums I like to read and some of them are talking about you."

"Me?"

"Not by name. But they make you sound like Bruce Willis. How you stormed into Estonia and took down the biggest, baddest cybercriminal in the world."

"You mean the biggest, baddest cybercriminal under five feet six inches, named Henry. That's the best I'll give that little twerp."

Eddie laughed out loud.

"Although," I corrected, "we haven't quite brought him down yet, just have him on the run."

"It's amazing you did everything you did without knowing computers very well. You didn't have to clone any phones or crack the security on any systems. The things cybercriminals do every day."

"I just did what *I* do every day. Simple police work. You know about cloning phones?"

"Only in theory. I've never tried it."

"Relax. This isn't an interrogation."

I listened as he explained several complicated high-tech processes. I had to wonder where this kid got his brains.

Finally I said, "Thanks for the insight. It would've helped me in Estonia. And I appreciate the compliments, but I did what any good cop would do."

"Either way, I've seen more than one person talk about the American cop who dismantled a major hacker. I guess it was even on the news in Estonia."

"I don't think it takes much to get on the local news in Tallinn. It's just a nice town with nice people. Mostly nice people."

Eddie turned from the computer and gave me a hug. That was somewhat un-Eddie-like. He was more reserved than most of the kids.

He said, "I'm just glad you're back. I missed you."

"I missed you, too."

"And from what I've read, you were lucky. That guy from Estonia, Henry, sounds like a really bad guy."

"I don't want to give him that much credit. I'm just glad to be home and with you guys."

And that was the God's honest truth.

CHAPTER 96

THE NEXT DAY I went to my office on the sixth floor of an unmarked building on the Upper West Side. I wasn't built to sit around my apartment and wait for things to happen. The kids were in school, and Mary Catherine was busy, so I decided to go in and get back to my real life.

I hadn't gotten official approval to return to my normal job, and I hoped no one would shout at me as I walked through the door. But everyone welcomed me back, even my lieutenant, Harry Grissom. If someone was going to tell me to get lost and take more time off, it was going to be Harry. His first concern was how well the squad operated. I'd trust him with my life, but if he thought I was going to be a detriment in any way, he'd send me home in a heartbeat.

Detective Terri Hernandez was in the building, checking

whether any information had developed on the suspect in her homicide, Tight. She surprised me with a hug.

I stepped back and looked at her. "You could pass for a college student."

"That's the idea, Slick."

I laughed and we caught up on what had happened since I left. The long and the short of her investigation was that she had no other leads except for the guy I'd met, Tight. The media had kept up a pretty good pace of coverage for three or four days after the murders. A young nurse and her daughter being killed in their own apartment captured people's attention for a little longer than most stories. But now interest had ebbed in what was quickly becoming a cold homicide.

Terri looked down. She was one of the most dedicated detectives I'd ever met. She checked in on a victim's family for months after a homicide, filling them in on progress. She looked at every murder as a personal quest to be solved, and she excelled in public service because she really cared.

I said, "We'll catch a break. This one won't haunt you."

"They all haunt me. Even the ones we've solved. They're murders. I think God wants them to haunt us."

"That's a good point. And you're right. We shouldn't get callous toward homicides. It's too easy to start taking shortcuts if we do."

I checked in with Harry and spent most of the day at my desk. In the midafternoon, my phone buzzed, telling me I had a text. I looked down and saw it was from the mayor's mobile phone. It said, I'm sending a car. Meet it at Riverside and 132nd Street, just a few blocks from your office. Don't say anything to anyone. The little fat prick.

I had to smile at his sense of humor.

I started to make my way out and nodded at Harry Grissom as I walked past his office.

I took a leisurely stroll, actually looking in storefronts for a change. I saw a rented Lincoln stretch limo right where the text said it would be. It was a little gaudy and obnoxious, but I didn't get to ride in the back of a limo very often.

The driver didn't get out to meet me, so I leaned down and waved to him. He gave me a thumbs-up, and I crawled into the back.

I was not the only passenger.

CHAPTER 97

I EASED INTO the seat and made a quick assessment of the giant passenger compartment of the limo. There was even a wet bar. Too bad I was on duty.

The driver lowered the glass partition, turned his head, and said, "Hello, Detective. It was lucky you two were in the same area. As soon as Natalie said she was nearby, the mayor said I could get you both at the same time."

The young woman's Yankees baseball cap and big sunglasses made her look like a celebrity trying to keep a low profile. A little of her hair had popped out from under the ball cap. She looked relaxed but didn't say anything.

I said, "Hey, Natalie. You doing okay?"

She nodded and said quietly, "Not thrilled about seeing my dad."

I noticed the driver was eavesdropping. "I'm sure it'll be fine. You just have to give him a chance."

"Like the chance to greet me at the airport?"

"That was disappointing."

She grunted but kept quiet after that.

The driver was still listening, I knew.

I asked him, "Do you work in the mayor's office?"

The tubby man with slicked-back, light-brown hair had a slight accent. He said, "No, sir, I help the mayor in his unofficial life. In other words, he contracted me. I guess Hizzoner wants this meeting to be low profile."

"It seems like he feels that way about most meetings."

I sat back and enjoyed the ride. At this time of the day, with traffic, it was going to take a while to get to City Hall. Then the driver cut east through Manhattan. It's not the way I would've gone, but he was a professional and no one had asked my opinion.

Ten minutes later, the driver made another turn and I realized he was headed for the Queensboro Bridge.

I leaned up and said, "Where are we going?"

The driver focused on traffic in front of us for a moment, beeping at a tourist from Delaware who was clearly unsure where he wanted to go. Then the driver called over his shoulder, "The mayor told me to bring you to an address in Queens. I didn't ask any questions. Let me call and see if I can get any answers you might need."

He pulled out his cell phone and started to speak. His conversation lasted until we were over the bridge.

We were on the upper level when the driver turned off to loop around back under the bridge onto Vernon Boulevard. We passed Queensbridge Park on our left. He was pulling past the sprawling Ravenswood power plant when he called over his shoulder, "I guess the mayor drove over here as well. He's anxious to see his daughter. He says we can meet him by Rainey Park just up here."

I looked across the seat and said, "You doing okay?"

She nodded, the ball cap pulled low over her face.

The limo was so big that any change in speed felt like a boat moving in water. We slowed and turned down a narrow street that ran along the north of Rainey Park, some blocks past the power plant and right along the backside of a big-box store. Cars were parked next to the building at first, probably those of the employees, but the driver continued to the nearly empty far end of the road, closer to the river, and stopped. I reached into my pocket for my phone.

As we came to a stop, the driver looked in the rearview mirror and said, "Please, sir, no calls."

"What? I'm sorry, I need to check in with my office."

"I don't think so."

When I looked up from my phone to see what would make the driver say something so crazy, I froze. He had turned around and held a small semiautomatic pistol in his left hand, pointed at my head.

Without the man saying a word, I knew to hand over my own pistol. I reached to my right hip and slowly unholstered my Glock. I handed it over the seat to the driver.

The driver said, "Phone, too."

I sighed as I tossed my phone over the seat as well.

The driver added, "And Natalie's purse."

She handed the purse to the driver.

I felt like I was back in Estonia, staring at the barrel of another gun. When was this shit gonna end?

CHAPTER 98

AS I CONTINUED to sit in the rear seat of the limo, staring at the gun, I took a moment to look at the driver more closely. He was about forty with the smooth face of someone who hasn't worked outdoors much their whole life. He had an accent, but I couldn't tell where he was from. In New York, you just rolled with any sort of accent. As long as you could make out the general meaning of what someone was trying to say, everyone was happy.

This guy worked for Henry. He hadn't said so in words, but someone holding a gun conveys a lot with just a look. I was in deep shit.

The driver kept the gun on me as he opened his door, stepped outside, and opened my door. He said, "C'mon, out of the car, Detective Bennett."

When I was standing with him on the asphalt, he reached into the car and raised the privacy glass. Then he hit a button that locked the doors. Before he shut my door, he leaned into the car and said, "Natalie, you sit tight for a little while. Don't even try to slip out of the car."

Now it was just the two of us. I knew that wasn't going to last for long. I asked the driver, whose head didn't come up to my nose, "What exactly is this bullshit?"

The driver said, "Henry isn't finished with you yet. He thought it was rude the way you left him in Estonia. He says you're the kind of man who should understand payback."

"What's the girl got to do with this? He could've left her alone."

"Henry doesn't consult me about those kinds of decisions. I just handle problems in New York."

"What's he gain from this? How is this good for business?"

The driver shrugged. "I'd save those kinds of talking points for Henry. He'll be here in a minute."

"Are you saying you don't think this is bullshit?"

"I just understand you embarrassed Henry and now he needs to make a statement so people know he's serious. He keeps all these cyber people in line with fear."

In a crazy kind of way, that made sense. And because we were talking about a crazy person, I'm sure it made perfect sense to Henry.

I noticed a new Audi rolling toward us along the street and parking maybe fifty feet away. I turned toward it, then glanced over my shoulder at the limo. There was a lot to think about in this encounter.

I worked hard at keeping a disinterested expression when Henry popped out of the Audi wearing a gray Armani suit. He looked like one of the young investment bankers down on Wall

Street, except for the Walther .380 pistol in his right hand. He smiled and said, "Detective Bennett, nice to see you again."

"Wish I could say the same. But I'll say this, Henry, you have definitely impressed me this time. I've only been back a day and you were able to travel across the Atlantic, use the phone you cloned from the mayor, and trick me with the fake text. By the way, the 'little fat prick' comment on the text was inspired."

"Since we're complimenting each other, let me tell you how impressed *I* am that you were able to figure all that out on the ride over here."

Now I gave him a sly smile. The guys who think they're smarter than everyone else never really see it coming. I said, "I didn't figure it out on the ride. My son pointed me in the right direction last night. The NYPD tech people confirmed it all this morning."

That got Henry's attention. But it didn't seem to have quite the impact I was hoping it would.

He said, "Then I guess we'll make this fast." He racked the slide on his Walther.

I knew racking the gun was more to scare me. But I could tell he wasn't particularly comfortable holding the pistol.

Henry looked at the driver and said, "Go get Natalie."

CHAPTER 99

HENRY AND I stood in the wide gap between the two vehicles in the middle of the road, with the sun on us but the park's large trees masking us somewhat from any afternoon runners or dog walkers. A gunshot might change all that, of course. A few cars trickled by on Vernon Boulevard several hundred yards back, too far away to see what was going on down here. And probably no one from the store came back here. Plus, Henry would've easily disabled any CCTV cameras on the building. In short, it was perfect for Henry and whatever his crazy plan was.

I was waiting for the driver. I'd know when it was time to act.

Henry said to me, "I don't know how you convinced Natalie to betray me, but it ruined a pretty good thing."

"Aww, did she break your heart?" I enjoyed watching him change colors like some kind of screwed-up chameleon. He went from his normal flesh tone to a dark red, then a purple. After a few seconds, his color returned to normal.

In a much sharper tone than usual, he said, "You'll learn— how do you Americans say it?—not to run your mouth."

"When?"

"Today."

When he smiled, I realized he was back to his usual, pompous self. Good. That made things more enjoyable and interesting.

That also made me throw in, "What if I don't learn?"

Henry shook his head and mumbled, "It won't matter."

"Henry, I've been around a lot of criminals in my life. The successful ones are all business. How does this help your business?"

"What's the point of being as successful as me if I can't do things that make me feel better? This will make me feel better. In fact, I'm already enjoying it. I wish I could slip you back to Estonia so I could make it last."

I smiled. "I don't see you having the stomach to torture anyone. Even me."

"I don't have to torture anyone. I could just let you watch as your family suffers and destroys itself while you're away."

"You don't know my family. They're resilient."

"Even if I ruined your credit and drained your bank accounts? What about if I add things to your son's record and he doesn't get out of jail for ten more years?"

I tried to hide the fact that this asshole had just hit a nerve. I didn't do a very good job.

Henry chuckled. "See, everyone has a weakness. Virtually all weaknesses can be exploited by something online. That's where I rule."

"This isn't the internet, it's real life."

"Yes, this is real. Sometimes that's more satisfying." He looked past me and said, "Here comes our other contestant."

I turned my head and had to smile at the way the driver kept a couple of feet away from his prisoner. They stopped a few steps from us. The look on Henry's face was spectacular. He stared silently for a moment. I hoped he might change colors again.

Henry said, "Who the hell is that?"

The confused driver held up his hands and said, "It's the mayor's daughter. She was waiting right where you told me she would be."

Henry walked over and ripped off the Yankees cap. Dark hair flopped out from under it and spread out across her shoulders.

I let out a laugh. It was partially to distract the two men, but there was a genuine element to it as well. I said, "I thought you were too smart to be tricked by anyone. You fell for this like an eight-year-old. Allow me to introduce you to NYPD detective Terri Hernandez. She looks a little like Natalie, I mean in a general way, right? Your driver fell for it."

Henry worked his jaw for a moment as he backed away a few paces and then said, "You forget something, Detective."

"What's that?"

"I still have a gun." He raised it next to his face, like he was showing it to us for the first time.

This time it was Terri Hernandez who let out a laugh. She said, "So what? Your driver has a pistol, too."

Henry said, "Why do you find that so funny, Detective?"

She kept a smile on her pretty face. Then she threw me a wink. She said, "You think I wasn't ready for that?" Without any warning, she stepped right next to the driver and hit the trigger of a Taser she had hidden under her dress. She used it like an old-style stun gun by jamming it into the driver's side and pulling the trigger.

He let out a squawk and immediately dropped to the ground. His pistol skittered away from his outstretched arms. He convulsed for a few seconds, drawing everyone's attention. A thin line of spit dribbled out of his open mouth. His eyes rolled back, giving him the look of a quivering zombie.

Henry was distracted for a moment. Most people have never seen a Taser deployed. It's an interesting show.

Then he regained his common sense and faced me with the pistol once again.

CHAPTER 100

THE AFTERNOON SUN was over my shoulder now and in Henry's eyes. Good. I needed any advantage. I wasn't about to let Henry point that gun at me again. Before he'd even brought it on target, I stepped closer and slapped it out of his hand. I have to admit, my initial response was to punch him in the face, but at the last second, I realized I needed to eliminate the pistol from the equation.

I wasn't worried about Terri Hernandez. She was as smart and as tough as any cop I had ever met. She was also impressively efficient. She was on top of the stunned driver even before I'd slapped the pistol away from Henry.

I did something I never do. I gave a prisoner a chance to fight his way into an escape. I faced off against Henry and let him see that my hands were empty. It's not a smart tactical move and not what a cop *should* do. But this little son of a bitch had caused me a lot of heartache. And I'd let him run his mouth on two different continents. Now it was time that *he* learned a lesson.

We squared off. I was going to give the young Estonian a chance to show me just how his showy beach muscles would help him in a fight. Big biceps had never helped in a street fight.

Henry raised both of his hands and balled them into fists. Then he started to dance like a boxer. He was loose and casual. It looked pretty good. He danced and circled away from me a few feet, throwing a quick left jab out into space.

I turned and adjusted to close the distance between us.

He danced a little farther.

Then I lunged at him. I used my long legs to really cover some distance. But Henry easily skipped backward and somehow now there was even more room between us.

Terri Hernandez shouted something at me. She sounded muffled and far away, but I couldn't take my attention off the feisty young Estonian.

For another twenty seconds, all of it spent in frustration, Henry kept dancing just outside the range of my fists. We covered the majority of what was left of the road, and now the East River was not far from me. I was close enough to smell it. I also had sweat trickling into my eyes. This was turning into a regular workout. The only problem was that Henry didn't look like he was working as hard as me.

Henry planted his feet, and right at that moment I realized the joke was on me. He had purposely led me away from any backup. I realized immediately that Terri Hernandez had shouted for me to keep close just in case.

I was an idiot, and Henry's smug smile didn't make me feel any better.

Now he cracked his knuckles and peeked over my shoulder to make sure we were far enough away from Terri. Then Henry said, "I love so many things about America." He almost shouted it. He was showing me he wasn't nervous.

Oddly, I felt a flutter of nerves. But I stayed in his game and said, "It's nice when visitors appreciate the country." I sucked in a little extra oxygen. This would be a longer fight than I had anticipated.

Henry said, "I love the freedoms and wealth as much as I love the hypocrisy of Americans. You have this vast continent, yet everyone crams onto an insignificant little island like Manhattan. Why is that? It feels like something lemmings would do."

He slowly circled me as he kept talking. Now it was Henry who was looking for an opening. "I also like how you let lawyers and the threat of lawsuits govern your behavior more than the government. And especially I like how you are all utterly convinced that the world needs you. Like you'll ride to the rescue if there's a problem." He threw a few more punches in the air.

Then he looked right at me and changed his tone. "You know what else I love?"

"What's that?"

"Your media outlets have to fill time with drivel. Every detail of the lives of celebrities is broadcast at all hours. Every aspect of police investigations is reported. Like the stories of your recent shooting. The one where you gunned down an innocent youth for no reason. You know what that tells me?"

"That you watch too much TV?"

He gave me a polite smile and shook his head. "No, it tells

me that no matter what happens between us, you won't use a gun, even if you grabbed one. It would look too bad for you."

"The day I need a gun to deal with a little punk like you is the day I retire."

"If you ever get a chance to retire."

CHAPTER 101

I HAD LISTENED to this bullshit long enough. The smart-ass had been asking for a lesson in manners for a long time and had traveled a long way to get it.

I didn't have thoughts like that often, but this was a fight I had been waiting for. I held my right hand just behind my right leg as I balled it into a fist. I pictured hitting the computer genius so hard I knocked him into the river behind him.

Maybe my expectations were a little high.

Henry feinted with his left hand, then threw a hard, round kick right into my ribs. It knocked the wind out of me and shook my confidence at the same time.

As I sucked in air hard, I realized I hadn't expected him to be so good with his feet.

Henry gave me a smile and said, "I do a lot to stay in shape. Lift weights, run, and I've been studying Tae Kwon Do with a master in Estonia. I finally get to use it. Too bad I couldn't find a more worthy opponent." To emphasize his comment, he made a quick turn and caught me in the stomach with a spinning back kick.

I took a few steps back to give me some distance. I had to suck in as much air as possible. This guy was full of surprises. I didn't want this to be his final one. But it wasn't like I'd never been in a fight. I was a New York City police detective.

I had a great reach advantage, if I could just keep him from using his feet. I had to think.

Henry charged me and leapt into the air to deliver a kick to my head. I swung hard with my left arm and knocked him onto the asphalt half a dozen feet from me. He didn't scramble to get up like I thought he might. But he did make it to his feet and faced me again.

I said, "Maybe your time would've been better spent studying a Japanese martial art like Shotokan. More practical, lower to the ground. No fancy moves like that. But it might not work with a little short guy like you."

Again I noticed his face change color. My comment had exactly the effect I wanted it to.

He let out a low growl as he stepped toward me and raised his right fist like he was going to punch me. This time I was ready for the fake. I moved my left arm slightly, but as soon as his foot came off the ground, I shifted my weight and used both of my forearms to block the kick. I didn't know how a guy that size generated so much power. Maybe it was from his anger. Either way, I was glad the kick hadn't landed on a rib or my chin.

He danced away from me and we squared off again.

I said, "Aren't you getting tired yet? I'd like to wrap this up. I have a lot left to do today."

This time, as he came at me, he kicked low. Very low. It caught me right on the shin. I was shocked how much pain shot through my system. I tried to hop back, but he was on me. An elbow crashed into my temple.

This fight was definitely not unfolding the way I had expected.

CHAPTER 102

AS I BREATHED hard and did my own dancing to get a little farther away from Henry, I glanced around the street, wondering where the reinforcements were. Then Henry forced me to focus on the fight again.

I managed to parry two hard punches aimed at my face. Now sweat was starting to pour into my eyes, and the pain from the kicks to my ribs and my shin intensified. I felt my breath become labored. My vision blurred.

I needed a change in tactics. I gained a little more distance, backing farther away from Henry.

He had a real swagger about him now. He was enjoying this. Maybe he thought he was putting on a show. Too bad for him there was no one around to see it. I would have gladly led him back to Terri Hernandez if I thought he'd bite on that idea. I also realized that if I went for my gun, with his speed he'd be all over me.

Henry took a big step to his left, then spun and kicked me with his right foot. It hit me high. Just above the solar plexus. At least a blow like that in my chest didn't knock the wind out of me. I took the kick and stepped back, then slipped to one knee. This was not the position I wanted to be in.

Henry let out a laugh. "This feels about right. You kneeling before me. Now all you need to do is ask for mercy."

"Does that mean you'll *show* me mercy?"

"What do you think?" He swung his left leg high over his head to bring an ax kick down on my shoulders. It was a lot easier to do something like that when your opponent was on his knee. At the last moment, I rolled to one side and avoided the kick. But I could feel the effects of the fight catching up to me. I tried to clear my head.

I was still on the ground, and now my limbs were shaky. Henry jumped to one side so he could attack me from behind. This time, instead of blows, he wrapped his arm around my neck. I felt his other arm brace my head. He had me in a solid choke hold. This was the last place a cop wanted to be.

He leaned in close as he used his arms to slowly cut off my air. He whispered in my ear, "Not what you expected, is it? I don't know about you, but I don't like surprises."

That's when I reverted to what we like to call nonconventional street tactics. It really wasn't that hard, either. As he shifted to get a better position on his choke, his groin ended up next to my shoulder. I wasted no time in making a fist and punching him in the balls as hard as I could.

I could tell by the way he released me instantly and the sound he made that I had been right on target. I rose to my feet as he staggered back, holding his crotch the entire way.

He worked hard to shake off the blow. I used the time to catch my breath. He came at me again, only this time much slower. I blocked a right cross, and while he was close to me, I head-butted him in the face.

I felt his nose shatter. I'd caught him with the top of my forehead, just the way you're supposed to. He staggered back. His eyes weren't focused. After three steps, he flopped onto the ground, then lay down, like he needed a nap.

I resisted the urge to kick him while he was on the ground. But I wasn't a big enough man to resist standing over him, with my hands on my knees so we were looking at each other, and saying, "I guess all those brains couldn't cushion a good head butt. You're under arrest."

Terri Hernandez led her dazed prisoner over to me. She held two of his interlocked fingers on his head, an old trick for holding people if you didn't have handcuffs close by.

She said, "You okay?"

All I could do was nod.

Terri said, "He wasn't a bad fighter. Clearly he was never a street fighter."

I couldn't even answer verbally. I just nodded.

Three cars turned from Vernon Boulevard and came in a line down the street, then angled in different directions as they stopped, blocking off the street completely. I knew it was Harry Grissom and the rest of our squad.

I was happy to sit with my prisoner and let my colleagues handle the rest.

CHAPTER 103

I BRUSHED MYSELF off and wiped some blood from my nose. Two junior detectives took custody of Henry. One of them checked his eyes and made sure he was fully conscious and coherent. When the detective nodded, the other detective said, "Do you speak English?"

When Henry didn't answer, the detective repeated the question in a much louder voice. Somehow NYPD personnel viewed that as a universal language.

This time, Henry nodded as he stared at the ground. A few drops of blood leaked from a cut on his lip.

The detective immediately said, "You have the right to remain silent."

I tuned out the rest of the Miranda warning as Harry Grissom joined me and put an arm around my shoulders. As we started to walk away from Henry and the two detectives, I had to say to Harry, "Just a little late, huh, Harry?"

The lieutenant laughed. "I'll admit the move to Queens threw us off. I can't believe I let you talk me into this crazy plan. You and Hernandez could've been killed."

"We could be killed every day. The plan worked. That's what's important."

"Thank God your brainiac kid knew about cloned phones. The GPS unit in your pocket worked pretty well. At least now we can let Natalie Lunden out of protective custody and give her back her phone. The mayor should be thrilled."

I shook my head. "The mayor was nothing like I expected him to be, but I don't give a damn if he's thrilled or not. Turns out, I didn't do this for him. Natalie is a sweet kid. She's got a bright future. I'm just glad she didn't waste it on an asshole like Henry."

A few minutes later, as the two detectives were about to transport Henry to booking, I couldn't resist taking a moment to chat with my Estonian friend.

I opened the rear door and kneeled down so I could look in on the handcuffed computer genius. He looked beaten, with his hands secured behind him, sitting in the back of a Crown Vic with a plexiglass shield separating the front seat from the rear.

He surprised me by speaking first. He said, "I underestimated you."

I said, "And I *overestimated* you. Let's call it even."

"What now?"

"You'll face a slew of federal charges and then we'll throw in the attempted murder. Plus all the murders you've ordered. So I wouldn't plan any exotic trips. You're going to be occupied for a good long time."

Henry smiled. "I'm glad you feel satisfied. I hope it lasts."

"What's that supposed to mean?"

"You've made a huge mistake. It's funny that you think I'll be in prison for a long time. Last I checked, prisons had computers. I still have friends. I have more money than you can comprehend. I won't be out of circulation long."

"Should I be scared? I don't feel it right now."

"You will. Trust me. No one will keep me locked up for very long."

I patted him on the shoulder. "You keep those positive thoughts. Frankly, it's a nice change from the 'I'm innocent' excuse I usually hear."

I shut the door and watched the car pull away.

CHAPTER 104

A COUPLE OF days later, when I walked into the mayor's office, I still carried a few cuts on my face and a black eye. That's what was obvious; I also had a cracked rib and a broken finger. It doesn't sound like much, but it was enough to remind me of what had happened more than once a minute.

Of course, as soon as I confirmed that the mayor's phone and email had been compromised, the NYPD cybercrime unit had gone into overdrive. Every city phone and computer had to be checked and double-checked. It was as if no one had ever heard of cybercrime, and now that some asshole from Estonia had broken the meager security on the mayor's phone, the government's role was to overreact. It felt familiar.

Now, as I sat in an overstuffed leather chair waiting for the mayor to come into his office, the past few weeks seemed to catch up with me all at once. This felt like real closure. With any luck, this would be the last time I ever had to talk to the mayor face-to-face. That was the sincere wish of most NYPD employees.

I heard the mayor before the inner door to his office opened. He wore his usual tailored suit, which did nothing to hide his belly. He greeted me with a big smile and came right to my chair to shake my hand.

He said, "Look, it's my favorite NYPD detective." After he shook my hand, he held it for extra, awkward seconds. I guess he was trying to show me how much he appreciated everything I'd done. "You did a great job in Estonia. And the way you figured out that my phone had been hacked was brilliant. Thank you so much for bringing Natalie back to us."

"How's she doing? I know she wasn't very happy about being held in protective custody or whatever we called it."

The mayor plopped into the plush leather chair behind his wide oak desk. He looked down and was silent for a few moments. When he looked up at me again he said, "I'm sure Natalie told you we have a few issues. She's not ready to talk to me just yet. I'm trying to be patient. But her mother tells me she's doing quite well.

"The reason I asked you to visit today was to show my appreciation. I can tell you that officially you've been cleared of any wrongdoing in your shooting. In connection to that, I spoke to the esteemed Reverend Franklin Caldwell. He's agreed to stop his protests directed at you."

"How did you manage that?"

"The reverend and I have a good working relationship. I assured him that backing off your case will help him in the future. His living depends on getting a cut of all the settlements the city makes on cases he's involved in. It's not a great system, but it's worked in the past."

I almost asked the mayor why he hadn't had the reverend stop the protests as soon as the mayor knew my shooting was justified. I figured he'd just have some slick reply like "We have to pick our battles." And this wasn't the battle I wanted him to fight.

Now I had the real question, the one that had floated just below the surface since my last chat with the mayor. I said, "Were you able to talk to anyone about my son Brian? That's all I really care about."

The mayor patted his belly. "So it comes back to children. Seems like that's always the case. My daughter brought me to you. Your son motivates you."

"Did I motivate *you* enough to make some phone calls?"

The mayor smiled. "I can see why you're so effective. So I won't beat around the bush. I did talk to some Department of Corrections people and the attorney general. The responses were not overly optimistic. They don't want it to look like favoritism by releasing the son of a prominent police officer."

"So that's it?"

"I'm still trying. Let's give it a little time."

"May I speak freely, Mr. Mayor?"

"I didn't think you had any other way of speaking. But please say anything you want. It won't leave this room."

"I didn't just *try* to find your daughter. I did it. I didn't give up. Now you know what it's like to have a child returned to you. Please consider that in your efforts to get Brian released. I don't need you to *try* to get Brian released. I need you to put as much effort into it as I did in finding your daughter."

The mayor stared straight ahead silently, nodding his head slowly. "Well said, Detective. Well said."

CHAPTER 105

MY CELL PHONE rang on the nightstand, waking me from a dream about playing basketball with LeBron James. And I was winning. Startled, I automatically reached out with my left hand and fumbled for the phone before it rang again.

Mary Catherine barely stirred next to me as I said, "Bennett. This better be good." I managed a quick peek out the window. It was still pitch-black outside. I glanced at my alarm clock and realized it was only five thirty in the morning.

The call was important enough to get me moving quickly.

Mary Catherine called from the bed when she started to stir.

I said, "I want to take a day trip. You guys have been cooped up in the city too long. I'll get the kids moving. You get dressed."

Her voice was still scratchy with sleep. "A day trip? Where? Michael, what are you talking about?" Even without me answering, she got up and started to get dressed. That's trust.

It took a little longer to get the kids in order, but that allowed me to call my grandfather. And even though it was by then after six in the morning, he was still quite annoyed. But he agreed to be ready to go in twenty minutes.

It wasn't even seven o'clock by the time we were pulling away from Holy Name in the van.

The rapid-fire questions started coming from everyone.

"Where are we going?"

"Why couldn't we keep sleeping?"

"When will we get there?"

"When can we eat?"

I shut everyone up with a quick run to McDonald's, then let nature take its course, and I gave a satisfied smile once everyone fell back to sleep. Everyone except Seamus. And he was smart enough to not ask any questions.

A little over an hour and a half after we'd eaten, about half the kids woke up.

Jane, my second oldest daughter, looked out the window of the van and said, "Isn't this the way to Fishkill?"

Trent said, "Where the prison is?"

Fiona, with a higher pitch of excitement in her voice, said, "We're going to visit Brian, right?"

I smiled and said, "Do I ever have some bright kids."

Now everyone was awake, and excitement rippled through the van.

There were no more complaints now that they all knew the reason we'd gotten moving so early. But the real surprise for my family was yet to come.

They knew the drill. Go into the prison. Check in. Wait. Move to the visiting area. Wait. Get to see Brian.

Today, the drill was thrown off. We were immediately led to a community room with no guards, partitions, or closed-circuit telephones. There were more questions, but everyone filed into the room dutifully.

That's why, when a door on the other side of the room opened, everyone just stood in shock.

Three corrections officers entered the room, followed by Brian. He was wearing jeans and a collared shirt, holding a duffel bag crammed with everything he owned.

Mary Catherine said, "What's this?"

Brian dropped his bag and ran right to me for a big hug. All I could manage to say as the weight of my grown son pushed me back onto a couch was "Brian's coming home." I would've given more explanation, but I started to cry.

Before I could be self-conscious about crying in front of corrections officers, everyone in my family started to cry. And they piled on me and Brian.

My glimpse of the corrections officers told me they liked the happy scene. They all smiled and clapped.

My grandfather had to sit at the end of the couch just to catch his breath. The combination of excitement and joy had worn out the old man. Seamus asked, "How did this happen? It has to be the hand of God."

I couldn't speak with everyone piled on top of me, but it was better that way. Because Brian *was* released with the help of God. That's the only way I could view it. God helped me find Natalie and rescue her. He certainly protected us during our escape. And that led the mayor to work extra hard and push for Brian's release. The mayor's pressure, and the work Brian had done on a drug case against the cartel, had led to an early parole.

Part of it might've been the failure of the Department of Corrections to keep Brian safe when he was attacked by cartel members last year. But it didn't matter. Only one thing mattered at this moment.

Brian was coming home.

CHAPTER 106

ONCE WE GOT Brian home, I took a few extra days off. It might've been the most joy-filled week of my life, and that includes the week before every Christmas as a kid. Brian was home and was still himself, although he was not the boy who'd left us. Prison can do crazy things to people. It can twist them and distort their view of reality, or cause a depression that never leaves.

One of the common threads I'd seen among convicted felons was a victim mentality. It's counterintuitive but prevalent. Released felons believe they were unfairly targeted by the police while others get away with everything. Brian accepted his mistakes and was ready to move on. He'd taken what the corrections system had offered in classes and training. It had made me proud in an odd kind of way.

He was already looking for air-conditioning companies he

might be able to work for. And he blended back into the family fairly easily. The boys played basketball at Holy Name, where the faculty seemed thrilled to see Brian home. My grandfather and I sat in the bleachers and watched Brian, Trent, Eddie, and Ricky play for hours.

On the third day after Brian's release, Seamus turned to me in the bleachers and said, "You did a great job raising these kids. I'm proud to be part of *your* family."

I waited for the punch line. Then I realized the old man was sincere. I draped my arm around his bony shoulders and said a silent prayer of thanks. What else is there to do when you realize all the blessings God has given you?

I went back to work a couple of days before I'd intended to. But it was for a good reason. My informant Flash had gotten word to me that he might have found the suspect in the murder of the nurse and her daughter—the elusive Tight.

Usually a suspect like Tight would have some kind of record. An assault charge is common. Those kinds of charges always get pleaded down, but there would still be a record. But we had nothing on him, not in either police intelligence or arrest files.

Flash told me he was supposed to meet Tight at Convent Garden on 151st Street up near Washington Heights, one of the places where Flash and I usually met. It was quiet and comfortable and, from a tactical standpoint, suitable for a quick arrest.

Even though I had worked with Flash for a few years and I knew his real name was Evis Tolder, I didn't tell anyone else what was going on. Informants are notoriously unreliable, and I didn't want to waste anyone's time.

I thought about calling Terri Hernandez, but if things went

south, I didn't want her in the trick bag. She had a bright future ahead of her. I decided if I was able to grab Tight, I'd call her, and she could take the collar.

The second reason, as important as the first, was my overwhelming need to be the cop who put cuffs on this killer. I thought back to the murder scene of the nurse and her daughter, with those giant holes the .45 slugs had made in their heads. I saw them at night when I started to fall asleep. I also remembered Tight goading the young man who'd robbed me. Without Tight, it would've been a simple robbery and we both would've walked away.

As soon as I met Flash, he said, "Did you bring the 2K for the pills he wants to sell?"

"Nice try. This is not a dope case. We don't have to do any kind of deal. As soon as I see him, I'm going to grab him. That's the end of this caper today. Understood?"

Flash looked troubled. Finally he said, "Then you'll throw some cash my way afterward?"

I said, "Have I ever stiffed you on information you gave me?" That seemed to satisfy my informant. He told me everything he'd done to find Tight. It wasn't much. He had been lucky and had met the pill addict at a Narcotics Anonymous meeting. Now he was supposed to buy a few thousand dollars' worth of pills from Tight.

Once we got to Convent Garden, I made Flash wait at the far end of the park. No one was inside the fence, and I was able to sit on a bench across the park without being seen easily. I ran through the drill in my head quickly. Once I grabbed Tight, I could charge him with attempted robbery. I could articulate how he had been part of the robbery with RJ and had fled after the shooting. Then Terri Hernandez would have to tie him to the homicide. If he had his pistol on him, we could match the slugs. Otherwise, it might be up to DNA.

I sat quietly, looking across the park, until about three twenty. I wasn't worried that our target hadn't shown up yet. He was working on DST, doper standard time. Addicts rarely stuck to schedules. It was one of the things that made it so hard to work in the Narcotics unit.

Then I looked up and he was there. Standing by the entrance to the park, the tall black man was all shakes and jitters. The time since the murder had not been kind to him. A threadbare coat over ripped sweatpants hardly made the profession of drug dealer look glamorous.

His eyes darted in every direction, and he never stopped moving. He noticed Flash and began shambling toward him.

I immediately stood up and started to stroll through the park, headed in the general direction of the two men. I had already told Flash to just walk away once I showed up. No chitchat, no staying to watch, just leave the area. It was the safest thing to do, and that way I didn't have to worry about Flash getting hurt.

I approached the two men at an angle where Tight couldn't see me. They talked for a few seconds. I stood directly behind them. As soon as Tight turned around, Flash started to walk away. I couldn't believe an informant had actually listened to directions.

I smiled at Tight. "Remember me?"

His right hand reached for his waistband.

But I was ready. My Glock was in my right hand behind my back. I reached out and pinned his arm with my left hand, then brought my pistol up to where it was almost touching his nose.

I said, "I guess that means you do remember me. Do you remember Sondra Evans and her daughter, Alicia?"

I yanked the pistol from his waistband. I stuck it in the back of my belt before I shoved him to the ground and put cuffs on him.

When he was securely in custody, I carefully pulled the pistol from my back. It was the same Colt .45 I had seen the day I was in the shooting.

I had the right man.

Tight screamed, "Police brutality. Help me, help me."

I pulled him to his feet and dusted him off. "Relax, Tight. The whole park has video surveillance. You need to find a new excuse."

Instantly he shifted gears and said, "I been framed. I been framed."

"That's why we have a judicial system. If I'm wrong, you go free and can sue me. But if I'm right, you're done."

That's when he tried to wiggle free and run.

I had to catch him hard by the elbow, then swing him onto a bench a few feet away.

Finally the fight went out of him. He sighed and started to cry. Through the tears, he said, "I need help, man. I don't even know who I am no more."

"I'll be sure to tell Mrs. Evans that."

"Who?"

"The woman whose daughter and granddaughter you shot. The nurse. Do you remember her? I've seen a lot of murders, but this is one where I just have to ask you: why? It made no sense to me."

He sat there staring straight ahead into the park, deep in

thought. Finally he turned his head to look at me and said, "She had access to pills."

I said, "Excuse me?"

Tight said, "She was the nurse in charge of securing the painkillers 'n' such. I thought she could load me up. She didn't like the idea of doing something like that."

"So you killed her and her daughter?"

He hung his head and said, "I don't remember it so clearly. I don't remember nothin' so clearly. And I don't really care. I don't care if you shoot me right here, take me to jail, or let me go. Nothin' matters no more."

"It may not matter to you, but it matters a lot to the Evans family. And they're going to be happy to see you behind bars."

"Good. Make those people happy for a few minutes, seein' me behind bars."

"I'm sure that's what everyone will say about you. That he just wanted to make the world a better place."

I walked him through the park in handcuffs. I called Terri Hernandez and told her to meet me in front of the Manhattan North Homicide building. I wanted to dump this mope and get on with my real life.

There were ten kids at home waiting to see me.

ACKNOWLEDGMENTS

Lieutenant Luke Miller, NYPD, for his patience and diligence in answering questions and making sure the NYPD's reputation remains positive.

ABOUT THE AUTHORS

JAMES PATTERSON is one of the best-known and biggest-selling writers of all time. His books have sold in excess of 385 million copies worldwide. He is the author of some of the most popular series of the past two decades – the Alex Cross, Women's Murder Club, Detective Michael Bennett, and Private novels – and he has written many other number one bestsellers including romance novels and stand-alone thrillers.

James is passionate about encouraging children to read. Inspired by his own son who was a reluctant reader, he also writes a range of books for young readers including the Middle School, I Funny, Treasure Hunters, Dog Diaries and Max Einstein series. James has donated millions in grants to independent bookshops and has been the most borrowed author of adult fiction in UK libraries for the past twelve years in a row. He lives in Florida with his wife and son.

JAMES O. BORN is an award-winning crime and science-fiction novelist as well as a career law-enforcement agent. A native Floridian, he still lives in the Sunshine State.

Have You Read Them All?

STEP ON A CRACK

The most powerful people in the world have gathered for a funeral
in New York City. They don't know it's a trap devised by a
ruthless mastermind, and it's up to Michael Bennett to
save every last hostage.

RUN FOR YOUR LIFE

The Teacher is giving New York a lesson it will never forget,
slaughtering the powerful and the arrogant. Michael Bennett
discovers a vital pattern, but has only a few hours to save the city.

WORST CASE

Children from wealthy families are being abducted. But the captor
isn't demanding money. He's quizzing his hostages on the price
others pay for their luxurious lives, and one wrong answer is fatal.

TICK TOCK

New York is in chaos as a rash of horrifying copycat crimes
tears through the city. Michael Bennett investigates, but
not even he could predict the earth-shattering enormity
of this killer's plan.

I, MICHAEL BENNETT

Bennett arrests infamous South American crime lord Manuel
Perrine. From jail, Perrine vows to rain terror down upon
New York City – and to get revenge on Michael Bennett.

GONE

Perrine is back and deadlier than ever. Bennett must make an impossible decision: stay and protect his family, or hunt down the man who is their biggest threat.

BURN

A group of well-dressed men enter a condemned building. Later, a charred body is found. Michael Bennett is about to enter a secret underground world of terrifying depravity.

ALERT

Two devastating catastrophes hit New York in quick succession, putting everyone on edge. Bennett is given the near impossible task of hunting down the shadowy terror group responsible.

BULLSEYE

As the most powerful men on earth gather for a meeting of the UN, Bennett receives shocking intelligence that there will be an assassination attempt on the US president. Are the Russian government behind the plot?

HAUNTED

Michael Bennett is ready for a vacation after a series of crises push him, and his family, to the brink. But when he gets pulled into a shocking case, Bennett is fighting to protect a town, the law, and the family that he loves.

AMBUSH

When an anonymous tip proves to be a trap. Michael Bennett believes he personally is being targetted. And not just him, but his family too.

OFFICER RORY YATES IS TRACKING TWO KILLERS. THE TEXAS RANGERS ARE TRACKING HIM . . .

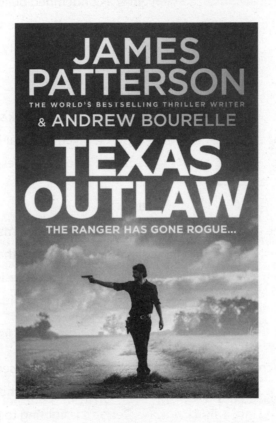

READ ON FOR A SNEAK PEAK OF *TEXAS OUTLAW*, COMING APRIL 2020

I PULL MY Ford F-150 into the small parking lot at the Rio Grande Bank and Trust in Waco. A big Dodge pickup, even bigger than mine, is taking up two handicapped spaces right in front. I drive around to the shady side and find an opening far from the door.

It's my lunch break, and I need to deposit a check for my girlfriend.

"Tell me again, Rory," my lieutenant and new boss says from the passenger seat, "why your girlfriend doesn't get a bank account in Tennessee."

Kyle Hendricks and I became Rangers right around the same time and have always been competitive. Up until about a month ago, Kyle and I were the same rank. Then my old boss, friend, and mentor, Lieutenant Ted Creasy, retired and Kyle got promoted. A lot of Rangers wanted me to take the lieutenant's

2

exam, but I wasn't in the right headspace to apply for the job. I've been through hell and back in the last year.

Now that Kyle's my boss, I remind myself to be respectful of his position. After all, he's in his late thirties, a few years older than me. The Texas-bred good old boy has hair the color of straw and the long, lean body of the baseball pitcher he was back in high school and college. Since football was my sport, I thought of Kyle and me as two quarterbacks vying for the starting spot, fueled by a mix of mutual respect and distaste—then suddenly one of them became the coach.

"Coach" invited me to lunch at a local restaurant called Butter My Biscuit, which I took as a good sign that he wants to smooth this transition. But the way he's been ribbing me about Willow makes me think that maybe he hasn't changed much after all.

"Hell," Kyle says, "it's the twenty-first century. They got national banks now, you know. Wells Fargo. Capital One. You might have heard of 'em."

I ignore him. The guys at work tease me all the time about Willow, who moved to Nashville a good eight months ago. She's a country singer—a hell of a good one, too. Through most of her twenties, she played in bars and roadhouses from Texas to Nashville. But she never got her big break—until last fall, when she broke her ankle and a video of her singing on a barstool in a leg cast went viral. Suddenly producers and talent scouts were asking for demos of her songs, inviting her to fly out to Nashville for auditions. She and I had really only just started dating. But I encouraged her to go and pursue her dreams. Take her shot.

She's done well so far. A couple of songs she wrote were recorded by Miranda Lambert and Little Big Town, and are already earning her royalty checks. Her own album is due out later this summer. People are saying Willow is going to be the next big thing, but she knows every new artist is next up for fame, though fame passes most of them by.

She's been cautiously optimistic, and maybe a little superstitious. She doesn't want to open a bank account in Nashville until she feels sure this is a permanent move. Which also has a little something to do with me. The Nashville Police Department has a job opening for a detective, and she's asked me to consider applying.

I'm honored to be a Texas Ranger, born and raised in Texas, and the thought of leaving the top division of state law enforcement isn't a decision I take lightly. Times have changed since the Wild West days, but not the legendary status of Texas Rangers. The badge still carries a mystique.

"How much is that check for anyway?" Kyle says, gesturing to the sealed envelope in my hand.

I ignore this question, too. "I'll be right back," I say.

"Take your time," he says, leaning his head back and tilting his Stetson down over his eyes. "I'm going to take me a little nap."

It's early June, but already the air is hot and thick with humidity. My clothes stick to my skin. I'm wearing the typical Texas Ranger attire: dress slacks, button-down shirt, tie, cowboy hat, and cowboy boots. And a polished silver star pinned to my shirt.

I'm wearing my gun, too, a SIG Sauer P320 loaded with .357 cartridges, sheathed in a quick-draw holster. *A Texas Ranger should always be ready for anything.*

I walk into the bank head down, not paying attention to my surroundings as I open the envelope Willow sent me. I'm caught off guard by the amount of the check. I'm glad I didn't tell Kyle—I'd never hear the end of it.

Not until I hear the unmistakable click of a gun being cocked no more than a foot from my head do I sense anything is wrong. *Today I'm not ready.*

"Hold it right there, Ranger," a voice says from behind me. "One move and I'll put a bullet right through your skull."

I SLOWLY RAISE my head and take in the scene. Besides the guy holding a gun to my head, I see only one other robber. He rises from a crouch behind the counter, where the half dozen tellers are standing. The AR-15 assault rifle he carries is equipped with a bump stock to effectively turn it from semiautomatic to fully automatic.

"No sudden movements," he yells at me, "or I'll light this place up like the Fourth of July."

The big Dodge parked out front, blocking the view into the bank, is probably the robbers' getaway car.

The guy behind me swivels around, keeping the pistol— a 9mm Beretta—leveled at my head. "Put those hands up," he says. "Slowly."

I do as he says, quickly counting the six customers standing in the bank lobby. The last thing I want is to put innocent bystanders in the midst of a gunfight.

These guys look like pros. They're wearing black tactical gear from head to toe, including masks and bulletproof vests, standard issue for law enforcement or military personnel (though your average citizen can get this stuff on the internet).

Even if these guys are professionals, I still have one question.

"Why the hell are you guys robbing a bank at lunchtime?" I say. "There probably wouldn't be a soul in here at any other time of day."

"Not that we owe you any goddamn explanation," the guy with the AR-15 says, "but the vault's on a time lock." He checks his watch. "And it's just about time."

With that, he disappears into a back room. Now is the time for me to make a move. But even if I could get the drop on the guy with a gun to my head, Mr. AR-15 would hear the gunshot and come running. He'd open fire with the assault rifle and tear the place apart. He could kill everyone in the room before he needed to reload.

The eyes of the guy with the Beretta dart to the pistol on my hip, then back up to my face. I can tell what he's thinking. He's wondering how to disarm me. If he gets close enough to reach for the pistol, maybe I can disarm and disable him. Asking me to remove it from the holster and drop it will risk putting a gun into one of my hands, even if he insists I use the left one. Or I could leave my hands right where they are, shoulder high and far from my gun belt.

"I don't want any trouble," I say to the guy. "I'm going to let you walk right out of here. You don't want to hurt anyone."

"If anyone's gonna get hurt, Ranger, it's you. I hate the fucking Texas Rangers. I might kill you just 'cause I feel like it."

The guy's voice is rough and strained. These guys might be

7

professionals, but this one's nerves are shot. I need to find a way to keep him under control.

"Let me remind you," I say, maintaining a steady, calm voice, "killing a Texas Ranger is capital murder. They'll give you the needle for it."

In other states, death-row inmates die of old age while their lawyers delay their sentences with endless appeals. But this is Texas, which executed more people last year than every other state combined.

The hand holding the gun trembles slightly.

"It's also capital murder," I say, "to kill someone during the execution of a robbery. If you shoot anyone today, anyone at all, that's a death sentence. Automatically."

I've scared him, which isn't necessarily a good thing.

"You and your partner are free to go," I assure him. "I don't care about the money you're stealing. Maybe you'll get caught at a later date. Maybe you'll get away with it. That's not my problem today. What I care about is that no one gets hurt."

I can't gauge the impact of my words. The guy watches as his partner lugs two loaded duffel bags, one on each shoulder. He hauls them up onto the counter and then, like a bank robber in a movie, climbs atop the marble. He stands and shoulders the assault rifle, swinging it around at the people standing in the lobby.

Some are crying. Some are shaking. All of them look scared to death.

"All right," Mr. AR-15 announces, breath heaving from carrying the bags, "since we had the bad luck of a Texas Ranger walking in on us, we're going to have to take us a hostage."

"There's no need to take any hostages," I say. "I'm going to let you walk right out of here."

"We seen you circle the parking lot," he says. "We know there's another Ranger out there. We need some insurance we won't be followed."

Mr. AR-15 looks overly confident, crazed almost. But his partner, Mr. Beretta—I can tell he's spooked. His eyes bulge in his mask. And his arm is getting tired, too. His gun hand is shaking more and more.

"If you have to take anyone," I say, "take me."

Also by James Patterson

ALEX CROSS NOVELS

Along Came a Spider • Kiss the Girls • Jack and Jill • Cat and Mouse • Pop Goes the Weasel • Roses are Red • Violets are Blue • Four Blind Mice • The Big Bad Wolf • London Bridges • Mary, Mary • Cross • Double Cross • Cross Country • Alex Cross's Trial (*with Richard DiLallo*) • I, Alex Cross • Cross Fire • Kill Alex Cross • Merry Christmas, Alex Cross • Alex Cross, Run • Cross My Heart • Hope to Die • Cross Justice • Cross the Line • The People vs. Alex Cross • Target: Alex Cross • Criss Cross

THE WOMEN'S MURDER CLUB SERIES

1st to Die • 2nd Chance (*with Andrew Gross*) • 3rd Degree (*with Andrew Gross*) • 4th of July (*with Maxine Paetro*) • The 5th Horseman (*with Maxine Paetro*) • The 6th Target (*with Maxine Paetro*) • 7th Heaven (*with Maxine Paetro*) • 8th Confession (*with Maxine Paetro*) • 9th Judgement (*with Maxine Paetro*) • 10th Anniversary (*with Maxine Paetro*) • 11th Hour (*with Maxine Paetro*) • 12th of Never (*with Maxine Paetro*) • Unlucky 13 (*with Maxine Paetro*) • 14th Deadly Sin (*with Maxine Paetro*) • 15th Affair (*with Maxine Paetro*) • 16th Seduction (*with Maxine Paetro*) • 17th Suspect (*with Maxine Paetro*) • 18th Abduction (*with Maxine Paetro*) • 19th Christmas (*with Maxine Paetro*)

PRIVATE NOVELS

Private (*with Maxine Paetro*) • Private London (*with Mark Pearson*) • Private Games (*with Mark Sullivan*) • Private: No. 1 Suspect (*with Maxine Paetro*) • Private Berlin (*with Mark Sullivan*) • Private Down Under (*with Michael White*) • Private L.A. (*with Mark Sullivan*) • Private India (*with Ashwin Sanghi*) • Private Vegas (*with Maxine Paetro*) • Private Sydney (*with Kathryn Fox*) • Private Paris (*with Mark Sullivan*) • The Games (*with Mark Sullivan*) • Private Delhi (*with Ashwin Sanghi*) • Private Princess (*with Rees Jones*)

NYPD RED SERIES

NYPD Red (*with Marshall Karp*) • NYPD Red 2 (*with Marshall Karp*) • NYPD Red 3 (*with Marshall Karp*) • NYPD Red 4 (*with Marshall Karp*) • NYPD Red 5 (*with Marshall Karp*)

DETECTIVE HARRIET BLUE SERIES

Never Never (*with Candice Fox*) • Fifty Fifty (*with Candice Fox*) • Liar Liar (*with Candice Fox*) • Hush Hush (*with Candice Fox*)

INSTINCT SERIES

Instinct (*with Howard Roughan, previously published as* Murder Games) • Killer Instinct (*with Howard Roughan*)

STAND-ALONE THRILLERS

The Thomas Berryman Number • Hide and Seek • Black Market • The Midnight Club • Sail (*with Howard Roughan*) • Swimsuit (*with Maxine Paetro*) • Don't Blink (*with Howard Roughan*) • Postcard Killers (*with Liza Marklund*) • Toys (*with Neil McMahon*) • Now You See Her (*with Michael Ledwidge*) • Kill Me If You Can (*with Marshall Karp*) • Guilty Wives (*with David Ellis*) • Zoo (*with Michael Ledwidge*) • Second Honeymoon (*with Howard Roughan*) • Mistress (*with David Ellis*) • Invisible (*with David Ellis*) • Truth or Die (*with Howard Roughan*) • Murder House (*with David Ellis*) • The Black Book (*with David Ellis*) • The Store (*with Richard DiLallo*) • Texas Ranger (*with Andrew Bourelle*) • The President is Missing (*with Bill Clinton*) • Revenge (*with Andrew Holmes*) • Juror No. 3 (*with Nancy Allen*) • The First Lady (*with Brendan DuBois*) • The Chef (*with Max DiLallo*) • Out of Sight (*with Brendan DuBois*) • Unsolved (*with David Ellis*) • The Inn (*with Candice Fox*) • Lost (*with James O. Born*)

NON-FICTION

Torn Apart (*with Hal and Cory Friedman*) • The Murder of King Tut (*with Martin Dugard*) • All-American Murder (*with Alex Abramovich and Mike Harvkey*)

MURDER IS FOREVER TRUE CRIME

Murder, Interrupted (*with Alex Abramovich and Christopher Charles*) • Home Sweet Murder (*with Andrew Bourelle and Scott Slaven*) • Murder Beyond the Grave (*with Andrew Bourelle and Christopher Charles*)

COLLECTIONS

Triple Threat (*with Max DiLallo and Andrew Bourelle*) • Kill or Be Killed (*with Maxine Paetro, Rees Jones, Shan Serafin and Emily Raymond*) • The Moores are Missing (*with Loren D. Estleman,*

Sam Hawken and Ed Chatterton) • The Family Lawyer (*with Robert Rotstein, Christopher Charles and Rachel Howzell Hall*) • Murder in Paradise (*with Doug Allyn, Connor Hyde and Duane Swierczynski*) • The House Next Door (*with Susan DiLallo, Max DiLallo and Brendan DuBois*) • 13-Minute Murder (*with Shan Serafin, Christopher Farnsworth and Scott Slaven*)

For more information about James Patterson's novels, visit
www.jamespatterson.co.uk